THE FARM

THE FARM

TOM ROB SMITH

**SIMON &
SCHUSTER**

London · New York · Sydney · Toronto · New Delhi

A CBS COMPANY

First published in Great Britain by Simon & Schuster UK Ltd, 2014
A CBS COMPANY

1 3 5 7 9 10 8 6 4 2

Simon & Schuster UK Ltd
1st Floor
222 Gray's Inn Road
London
WC1X 8HB

www.simonandschuster.co.uk
www.simonandschuster.com.au

Simon & Schuster Australia, Sydney
Simon & Schuster India, New Delhi

A CIP catalogue record for this book
is available from the British Library

ISBN HB 978-1-84737-569-8
ISBN TPB 978-1-84737-570-4
ISBN E-book 978-1-47111-067-2

Typeset by M Rules
Printed and bound by CPI Group (UK) Ltd, Croydon, CR0 4YY

THE FARM

U NTIL THAT PHONE CALL it had been an ordinary day. Laden with groceries, I was walking home through Bermondsey, a neighbourhood of London, just south of the river. It was a stifling August evening and when the phone rang I considered ignoring it, keen to hurry home and shower. Curiosity got the better of me so I slowed, sliding the phone out of my pocket, pressing it against my ear – sweat pooling on the screen. It was my dad. He'd recently moved to Sweden and the call was unusual; he rarely used his mobile and it would've been expensive to call London. My dad was crying. I came to an abrupt stop, dropping the grocery bag. I'd never heard him cry before. My parents had always been careful not to argue or lose their temper in front of me. In our household there were no furious rows or tearful fights. I said:

'Dad?'

'Your mother ... She's not well.'

'Mum's sick?'

'It's so sad.'

'Sad because she's sick? Sick how? How's Mum sick?'

Dad was still crying. All I could do was dumbly wait until he said:

'She's been imagining things – terrible, terrible things.'

A reference to her imagination, rather than some physical ailment, was so strange and surprising that I crouched down, steadying myself with one hand on the warm cracked concrete pavement, observing a patch of red sauce leaking through the bottom of the dropped grocery bag. Eventually I asked:

'For how long?'

'The whole summer.'

Months and I hadn't known – I'd been here, in London, oblivious, my dad maintaining a tradition of concealment. Guessing my thoughts he added:

'I was sure I could help her. Maybe I waited too long, but the symptoms started gradually – anxiety and odd comments, we can all suffer from that. Then came the allegations. She claims she has proof, she talks about evidence and suspects, but it's nonsense and lies.'

Dad became louder, defiant, emphatic, no longer crying. He'd recovered his fluency. There was more to his voice than sadness.

'I was hoping it would pass, or that she just needed time to adjust to life in Sweden, on a farm. Except it got worse and worse. And now . . .'

My parents were from a generation that wouldn't go to the doctor unless it was an injury you could see with your eyes or feel with your fingers. To burden a stranger with the intimate details of their lives was unfathomable.

'Dad, tell me she's seen a doctor.'

'He says she's suffering from a psychotic episode. Daniel . . .'

Mum and Dad were the only people in the world who didn't shorten my name to Dan.

'Your mum's in hospital. She's been committed.'

I heard this final piece of news and opened my mouth to speak with no idea of what to say, perhaps just to exclaim, but in the end said nothing.

'Daniel?'

'Yes.'

'Did you hear?'

'I heard.'

*

A bashed-up car passed by, slowing to look at me but not stopping. I checked my watch. It was eight in the evening, and there was little chance of making a flight tonight – I'd fly early tomorrow. Instead of becoming emotional, I took it upon myself to be efficient. We spoke for a little while longer. After the upheaval of the first few minutes both of us were returning to type – controlled and measured. I said:

'I'll book a flight for the morning. Once that's done I'll call you back. Are you at the farm? Or the hospital?'

He was at the farm.

With the call finished I rummaged through the grocery bag, taking out every item, lining them up on the pavement until I found the cracked jar of tomato sauce, carefully removing it, the shards of glass held in place only by the label. I discarded it in a nearby bin, returning to my disassembled shopping, using tissues to mop up the excess sauce, and perhaps this seems unnecessary – fuck the bag, my mum's sick – but the cracked jar might have broken apart completely, tomato sauce spread over everything, and anyway, there was comfort in the humdrum simplicity of the task. I picked up the bag and at a faster pace completed my journey home, to the top floor of a former factory, now a set of apartments. I stood under a cold shower and considered crying – shouldn't I cry? I asked myself, as if it were the same as deciding whether to smoke a cigarette. Wasn't it my duty as a son? Crying should be instinctual. But before showing emotion I pause. In the eyes of strangers I'm guarded. In this case, it wasn't caution – it was disbelief. I couldn't attach an emotional response to a situation I didn't understand. I wouldn't cry. There were too many unanswered questions to cry.

*

After the shower I sat at my computer studying the emails sent by my mum over the past five months, wondering if there were hints that I'd missed. I hadn't seen my parents since they moved to Sweden in April. At their farewell to England party we'd toasted their peaceful retirement. All of the guests had stood outside their old home and waved fond goodbyes. I have no brothers or sisters, there are no uncles or aunts, when I speak about family I mean the three of us, Mum, Dad, me – a triangle, like a fragment of a constellation, three bright stars close together with a lot of empty space around us. The absence of relatives has never been discussed in detail. There have been hints – my parents went through difficult upbringings, estranged from their own parents, and I was sure that their vow never to argue in front of me originated from a powerful desire to provide a different kind of childhood to their own. The motivation wasn't British reserve. They never skimped on love, or happiness, those were expressed at every opportunity. If times were good they'd celebrate, if times weren't so good they'd be optimistic. That's why some people consider me sheltered – I've only seen the good times. The bad times were hidden. I was complicit in the arrangement. I didn't probe. That farewell party had been a good time, the crowd cheering as my mum and dad set off, embarking on a great adventure, my mum returning to the country she'd left when she was just sixteen years old.

Shortly after their arrival at the remote farm, located in the very south of Sweden, my mum had written regularly. The emails described how wonderful their life on the farm was, the beauty of the countryside, the warmth of the local people. If there was a hint of something wrong it was subtle, and one I'd misconstrued. Her emails dwindled in length as the weeks went on, the lines expressing wonder grew briefer. In my mind, I'd interpreted this as positive. My mum must have settled in and didn't have a moment to spare. Her last email to me flashed up:

Daniel!

Nothing else, just my name, an exclamation mark – my response had been to shoot back a quick-fire reply telling her that there'd been a glitch, her email hadn't come through and could she please resend, dismissing her one-word email as a mistake, never considering the possibility that this email might have been fired off in distress.

I worked through the entire chain of correspondence, unsettled by the notion that I'd been blind and troubled by the question of what else I might have overlooked. However, there were no telltale signs, no baffling flights of fancy; her writing style remained regular, using mostly English since, shamefully, I'd let slip much of the Swedish she'd taught me as a child. One email contained two large attachments – photographs. I must have looked at them before, but now my mind was blank. The first appeared onscreen – a bleak barn with a rusted steel roof, a grey sky, a tractor parked outside. Zooming in on the glass of the cabin I saw a partial reflection of the photographer – my mum – her face obscured by the flash so that it appeared as if her head had exploded into bright spikes of white light. The second showed my dad standing outside their farmhouse in conversation with a tall stranger. The photograph seemed to have been taken without my father's

knowledge. From a distance, it was more like a surveillance photograph than a family snap. Neither tallied with descriptions of great
beauty, although, of course, I hadn't queried this anomaly, replying
that I was excited to visit the farm myself. That was a lie. I wasn't looking forward to my visit and had already postponed it several times,
moving it back from early summer to late summer to early autumn,
offering vague half-truths in explanation.

The real reason for the delay was that I was scared. I hadn't told my
parents that I lived with my partner and that we'd known each
other for three years. The deceit dated back so far that I'd become
convinced I couldn't unravel it without damaging my family. I dated
girls at university, my parents cooked dinner for those girlfriends
and expressed delight at my choices – the girls were beautiful, funny,
and smart. But there was no quickening of my heart when they
undressed, and during sex I exhibited a professional concentration
on the task at hand, a belief that providing pleasure meant I wasn't
gay. Not until I was living away from home did I accept the truth,
telling my friends but excluding my mum and dad, not out of
shame but well-intentioned cowardice. I was terrified of damaging
the memory of my childhood. My parents had gone to extraordinary lengths to create a happy home, they'd made sacrifices,
they'd taken a solemn vow of tranquillity, sworn to provide a sanctuary free from trauma, and they'd never slipped up, not once, and
I loved them for it. Hearing the truth they'd be sure to conclude that
they'd failed. They'd think upon all the lies that I must have told.
They'd imagine me as lonely and tortured, bullied and ridiculed,
when none of that was true. Adolescence had been easy for me. I'd
transitioned from childhood to adulthood with a skip in my step –

my bright blond hair dulling only slightly, my bright blue eyes not dulling at all – and with good looks came unearned popularity. I floated through those years. Even my secret I'd worn lightly. It didn't make me sad. I just didn't think about it too deeply. In the end it came down to this: I couldn't stand the thought of my parents wondering if I'd ever doubted their love. It felt unfair to them. I could hear myself saying in a desperate voice, not believing my own words:

'It changes nothing!'

I was sure they'd embrace my partner, celebrate our relationship as they'd celebrated everything, but a trace of sadness would remain. The memory of a perfect childhood would die, and we'd mourn it as surely as we would the passing of a person we loved. So the real reason I'd postponed my visit to Sweden was because I'd promised my partner it would be the opportunity when I'd tell my parents the truth, when, finally, after all these years, I'd share with them my partner's name.

Mark came home that night to find me at the computer browsing flights to Sweden, and before I could say a word he smiled, presuming the lies were at an end. I was too slow to pre-empt his mistake and instead was forced to correct him, adopting my dad's euphemism:

'My mum's sick.'

It was painful watching Mark adjust, burying his disappointment. He was eleven years older than me, he'd just turned forty and it was his apartment, the spoils of being a successful corporate lawyer. I tried my best to play an equal role in the relationship, making a point of paying as much rent as I could afford. But in truth, I couldn't afford much. I worked freelance as a designer for a company that converted roof space into gardens and was only paid when there was a commission. Struggling through the recession, we had no jobs lined up. What did Mark see in me? I suspected he craved the kind of calm home life in which I was expert. I didn't argue. I didn't row. Following in my parents' footsteps, I worked hard to make our home a refuge from the world. Mark had been married to a woman for ten years, ending in an acrimonious divorce. His ex-wife declared that he'd stolen the best years of her life and that she'd squandered her love on him, and now, in her mid-thirties, she'd be unable to find a real partner. Mark accepted the notion and the guilt sat heavily on him. I wasn't convinced it would ever go away. I'd seen photos of him in his twenties, full of bullish confidence, looking slick in expensive suits – he used to work out a lot in the gym, and his shoulders were broad, his arms thick. He'd go to strip clubs and plan lurid stag parties for his colleagues. He'd laugh loudly at jokes and slap people on the back. He didn't laugh like that any more. During the divorce his parents sided with his ex-wife. His father, in particular, was disgusted with Mark. They were no longer speaking. His mum sent us musical Christmas cards as if she wanted to say more but didn't quite know how. His dad never signed them. Part of me wondered whether Mark saw my parents as a second chance. Needless to say, he had every right to ask that they be part of his life. The only reason he accepted the delay was because after he'd taken so long to come out he felt unable to demand anything on the subject. On some level I must have exploited this fact. It took the pressure off me. It allowed me to nudge the truth back time and again.

*

Without any work on the horizon there was no problem flying to Sweden at such short notice. There was only the issue of how I could afford the ticket. It was out of the question that Mark should pay when I hadn't even told my parents his name. I emptied the last of my savings, extending my overdraft, and with my ticket booked, I phoned my dad with the details. The first available flight departed Heathrow at nine-thirty the next morning, arriving at Gothenburg in the south of Sweden at midday. He said no more than a few words, sounding moribund and defeated. Concerned with how he was coping alone on the isolated farm, I asked what he was doing. He replied:

'I'm tidying up. She went through every drawer, every cupboard.'

'What was she looking for?'

'I don't know. There's no logic to it. Daniel, she wrote on the walls.'

I asked what she wrote. He said:

'It doesn't matter.'

There was no chance I'd sleep that night. Memories of Mum played on a loop in my head, fixating on the time when we'd been together in Sweden, twenty years ago, alone on a small holiday island in the archipelago north of Gothenburg, sitting side by side on a rock, our feet in the sea. In the distance an ocean-bound cargo vessel navigated the deep waters, and we watched the wave created by the bow travel towards us, a crease in the otherwise flat sea, neither of us moving, taking each other's hands, waiting for the inevitable impact, the wave growing in size as it passed over shallow water until it smashed against the base of the rock, soaking us to the skin. I'd picked the memory because that had been around the time Mum and I had been closest, when I couldn't imagine making an important decision without consulting her.

Next morning Mark insisted on driving me to Heathrow even though we both knew it would be faster on public transport. When the traffic was congested I didn't complain, or check my watch, aware of how much Mark wished that he was coming with me and how I'd made it impossible for him to be involved beyond this car journey. At the drop-off point he hugged me. To my surprise he was on the verge of crying – I could feel the stifled vibrations through his chest. I assured him there was no point in him showing me through to the departure gate, and we said goodbye outside.

Ticket and passport ready, I was about to check in when my phone rang:

'Daniel, she's not here!'

'Not where, Dad?'

'The hospital! They've discharged her. Yesterday I brought her in. She wouldn't have come in on her own. But she didn't protest, so it was a voluntary admission. Then, once I left – she convinced the doctors to discharge her.'

'Mum convinced them? You said the doctors diagnosed her as psychotic.'

My dad didn't reply. I pressed the point:

'The staff didn't discuss her release with you?'

His voice dropped in volume:

'She must have asked them not to speak to me.'

'Why would she do that?'

'I'm one of the people she's making allegations against.'

He hastily added:

'None of what she claims is real.'

It was my turn to be silent. I wanted to ask about the allegations but couldn't bring myself to. I sat on my luggage, head in hands, ushering the queue to move around me.

'Does she have a phone?'

'She smashed hers a few weeks ago. She doesn't trust them.'

I hesitated over the image of my frugal mother irrationally smashing a phone. My dad was describing the actions of a person I didn't recognise.

'Money?'

'Probably a little – she carries around a leather satchel. She never lets it out of her sight.'

'What's in it?'

'All kinds of junk she believes to be important. She calls it evidence.'

'How did she leave the hospital?'

'The hospital won't even tell me that. She could be anywhere!'

Feeling panic for the first time, I said:

'You and Mum have joint accounts. You can phone the bank and ask about recent transactions. Track her through the card.'

I could tell from the silence that Dad had never phoned the bank before: he'd always left money matters to my mum. In their joint business she'd balanced the books, paid the bills, and submitted the yearly tax accounts, gifted with an aptitude for numbers and the focus required to spend hours piecing together receipts and expenses.

I could picture her old-fashioned ledger, in the days before spread-sheets. She'd press so hard on it with a pen that the numbers were like Braille.

'Dad, check with the bank and call me straight back.'

While waiting I stepped out of the line and exited the terminal building, pacing among the congregation of smokers, struggling with the thought of Mum lost in Sweden. My phone rang again. I was surprised that my dad had managed his task so quickly, except it wasn't Dad:

'Daniel, listen to me carefully—'

It was my mum.

'I'm on a payphone and don't have much credit. I'm sure your father has spoken to you. Everything that man has told you is a lie. I'm not mad. I don't need a doctor. I need the police. I'm about to board a flight to London. Meet me at Heathrow, Terminal . . .'

She paused for the first time to check her ticket information. Seizing the opportunity, all I could manage was a pitiful '. . . Mum!'

'Daniel, don't talk, I have very little time. The plane comes in at Terminal One. I'll be landing in two hours. If your father calls, remember—'

The phone cut off.

I tried calling the payphone back in the hope that my mum would pick up, but there was no answer. As I was about to try again, my dad rang. Without any preamble he began to speak, sounding like he was reading from notes:

'At seven-twenty this morning she spent four hundred pounds at

Gothenburg airport. The vendor was Scandinavian Airlines. She's in time for the first flight to Heathrow. She's on her way to you! Daniel?'

'Yes.'

Why didn't I tell him that Mum had just called and that I already knew she was on her way? Did I believe her? She'd sounded commanding and authoritative. I'd expected a stream of conscious- ness, not clear facts and compact sentences. I was confused. It felt aggressive and confrontational to repeat her assertions that my dad was a liar. I stuttered a reply:

'I'll meet her here. When are you flying over?'

'I'm not.'

'You're staying in Sweden?'

'If she thinks I'm in Sweden she'll relax. She's got it into her head that I'm pursuing her. Staying here will buy you some time. You need to convince her to get help. I can't help her. She won't let me. Take her to the doctor's. You have a better chance if she's not worrying about me.'

I couldn't follow his reasoning.

'I'll call you when she arrives. Let's work out a plan then.'

I ended the conversation with my thoughts pinched between interpretations. If my mum was suffering from a psychotic episode, why had the doctors discharged her? Even if they couldn't detain her on a legal technicality they should've notified my dad, yet they'd refused, treating him as a hostile force, aiding her escape not from hospital but from him. To other people she must seem okay. The airline staff had sold her a ticket, security had allowed her through airport screening – no one had stopped her. I started to wonder what she'd written on the walls, unable to shake the image that Mum had emailed me, showing Dad in conversation with a stranger.

Daniel!

In my head it began to sound like a cry for help.

The screen updated; Mum's plane had landed. The automatic doors opened and I hurried to the front of the barriers, checking the baggage tags. Soon the Gothenburg passengers began to trickle through. First were the executives searching for the laminated plastic sign with their name, followed by couples, then families with bulky luggage piled high. There was no sign of my mum, even though she was a brisk walker and I couldn't imagine that she'd checked luggage into the hold. An elderly man slowly passed by me, surely one of the last passengers from Gothenburg. I gave serious consideration to phoning my dad, explaining that something had gone wrong. Then the giant doors hissed open and my mum stepped through.

Her eyes were turned downwards, as though following a trail of breadcrumbs. There was a beat-up leather satchel over her shoulder, packed full and straining at the strap. I'd never seen it before: it wasn't the kind of thing my mum would normally have bought. Her clothes, like the satchel, showed signs of distress. There were scuffs on her shoes. Her trousers were crumpled around the knees. A button was missing from her shirt. My mum had a tendency to overdress – smart for restaurants, smart for the theatre, smart for work even though there was no need. She and my dad had owned a garden centre in north London, set on a slip of T-shaped land between grand white stucco houses, bought in the early 1970s when land in London was cheap. While my dad wore torn jeans, clumpy boots and baggy jumpers, smoking roll-up cigarettes, my mum selected starched white shirts, wool trousers in the winter, and cotton trousers in the summer. Customers would remark on her immaculate office attire, wondering how she kept so pristine because she'd carry out as much of the physical labour as my dad. She'd laugh when they asked and shrug innocently as if to say, 'I have no idea!' But it was calculated. There were always spare changes of clothes in the back room. She'd tell me that, as the face of the business, it was important to keep up appearances.

I allowed my mum to pass by, curious as to whether she'd see me. She was notably thinner than when we'd said goodbye in April, unhealthily so. Her trousers were loose, reminding me of clothes on a wooden puppet, hanging without shape. She seemed to have no natural curves, a hasty line drawing rather than the real person. Her short blonde hair looked wet, brushed back, slick and smooth, not with wax or gel but water. She must have stopped off at a washroom after leaving the plane, making an effort to fix her appearance to be sure a hair wasn't out of place. Normally youthful in appearance, her face had aged over the past few months. Like her clothes, her skin carried marks of distress. There were dark spots on her cheeks. The lines under her eyes had grown more pronounced. In contrast her watery blue eyes seemed brighter than ever. As I moved around the barrier, instinct stopped me from touching her, a concern that she might scream.

'Mum.'

She looked up, frightened, but seeing that it was me – her son – she smiled triumphantly:

'Daniel.'

She uttered my name in the same way as when I'd made her proud – a quiet, intense happiness. As we hugged she rested her face against the side of my chest. Pulling back, she took hold of my hands and I surreptitiously examined her fingers with the edge of my thumb. Her skin was rough. Her nails were jagged and not cared for. She whispered:

'It's over. I'm safe.'

I quickly established that her mind was sharp as she immediately noticed my luggage:

'What's that for?'

'Dad called me last night to tell me you were in the hospital—'

She cut me short:

'Don't call it a hospital. It was an asylum. He drove me to the madhouse. He said this is where I belong, in rooms next to people howling like animals. Then he phoned you and told you the same thing. Your mum's mad. Isn't that right?'

I was slow to respond, finding it difficult to adjust to her confrontational anger:

'I was about to fly to Sweden when you called.'

'Then you believed him?'

'Why wouldn't I?'

'He was relying on that.'

'Tell me what's going on.'

'Not here. Not with these people. We have to do it properly, from the beginning. It must be done right. Please, no questions? Not yet.'

There was a formality in the way she spoke, an excessive politeness, overarticulating each syllable and clipping each point of punctuation. I agreed:

'No questions.'

She squeezed my hand appreciatively, softening her voice:

'Take me home.'

She didn't own a house in England any more. She'd sold it and relocated to a farm in Sweden, a farm intended to be her last and happiest home. I could only assume she meant my apartment, Mark's apartment, a man she'd never even heard about.

I'd already spoken to Mark while waiting for Mum's plane to land. He was alarmed at the turn of events, particularly with the fact that there would no longer be any doctors supervising. I'd be on my own. I told him that I'd phone to keep him updated. I'd also promised to phone my dad, but there was no opportunity to make that call with my mum by my side. I didn't dare leave her alone and feared that reporting openly back to my dad could make me appear partisan, something I couldn't risk; she might begin to mistrust me or, worse, she might run away, an idea that would never have occurred to me if my dad hadn't mentioned it. The prospect terrified me. I slipped my hand into my pocket, silencing my phone.

Mum remained close by my side as I bought train tickets to the centre of town. I found myself checking on her frequently, smiling in an attempt to veil the fact that she was under careful observation. At intervals she'd hold my hand, something she'd not done since I was a child. My strategy was to behave as neutrally as possible, making no assumptions, ready to hear her story fairly. As it happens I didn't have any history of siding with my mum or my dad simply because they'd never given me a conflict where I'd needed to pick sides. On balance I was closer to my mum only because she'd been more involved in the everyday details of my life. My dad had always been content to defer to her judgment.

Boarding the train, my mum selected seats at the rear of the carriage, nestling against the window. Her seat, I realised, had the best vantage point. No one could sneak up on her. She placed the satchel on her lap, holding it tight – as if she were the courier of a vitally important package. I asked:

'Is that all you have?'

She solemnly tapped the top of the bag:

'This is the evidence that proves I'm not mad. Evidence of crimes that are being covered up.'

These words were so removed from ordinary life that they sounded odd to my ear. However, they were spoken in earnest. I asked:

'Can I look?'

'Not here.'

She raised a finger to her lips, signalling that this was not a topic we should talk about in a public place. The gesture itself was peculiar and unnecessary. Even though we'd spent over thirty minutes together, I couldn't decide on her state of mind. I'd expected to know immediately. She was different, physically and in terms of her character. It was impossible to be sure whether the changes were a result of a real experience, or whether that experience had taken place entirely in her mind. Much depended on what she produced from that satchel – much depended on her evidence.

As we arrived at Paddington station, ready to disembark, Mum gripped my arm, possessed by a vivid and sudden fear:

'Promise that you'll listen to everything I say with an open mind. All I ask for is an open mind. Promise me you'll do that, that's why I've come to you. Promise me!'

I put my hand on top of hers. She was trembling, terrified that I might not be on her side.

'I promise.'

In the back of a cab, our hands knitted together like eloping lovers, I caught the smell of her breath. It was a subtle odour – metallic. I thought of grated steel, if there is such a smell. I saw that her lips were edged with a thin blue line as if touched by extreme cold. My mum followed my thoughts, opening her mouth and sticking out her tongue for examination. The tip was black, the colour of octopus ink. She said:

'Poison.'

Before I could query the astounding claim, she shook her head and pointed at the cab driver, reminding me of her desire for discretion. I wondered what tests the doctors in Sweden had carried out, what poisons had been discovered, if any. Most importantly, I wondered who my mum suspected of poisoning her.

*

The cab pulled up outside my apartment building only a few hundred metres from the spot where I'd abandoned my groceries last night. My mum had never visited before, held back by my protest that it was embarrassing to share a flat with other people and have my parents come round. I don't know why they'd accepted such a feeble lie or how I'd had the stomach to voice it. For the time being, I'd play along with the story I'd created for myself, not wishing to sidetrack my mum with revelations of my own. I guided her inside the apartment, belatedly realising that anyone paying attention would notice that only one bedroom was in use. The second bedroom was set up as a study. As I unlocked the front door I hurried ahead. My mum always removed her shoes upon entering a home, which would give me enough time to close the doors to the bedroom and study. I returned:

'I wanted to see if anyone else was home. But it's fine, we're alone.'

My mum was pleased. However, outside the two closed doors she paused. She wanted to check for herself. I put my arm around her, guiding her upstairs, and said:

'I promise, it's just you and me.'

Standing in the open-plan kitchen and living room, the heart of Mark's apartment, my mum was fascinated with her first look at my home. Mark had always described his taste as minimalist, relying on the view over the city to provide character. When I'd moved in there was barely any furniture. Far from stylish, the apartment had felt empty and sad. Mark had slept there, eaten there, but not lived. Bit by bit I'd made suggestions. His possessions didn't need to be hidden. Boxes could be unpacked. I watched my mum trace my line of influence with remarkable accuracy. She picked a book off the shelves, one she'd given me as a gift. I blurted out:

'I don't own this place.'

I'd lied for years, readily and easily, but today the lies were painful, like running on a twisted ankle. My mum took my hand and said:

'Show me the garden.'

Mark had hired the company I work for to design and plant a roof garden. He claimed he'd intended to do it, but it was a favour to me, a form of patronage. My parents had always been quietly baffled by my choice of profession, believing I'd do something different from them. They'd both left school at sixteen, while I'd attended university, only to end up doing the same job they'd done all their lives, more or less, except rubber-stamped by a degree and starting out with twenty thousand pounds of debt. But I'd spent my whole childhood around plants and flowers; I'd inherited my parents' gift for growing, and the work, when it trickled through, made me happy. Sitting on the roof, looking out over London, among those plants, it was easy to forget anything was wrong. I wanted to stay like this forever, basking in the sun, clinging onto the silence. However, I noticed my mum wasn't interested in the garden; she was assessing the layout of the roof, the fire exits, identifying escape routes. She checked her watch, a great impatience sweeping over her:

'We don't have much time.'

Before hearing her version of events I offered food. My mum politely declined, wanting to press on:

'There's so much I need to tell you.'

I insisted. One incontestable truth was that she'd lost weight. Unable to find out when she'd last eaten – my mum was evasive on the subject – I set about blending a drink of bananas, strawberries and local honey. She stood, studying the process:

'You trust me, don't you?'

Her instincts were extreme caution and heightened suspicion, only allowing me to use fruit that she'd examined. To prove the blended fruit was safe I tasted it before handing her the glass. She took the smallest possible sip. She met my glance, understanding that it had become a test of her state of mind. Her attitude changed and she began to take hasty long gulps. Finished with the drink, she declared:

'I need the bathroom.'

I was worried she was going to make herself sick, but I could hardly insist upon going with her.

'It's downstairs.'

She left the kitchen, clasping the satchel that never left her side.

I took out my phone to find thirty or more missed calls from my dad. I dialled him, whispering:

'Dad, she's here, she's safe. I can't speak—'

He interrupted:

'Wait! Listen to me!'

It was a risk speaking to him like this, and I was anxious about being caught. I turned, intending to move towards the top of the stairs so that I might hear when my mum was returning. But she was already there, at the edge of the room, watching me. She couldn't have been to the bathroom so quickly. She must have lied, setting a test of her own, to see how I'd make use of the time. If it was a test I'd failed. She was staring at me in a way that I'd never seen before. I was no longer her son but a threat – an enemy.

I was caught between the two of them. My mum said:

'That's him, isn't it?'

The formality was gone – she was accusatory and aggressive. My dad heard her voice in the background:

'Is she there?'

I couldn't move, paralysed by indecision, the phone against my ear – my eyes on my mum. My dad said:

'Daniel, she can become violent.'

Hearing my dad say this, I shook my head – no, I didn't believe it. My mum had never hurt anyone in her life. Dad was mistaken. Or he was lying. My mum stepped forward, pointing at the phone:

'Say another word to him and I'll walk out.'

With my dad's voice still audible, I cut him off.

As though I were surrendering a weapon, I offered the handset to my mum. My voice faltered as I pleaded my defence:

'I promised to ring Dad when you arrived. Just to let him know you were safe. Just like I promised to listen to you. Please, Mum, let's sit down together. You wanted to tell me your story. I want to listen.'

'The doctors examined me. Did he tell you that? They examined me, heard my story, and they let me go. The professionals believed me. They didn't believe him.'

She stepped towards me, offering her bag – her evidence. Granted a second chance, I met her in the middle of the room, taking hold of the cracked leather. It required an act of willpower for my mum to let go. I was surprised by how heavy the bag was. As I placed the satchel on the dining table my dad rang again, his image appearing on the screen. Mum saw his face:

'You can answer the phone. Or open the bag.'

Ignoring the phone, I placed one hand on the top of the satchel, pressing down in order to release the buckle, the leather creaking as I lifted the flap and looked inside.

•   •   •

MY MUM REACHED INTO THE SATCHEL, pulling out a small compact mirror, showing me my reflection as if it were the first article of her evidence. I looked tired, but my mum offered a different observation.

You're afraid of me, I can tell. I know your face better than my own, and if that sounds like a silly-sentimental exaggeration, consider how many times I've wiped away your tears or watched you smile. Daniel, in all those years you've never looked at me like this—

See for yourself!

But I mustn't become upset. It's not your fault. I've been framed, not as a criminal but as a psychotic. Your instincts are to side with your father. There's no point denying it, we must be honest with each other. On several occasions I've caught you staring at me nervously. My enemies declare that I'm a danger to myself and to others, even a danger to you, my son. That's how unscrupulous they are, vandalising the most precious relationship in my life, prepared to do anything in order to stop me.

Let me quickly remind you that the allegation of being mentally incapable is a tried and tested method of silencing women dating back hundreds of years, a weapon to discredit us when we fought against abuses and stood up to authority. That said, I accept that my appearance is alarming. My arms are wasted away, my clothes are tatty, my nails chipped, and my breath bad. I've spent my life striving to be presentable, and today you looked me up and down at the airport and you thought—

'She's sick!'

Wrong. I'm thinking more clearly than ever before.

At times you might find my voice unusual. You might decide that I don't sound like myself. But you can't expect me to speak with everyday ease when there are such serious consequences if I fail to convince you. Nor can you expect me to skip ahead to the most shocking incidents and tell you in a few quick words what is going on. If I outline in brief you'll be overwhelmed. You'll shake your head and roll your eyes. A summary won't do. You'll hear words like 'murder' and 'conspiracy' and you won't accept them. Instead, I must lay down the details one by one. You must see how the pieces fit together. Without the complete picture you'll consider me mad. You will. You'll escort me to some Victorian-built asylum in some forgotten corner of London and inform the doctors that I'm sick in the head. As though I were the criminal, as though I were the person who'd done awful wrongs, they'll imprison me until I'm so desperate to be released, so numb on their drugs I'll agree that everything I'm about to tell you is a lie. Bearing in mind the power you hold over me I should be afraid of you. And look at me, Daniel, look at me! I am afraid.

• • •

IT WAS LESS LIKE NORMAL SPEECH, more like words unleashed. Sentences dammed up in my mum's mind came tumbling out, fast but never uncontrolled. She was right: she didn't sound like herself – her voice was elevated, as strange as it was impressive. At times she sounded judicial, at other times intimate. She hadn't spoken in this way at the airport or during the train ride home. It was unlike anything I'd heard from her before, in terms of energy and breathless quantity. It was a performance more than a conversation. Was my mum really afraid of me? Her hands certainly trembled as she placed the mirror down on the table, not back in the satchel, signalling that she'd proceed through the contents one by one. If I hadn't been afraid before I was afraid now. On some level I must have been hoping that a simple resolution could be found in this room, between the two of us, without involving doctors or detectives – a quiet end, a soft landing and a gentle return to our lives as they had been. However, my mum's energies were so agitated that she was either very ill or something truly terrible had taken place in Sweden to provoke them.

A vast amount depends on you believing me, more than is fair to place on your shoulders. I'll admit that with so much at stake it's tempting to exploit our relationship and play on your emotions. However, I'll resist, because my case needs to stand on its own, supported by facts, not propped up by your devotion to me. For that reason you shouldn't think of me as your mother but as Tilde, the accuser—

Don't be upset! Be objective. That's your only duty today.

Throughout you'll be asking how Chris, a kind, gentle man, an excellent father to you, how can he be at the centre of such serious allegations? Consider this. There's a weakness in his character that other people can manipulate. He prefers compromise to conflict. He surrenders easily. He's susceptible to forceful opinions. And he has urges like everyone else. I believe he was led astray, manipulated in particular by one man – a villain.

*   *   *

M Y DAD WAS A MAN WHO could name every plant and flower, a man who never raised his voice, a man who loved wandering among forests – allegations of wrongdoing didn't hang easily off him. My mum sensed my hesitation and responded to it with impressive sensitivity:

You mistrust that word?

Villain.

You think it sounds unreal?

Villains are real. They walk among us. You can find them on any street, in any community, in any home – on any farm.

What is a villain? They're people who will stop at nothing in the pursuit of their desires. I know of no other word to describe the man I have in mind.

In this satchel is some of the evidence I've collected over the summer. There was more but this was all I could smuggle out of Sweden in such a rush. It makes sense to address each article of evidence in chronological order, starting with this—

• • •

FROM THE FRONT POCKET of the satchel my mum lifted a black leather-bound Filofax, the kind that was popular twenty years ago. It contained papers, photographs and clippings.

Originally intended as a place to jot down my thoughts, this has turned out to be the most important purchase I've ever made. Flicking through, you can see I took more and more notes as the months went by. Check the pages in April, when I first arrived at the farm. They contain only the occasional scribble. Compare that to July, three months later, writing squeezed into every line. This book was a way of figuring out what was going on around me. It became my companion, a partner in my investigation. No matter what others say, here are the facts written down at the time events took place, or at most a few hours after. If it were possible to analyse the aging of the ink then forensic science would support my claim.

Every now and then I'm going to pause and refer to these notes in order to prevent any mistakes. No artistic licence is allowed. If I'm unable to remember a particular detail and it isn't written down I won't attempt to fill in the blanks. You need to believe that every word I say is true. Even a harmless descriptive flourish is unacceptable. For example, I will not state that there were birds singing in the treetops unless I can be sure of it. If you suspect I'm embellishing rather than presenting the bare bones of what actually happened my credibility will suffer.

Finally let me add that I'd do anything for the troubles of these past months to exist solely in my mind. My God, that explanation would be easy. The horror of an asylum and the humiliation of being branded a fantasist would be a small price to pay if it meant that the crimes I'm about to describe never really took place.

• • •

So far we'd been standing with the satchel resting on the table. My mum gestured for me to sit down, indicating that her account would take some time. I obeyed, taking a position opposite her, the satchel between us as though it were the stakes in a poker game. She studied her journal, focused on finding the relevant entry. Briefly I was taken back to the many occasions when she'd read to me at bedtime, saddened by the contrast between the tranquillity of those childhood memories and the anxiety I was now feeling. It might seem that I lacked curiosity or courage, but my impulse was to implore her not to read.

Last time you saw me was on the day of our leaving party. 15 April. We hugged goodbye beside that old white van packed with all our worldly possessions. It was one of those days when everyone was in high spirits, laughing so much – a happy day, truly happy, honestly among the happiest in my life. Yet even that happiness is now the subject of dispute. Looking back, Chris claims I was chasing a perfect life in Sweden and a gap opened in my mind between expectation and reality, a gap that expanded as the months progressed, and out of my disappointment was born the belief that there was, in place of paradise, a hell of depravity and human disgrace. It's a seductive argument. And it's a lie, a clever lie, because underneath the laughter I understood better than anyone the difficulties ahead.

Here's what you don't know, Daniel. We're broke. Our family has no money. None. You knew there were

32

difficulties during the recession. It was far worse than we let on. Our business was in ruins. It was necessary to deceive you because Chris and I were embarrassed and didn't want offers of money. Let me be honest – today is a day for honesty and nothing else – I was ashamed. I'm still ashamed.

* * *

HEARING THE NEWS, I REACTED with a muddle of shame, sadness and shock. Mostly there was disbelief. I simply hadn't known. I hadn't even suspected. How was it possible I could be so ignorant of their circumstances? I was about to put the question to my mum, but she sensed that I intended to interrupt and touched the top of my hand to stop me.

Let me finish.

Please.

You can speak in a minute.

I'd always been in charge of the accounts. I'd run a tight ship for thirty years. We'd been okay. The garden centre never made much money. But we didn't hanker after wealth. We kept our heads above water. We loved our work. If we didn't holiday abroad for a couple of years, we'd go for day trips to the beach. We always got by. We were light on debt, low on overheads, and good at our jobs. Our customers were loyal. Even when the cheaper out-of-town garden centres opened up we survived.

You were living away from home when the letter landed on our doorstep from an estate agent. They explained the true value of our tiny garden centre. It was incredible. I could never have dreamed of such wealth. We'd spent our life working long hours, growing plants, and earning the slimmest of margins while underneath our feet the land which we'd done nothing to had increased in value so dramatically it was worth more than we'd ever earned through work. For the first time in our lives Chris and I were drunk on the idea of money. We bought you dinners in fancy restaurants. We gloated like fools. Rather than simply sell up, I made the decision to borrow hundreds of thousands against the value of our land. Everyone said it made sense. Why hold on to money? Property was like magic: it could produce wealth without work. Neglecting the garden centre, employing staff to half-heartedly do the tasks we'd always done passionately ourselves, we bought investment flats. On the face of it, Chris and I made the decisions jointly, but you know him – he's not interested in numbers. He took a back seat. I found the flats. I chose them. Within the space of six months we owned five and we were looking to own ten, a number I'd plucked from the air because it sounded better than nine. We started using phrases like 'our property portfolio'. I blush to think of it. We spoke of those flats as if we'd actually built them with our bare hands. We marvelled at how their value had increased by seven, eight, nine per cent in a single year. In my defence, it wasn't outright greed. I was planning for our retirement. Running a garden centre is backbreaking work. We couldn't do it forever. We weren't even sure we could manage another year. We didn't have any money saved up. We didn't have a pension. This was our way out.

They're calling me mad now, but five years ago I was mad, or touched with a kind of madness. That's the only way I can explain it. I lost my mind. I ventured into a business I knew nothing about, abandoning a livelihood that was in our blood and bones. When the recession hit, our bank was on the brink of collapse. The very institution that had convinced us to borrow and invest now looked upon us as if we were an abomination. We were their creation! They wanted their money back even faster than they'd been happy to give it to us. We were forced to sell everything, all five flats, you knew that, but you didn't appreciate the losses we were making on each. We'd put the deposit down on a new build. Since we couldn't complete the purchase the money was lost. Completely lost! Our backs were against the wall. We sold our home and the garden centre. We were pretending to everyone, not just to you, that it was part of a grand plan. We brought forward our retirement under the guise that we were sick and tired of the whole enterprise. That was a lie. There was no choice.

With what little money remained we bought the farm in Sweden. That's why we found somewhere remote and run-down. We presented it to you as the pursuit of the idyllic. True, but we also bought it cheap, for less than the price of a garage in London. Cheap as it was, once the costs of relocating were included, we were left with nine thousand pounds. Quote the figure to any financial adviser and they'd state categorically that it can't be done, there are two of us, four and a half thousand pounds each, we're in our sixties – we might live for another three decades. There was nothing to fall back on. We were betting our future on a far-flung farm in the middle of nowhere in a country unknown to me for fifty years.

Not having money in London is crippling. Board a bus and they charge you two pounds. A loaf of market bread can cost four pounds. On our farm we were going to rewrite the rules of modern living, happiness without the need of credit cards and cash. We'd cycle everywhere. Petrol would be saved for emergencies only. There'd be no need for holidays. Why take a holiday when you were living in one of the most beautiful locations in the world? In the summer there was the river to swim in, in the winter snow for skiing – activities that cost nothing. We'd reconnect our lives with nature, growing our own food, with plans for a vast vegetable garden supplemented with foraging, baskets of wild berries and chanterelle mushrooms, thousands of pounds' worth if you bought the equivalent in any delicatessen. Your father and I would go back to doing what we'd always done, what we did best, what we were put on this earth to do – to plant and grow.

Despite how it sounds, making these plans wasn't a miserable task. It didn't depress me. We were pruning our existence back to the essentials not out of some pious philosophy that austerity was good for the soul. To live within our means was the only way to be truly independent.

We were pilgrims seeking a new life, escaping the oppression of debt. On the boat to Sweden, Chris and I spent the evening seated on the deck looking up at the stars with a blanket over our knees and a Thermos of tea, strategising household economy as if it were a military operation because we vowed never to borrow money again, there'd never be another letter from the bank threatening us, no more suffocating helplessness at a stack of bills, never, never again!

• • •

FORCING A BREAK, I STOOD UP. Walking to the window, I rested my head against the glass. I'd been certain that my parents could comfortably support themselves through their retirement. They'd sold five apartments, the family home and the garden centre. The recession had hit the value of their properties, that was true, but their decisions never seemed troubled. They were always smiling and joking. It had been an act, one I'd fallen for. They'd presented their decision as part of a master plan. Moving to Sweden was a change of lifestyle, not a means of survival. In my mind, their life on the farm was one of leisure, growing their own food out of preference rather than desperate necessity. Most humiliating of all, I'd flirted with the idea of asking them for a loan, confident that a sum of two thousand pounds was insignificant to them. I shuddered to think of requesting the money with no idea of the anguish it would've caused. If I'd been rich I would've offered all my money to Mum, every penny, and begged forgiveness. But I had nothing to offer. I wondered whether I'd allowed myself to be casual about my own lack of money because I'd been certain that everyone close to me – my parents and Mark – was secure. My mum joined me at the window, misunderstanding my reaction:

'Right now, money is the least of our worries.'

That was only partly true. My family was in financial crisis, but it was not the crisis my mum wanted to talk about, it was not the crisis that had made her board a plane this morning. It struck me that if I didn't know about their finances, what else didn't I know? Just a few minutes ago I'd dismissed my mum's description of Dad. I was wrong to be so sure. I had no firm evidence yet as to the reliability of my mum's account, but I had concrete evidence that my insights were untrustworthy. The only logical conclusion, at this point, was that I wasn't up to the task at hand and I considered whether to seek help. However, I held my tongue, determined to prove that my mum had been right to turn to me in her hour of need. Since I had no right to be angry – after all, I'd lied to them over a great many years – I tried to keep my voice soft, asking the question:

'When were you going to tell me?'

When you visited the farm we planned to tell you everything. Our worry was that if we'd discussed being self-sufficient while we were still in London you'd have thought our plans far-fetched and unachievable. When you were on the farm, you'd see the vegetable garden, you'd eat food that had cost us nothing. We'd walk among our fruit trees. You'd pick baskets of mushrooms and berries that grow wild in the forests. You'd see a larder full of home-made jams and pickles. Your father would catch a salmon from the river and we'd feast like kings, with a stomach full of the most delicious food in the world and all of it free. Our cash poverty would seem an irrelevance. We'd be rich in other ways. Our lack of money wasn't a threat to our well-being. That's easier to demonstrate than explain. Which is why we were secretly pleased when you delayed your visit; it gave us time to make changes, to better prepare the farm and build a convincing case that we were going to be okay and you didn't need to worry.

•   •   •

M Y FIRST VISIT TO THE FARM would've been a feast of home-grown produce and home-grown deceit – theirs and mine. No wonder my parents hadn't pressed harder into my vague reasons for delaying my visit. It was to their advantage too, buying time, the three of us getting ready to undress our lies. My mum's insistence that I should be spared from worry was a further reminder of how incapable they considered me. Yet my mum's attitude had changed. She was no longer protecting me. Whether I was ready or not, she would not spare me any upsetting detail today. She took my hand, guiding me back to my seat, her impatience suggesting that this revelation was a small matter compared to the crimes she wanted to address. From her satchel she tugged free a crinkled map of Sweden, unfolding it on the table.

How did we come to live in this particular region of Sweden – a region unknown to me, an area where I have no family or friends, where I've never spent any time?

The farm's situated here—

Chris and I considered countless locations, mostly in the far north, beyond Stockholm, where prices were cheaper. During our search, Cecilia, the elderly woman who owned the farm, sought us out as buyers. I told you that it was a slice of remarkable good luck. We received a call from an estate agent asking if we wanted to view the property. More unusual, the seller wanted to personally meet us. We'd registered our details with the local agents, but the southern province of Halland is popular – many people have second homes there – and

41

it's expensive. After confessing to our limited budget we hadn't been sent the details of any farms until this call. We examined the particulars. It seemed perfect. There was bound to be a catch.

When we visited, our expectations were confounded. It was perfect! Do you remember how excited we were? The farm was close to the sea, less than thirty minutes by bicycle, a region with white sand beaches, old-fashioned ice cream parlours and summer hotels. The land included a small orchard, a pontoon on the Ätran River, famous for its salmon. Yet the price was incomprehensibly low. The owner, Cecilia, was a widow without children. There was a pressing medical need for her to move into a care home, therefore she wanted a quick sale. During our interview we didn't dig any deeper. I was so bewitched by the property that I interpreted it as a sign that my return to Sweden was blessed and that our fortunes had finally changed.

You must have wondered why I never got in touch with my father during this process. Part of me understands why you didn't ask the question. I've given the impression that my childhood wasn't a topic to be discussed. And you've always enjoyed the fact that it was just the three of us in our family. Perhaps you imagined three bonds were stronger than four or five. Nonetheless, I'm sorry that your grandfather is a stranger to you and has never been part of our family life. He still lives on the same farm where I grew up. That farm isn't in

Halland, where we'd bought our home, but in the province of Värmland, to the north of us, on the far face of the great Lake Vänern, between the cities of Gothenburg and Stockholm—

Here—

We'd be a six-hour car drive apart.

The distance speaks for itself. The sad truth is that I didn't want to attempt a reunion with him. Too much time had passed. My return was to Sweden, not to him. He's now in his eighties. Some might consider wanting to be far away cruel, but there's no mystery to our estrangement. When I was sixteen I asked for his help. He refused. And it became impossible to stay.

Don't concern yourself with my handwritten annotations. We'll come to those later. On second thoughts, since you've seen them now it would be worth noting the scale of these crimes. The conspiracy stretches across the entire region and touches many lives, including local authorities and institutions, politicians and police officers. There's so much to tell you and so little time. As we speak, Chris will be booking his flight to London. Very soon he'll be arriving at your apartment, hammering on your door, demanding—

• • •

I INTERRUPTED, RAISING MY HAND as if I were in class: 'Dad isn't flying over. He's staying in Sweden.'

Is that what he told you? He wants you to think that he doesn't need to be here and doesn't need to make his case because there's no doubt in his mind that you're going to dismiss everything I say. He's completely confident you'll come to the only possible conclusion – that I am insane. Well, no matter what he claimed about staying in Sweden, that man will be in frantic conference with his co-conspirators. Together they'll order him over to London at the first possible opportunity to make sure I'm institutionalised. Any minute now he'll call to say that he's changed his mind, he's bought a ticket, he's at the airport about to fly. He'll disguise this about-face with some noble-sounding excuse, pretending to be worried as to how you're coping. You wait and see! He'll prove me right, which is why that lie was a miscalculation. I'm sure he's kicking himself because soon you'll have incontestable evidence of his deception—

•   •   •

WITHOUT FINISHING HER SENTENCE, my mum rose up out of her chair and hurried downstairs. I followed her to the front door, fearing that I'd done something wrong and she was about to leave.

'Wait!'

Instead, she slid the chain across the door and turned to face me, determined to secure the apartment. I was so relieved she hadn't fled that I took a moment to steady my voice:

'Mum, you're safe here. Please take the chain off the latch.'

'Why not leave it on?'

I couldn't think of a reason to disagree apart from the fact that the chain made me uneasy. It was a tacit acceptance that my dad was a threat – something that hadn't yet been proved. To end the stalemate I gave in:

'Leave it, if you want.'

My mum shot me a knowing glance. She could win a minor victory but it would count against her. She lifted the chain off and let it drop. Irritated, she shooed me upstairs, trailing behind.

You're making the same mistakes I did. I underestimated Chris. Just like you, I gave him the benefit of the doubt, again and again, until it was too late. He's probably already on a flight. There was one departing only a few hours after mine. He might not give us any warning.

•   •   •

45

BACK AT THE TABLE, HER DISSATISFACTION with me still lingering, my mum folded the map, picking up her diary again, reorienting herself after the interruption. I picked a different seat, closer to her, without the bulk of the table between us. She showed me the entry marked 16 April, the date they'd first arrived at the farm. All that was written on the page was the note, 'what a strange fast-moving sky'.

On the drive to Sweden, in our white van, I was excited but I was scared too, scared that I'd set myself an impossible challenge trying to reclaim this land as my home after so many years. The responsibility rested on my shoulders. Chris didn't speak a word of the language. He had no more than a passing acquaintance with Swedish traditions. I'd be the bridge between our cultures. These issues didn't matter to him – he was a foreigner, his identity was clear. But what was I? Was I a foreigner or a national? Neither English nor Swedish, an outsider in my own country – what name is there for me?

Utlänning!

That's what they'd call me! It's a cruel Swedish word, one of the cruellest words, meaning a person from outside this land. Even though I'd been born and raised in Sweden, the community would consider me a foreigner, a foreigner in my own home – I'd be an *utlänning* there as I'd been in London.

Utlänning here!

Utlänning there!
Utlänning everywhere!

Looking out the window I was reminded of just how lonely this landscape was. In Sweden, outside the cities, the wilderness rules supreme. People tiptoe timidly around the edge, surrounded by skyscraping fir trees and lakes larger than entire nations. Remember, this is the landscape that inspired the mythology of trolls, stories I used to read to you about giant lumbering man-eating creatures with mushroom warts on their crooked noses and bellies like boulders. Their sinewy arms can rip a person in two, snapping human bones and using splinters to scrape the gristle out of their shrapnel teeth. Only in forests as vast as this could such monsters be hiding, yellow eyes stalking you.

Along the final stretch of deserted road before the farm, there were bleak brown fields, the winter snow had melted away but the topsoil was hard and jagged with ice. There was no sign of life, no crops, no tractors, no farmers – stillness, but overhead the clouds were moving incredibly fast, as though the sun were a plug that had been pulled out of the horizon and the clouds, along with the dregs of daylight, were being sucked down a sinkhole. I couldn't take my eyes off this fast-moving sky. After a short while I began to feel dizzy, my head began to spin. I asked Chris to stop the van because I felt nauseous. He carried on driving, arguing that we were almost there and it made no sense to stop. I asked again, less politely this time, to stop the van, only for him to repeat how close we were, and finally I banged my fists against the dashboard and demanded that he stop the van right this very second!

He looked at me like you're now looking at me. But he obeyed. I jumped out and was sick in the grassy verge, angry with myself, worried that I had ruined what should have been a joyful occasion. Too queasy to climb back into the vehicle, I instructed Chris to drive on, intending to walk the last distance. He refused, wanting us to arrive together. He declared the moment important symbolically. Therefore we decided that he'd drive at a snail's pace and I'd walk in front. As if I were leading a funeral procession I began the short walk to our new home, our farm, the van following behind – a ridiculous spectacle, I accept, but how else could we reconcile my need to walk, his need to drive the van, and the shared desire to arrive simultaneously?

Listening to Chris boohooing crocodile tears to the doctors at the Swedish asylum, he presented this episode as evidence of an irrational mind. If he were telling the story now he'd almost certainly have started his version of events here, omitting any mention of the strange fast-moving sky. Instead, he would've described me as baffling and fragile, unstable from the outset. That's what he claims, his voice strained with make-believe sadness. Who would have thought he was such an actor? Regardless of what he claims now, at the time he understood the emotions triggered by my return, an extraordinary feeling after fifty years, as extraordinary as the sky that welcomed me home.

Once we reached the farm he stepped out of the van, leaving it parked in the middle of the road. He took my hand. When we crossed over the threshold to our farm we did it together, as partners, as a loving couple starting an exciting new chapter in their life.

·   ·   ·

I REMEMBERED THESE PHRASES – 'shrapnel teeth' and 'bellies like boulders' – they were lifted from a Swedish collection of troll stories that we'd both loved. The book's cover had been missing and there was only one illustration of a troll near the front, a pair of dangerous dirty yellow eyes lurking in the depths of a forest. There were glossier books about trolls, sanitised child-friendly stories, but this tatty old anthology, long out of print, found in a secondhand bookstore, was filled with gruesome stories. By far it was my mum's favourite book to read at bedtime, and I'd heard each of the stories many times. My mum had kept the book among her collection, perhaps because it was in such a fragile condition that she feared it would fall apart in my hands. It was a contradiction that she'd always shielded me from trauma, yet when it came to fairy tales she'd wilfully sought out more disturbing stories, as if trying to compensate, giving me in fiction that which she'd tried so hard to take away from real life.

My mum unclipped three photographs from the journal and laid them side by side on the table in front of me. They matched up, forming a single panorama of their farm.

It is a pity that you never had a chance to visit. My task today would have been easier if you'd experienced the farm first-hand. Maybe with these photos you consider a description of the landscape unnecessary. That's exactly what my enemies hope you'll think, because they portray the countryside as being no different from the tourist-brochure stereotype of rural Sweden. They want you to conclude that anything other than an enthusiastic reaction is so bizarre that it could only be the product of sickness and paranoia. Be warned: they have a vested interest in presenting it as picturesque since beauty is easily mistaken for innocence.

Standing at the point where these photographs were taken, you're immersed in the most unbelievable quiet. It's like being at the bottom of the sea except instead of a rusted shipwreck there's an ancient farmhouse. Even the thoughts in my head sounded loud, and sometimes I found my heart beating hard for no reason except as a reaction against the silence.

You can't appreciate it from the photographs, but the thatched roof was alive, a living entity spotted with moss and small flowers, home to insects and birds – a fairytale roof in a fairytale setting – I use the word carefully, for fairy tales are full of danger and darkness as well as wonder and light.

The exterior of this ancient property hadn't been altered since its construction two hundred years ago. The only evidence of the modern world was the collection of red dots in the distance, beady rat eyes atop wind turbines, barely visible in the gloom, churning a morbid April sky.

Here's the crucial point. As the fact of isolation sinks into our consciousness we change, not at first but slowly, gradually, until we accept it as the norm, living day to day without the presence of the state, without the outside world chafing against our side, reminding us of our duty to each other, no passing strangers or nearby neighbours, no one peering over our shoulder – a permanent state of unwatched. It alters our notions of how we should behave, of what is acceptable, and, most important of all, what we can get away with.

* * *

THE MELANCHOLY IN MY MUM'S description didn't surprise me. There was always going to be more than straightforward happiness bound up in her return to Sweden. Aged sixteen she'd run away from her family home and carried on running, through Germany, Switzerland and Holland, working as a nanny and a waitress, sleeping on floors, until she'd reached England where she met my dad. Of course, this wasn't her first time back, we'd often holidayed in Sweden, renting remote cottages on islands or near lakes, never spending more than a day in the cities, partly due to expense but mostly because my mum wanted to be among the forests and wilderness. Within days of our arriving, empty jam jars would be filled with wildflowers. Bowls would be brimming with berries. Yet we'd never made an attempt to meet any relatives. Though I was content to spend the time with just my mum and dad, occasionally even I – naïve as I was – sensed sadness in the absence of other people.

My mum returned to the diary and seemed frustrated as she searched the pages.

I can't be sure of the exact day. It was roughly a week after we'd arrived. At that point I wasn't in the habit of taking many notes. The idea hadn't occurred to me that my word would be doubted as if I were a fanciful child making up stories for attention. Of the many humiliations I've experienced in these past few months, including having my hands and feet bound, by far the worst has been the disbelief in people's eyes as I make a statement. To speak, be heard, and not believed.

During our first week on the farm Chris's state of mind was cause for concern, not mine. He'd never lived outside a city and struggled to cope. April was far colder than we'd expected. The farmers have a term called Iron Nights, when winter clings on and spring can't break through. There's ice in the soil. Days are raw and short. The nights are bitter and long. Chris was depressed. And his depression felt like an accusation, that I was responsible for bringing him to a property with none of the modern conveniences, away from everything he knew, because I was Swedish and the farm was in Sweden. In reality, we'd made the decision together as a desperate fix to our circumstances. There was no choice. We were there, or nowhere. If we sold the farm we'd have money to rent a place for two or three years in England and then nothing.

One evening I'd had enough of his misery. The farmhouse isn't large – the ceilings are low, the walls are thick, the rooms are small – and we were spending all our time together, trapped inside by hostile weather. There was no central heating. In the kitchen there was a wrought-iron oven where you could bake bread, cook food and boil water – the heart of the house. When Chris wasn't sleeping he sat in front of it, hands outstretched, a pantomime of rural drudgery. I lost my temper, shouting at him to stop being such a glum bastard, before hurrying out, slamming the door—

• • •

I MUST HAVE REACTED TO THE IMAGE of my mum shouting at my dad.

Daniel, don't look so surprised. Your father and I argue, not often, not regularly, but like every other couple in the world we lose our tempers. We just made sure you never heard. You were so sensitive as a child. If we raised our voices you'd be upset for hours. You wouldn't sleep. You wouldn't eat. Once, at breakfast, I banged my hand against the table. You copied me! You started banging your little fists against your head. We had to hold your arms to stop you. Quickly we learned to control our tempers. Arguments were held back, stacked up, and we'd work through them when you were out.

.   .   .

I N NO MORE THAN A BRIEF ASIDE, my mum had swept away my entire conception of our family life. I'd no memory of behaving in this way – hitting my own head, refusing to eat, unable to sleep, disturbed by anger. I'd thought my parents had voluntarily taken a vow of tranquillity. The truth was that they'd been forced to shelter me not because they believed it for the best but because I demanded calm as though it were a requirement of my existence, the same as food or warmth. The sanctuary of our home was defined by my weakness as much as it was by their strength. My mum took my hand:

'Maybe I made a mistake coming to you.'

Even now she was worried I couldn't cope. And she was right to doubt me. Only a few minutes ago I'd felt an impulse to ask her not to speak, to cling on to silence.

'Mum, I want to listen – I'm ready.'

In an effort to conceal my anxiety, I tried to encourage her:

'You shouted at Dad. You walked out. You slammed the door. What happened next?'

It was shrewd to bring her focus back to events. Her desire to discuss the allegations was so powerful I could see her doubts about me disappearing as she was tugged back into the flow of her storytelling. Our knees touching, she lowered her voice as if imparting a conspiracy.

I set off towards the river. The waterfront was one of the most important parts of our property. We still needed a little cash to survive. We weren't producing our own electricity and there were annual land taxes. Our answer was salmon. We could eat the salmon in the summer, smoke and preserve it for the winter. We could sell some to fishmongers, but I saw the potential for more. We'd fix up the farm's outbuildings – they used to house live-stock but they could easily be converted into rustic guest accommodations. We'd carry out the work with minimal paid help since Chris and I were both handy with tools. Once that was complete, we'd open the farm as a holiday destination, guests lured to our obscure location with the promise of freshly grown food, a picturesque land-scape, and the prospect of catching some of the world's most beautiful salmon at a bargain price compared to fishing in Scotland or Canada. Despite its importance, in those early days Chris wouldn't spend any time down by the river. He said it was too bleak. He didn't see how our plans were possible. No one would ever pay to come to our farm. That's what he claimed. I admit that it wasn't picture-postcard-pretty when we arrived. The riverbank was overgrown, the grass was knee high, and I've never seen slugs so big, as fat as my thumb. But the potential was there. It just needed love.

At the river there was a small wooden jetty. In April it was entangled in reeds. Standing on it that evening, with a smudge of light in the sky, I felt tired and alone. After a few minutes I pulled myself together and decided it was time to swim and declare this river officially open for business! I stripped naked, dropping my clothes in a heap, and jumped into the water. The temperature was a shock. When I surfaced I gasped and started swimming frantically, trying to warm up until suddenly I stopped because on the opposite bank the low branches of a tree were moving. It can't have been the wind because the tops of the trees were motionless. It was something else – a person watching me, clasped around the branch. Alone and naked in the water, I was vulnerable. From this distance Chris couldn't hear me even if I screamed. Then the branches on the riverbank began to move again, breaking from the tree, sliding towards me. I should have swum away, as fast as I could, but my body wouldn't obey and I remained where I was, treading water as the branches drew closer. Except they weren't branches! They were the antlers of a giant elk.

Never in my childhood years in Sweden had an elk been this close to me. I was careful not to splash or make a noise as the elk passed so close I could've reached out and hooked my arms around its thick neck, lifted myself up and mounted its back, just like in those stories I'd read to you where a forest princess rides naked on the back of an elk, her long silver hair catching the moonlight. I must have exclaimed in wonder, because the elk swung around, turning its face towards me – black eyes staring into mine, its warm breath on my face. Around my thighs I could feel the water disturbed by its powerful legs. Then it snorted and swam to our side of the river, walking out onto our farmland beside the jetty and revealing its mighty proportions, truly a king of this land. It shook the water off its coat, steam rising from its skin, before slowly heading back towards the forests.

I remained in the middle of the river for several minutes, treading water, no longer cold, blessed with absolute certainty that we'd made the right decision in moving here. There was a reason we were at this farm. We belonged here. I closed my eyes, imagining thousands of brightly coloured salmon swimming around me.

• • •

M Y MUM REACHED INTO THE SATCHEL and pulled out a knife. Instinctively I recoiled, a reaction that concerned my mum: 'I startled you?'

It was an accusation. The manner in which she'd abruptly brandished the knife, without warning, made me wonder whether she was deliberately testing me in the same way as before, when she'd left me alone, and I made a mental note to be on my guard against any future attempts to provoke me. She flipped the knife around, offering me the handle:

'Hold it.'

The entire knife was carved from wood, including the blade, painted silver to resemble metal. It was quite blunt and harmless. On the handle there were intricate engravings. On one side there was a naked woman bathing by the rocks of a lake, with large breasts and long flowing hair, her vagina marked by a single notch. On the other side there was a troll's face, his tongue hanging out like a panting dog and his nose mischievously shaped like a grotesque phallus.

It's a type of humour you probably recognise, popular in rural Sweden, where farmers craft crude figures such as a man relieving himself, a thin curve of wood chiselled to represent the arc of piss.

Rotate the knife on your palm, backwards and forwards—

Spinning it like this—

Faster! So you can see both figures at the same time, the troll lusting after the woman, the woman unaware she's being watched – the two blurred together. The implication is clear. The fact of the woman being blind to her danger heightens the sexual pleasure of the troll.

The knife was a gift, a strange gift, I'm sure you'd agree, given to me by my neighbour the first time we met. Despite him being only a ten-minute walk from our farm, that meeting didn't take place until we'd lived in Sweden for two weeks – two weeks, and in all that time, not a single introduction from any of the nearby farmers. We were being ignored. Instructions had been given not to approach us. In London there are countless neighbours who never speak to each other. But anonymity doesn't exist in rural Sweden. It isn't possible to live that way. We required the consent of the community to settle in that region, we couldn't sulk in our corner of the countryside. There were practical considerations. The previous owner – brave Cecilia – had informed me that our spare land could be leased to local farmers. Typically they'd pay a nominal sum, however, I was of the opinion that we could persuade them to provide the foodstuffs we couldn't produce.

Deciding that two weeks was long enough, I woke up one morning and told Chris we'd knock on their door if they wouldn't knock on ours. That day I took great care over my appearance, selecting a pair of cotton trousers since a dress would've implied I was incapable of manual labour. I didn't want to play poverty. We couldn't admit the extent of our financial problems. The truth might make us seem pitiful, and they'd interpret the information as an insult, deducing that we'd only moved into the region because we couldn't afford to be anywhere else. Equally we couldn't give off the impression that we believed we could buy our way into the community. On the spur of the moment I took down the small Swedish flag hanging from the side of our house and turned the flag into a bandana, using it to tie back my hair.

Chris refused to accompany me. He couldn't speak Swedish and was too proud to stand beside me waiting for a translation. To tell the truth, I was pleased. First impressions were vital and I was sceptical they'd react warmly to an Englishman who barely spoke a word of their language. I wanted to prove to these farmers that we weren't hapless foreign city folk who placed no value on tradition. I couldn't wait to see their faces light up when I spoke to them in fluent Swedish, proudly declaring that I'd been brought up on a remote farm, just like the one we now owned.

The farm nearest to us belonged to the largest landowner in the region and it was with this particular farmer that Cecilia had struck an arrangement to lease the fields. It was obvious that I should begin with him. Walking up the road I arrived at an enormous pig barn, no windows, a bleak steel roof with narrow black chimneys jutting out the top and a smell of pig shit and pig-fattening chemicals. Qualms about intensive farming were not going to win over the locals. What's more, Chris had stated clearly that he couldn't survive as a vegetarian. There was very little protein in our diet and almost no money in the bank, so if this was our only source of meat, aside from the salmon, then I couldn't afford to turn it down on the basis of food ethics. A moral position would make me seem superior, fussy and, worst of all, foreign.

Their house was situated at the end of a long gravel drive. Every window on the front looked out onto the pig barn, odd when you consider that there were fields and trees in the other directions. Unlike our farmhouse, which was built two hundred years ago, they'd torn down the original property and put in its place a modern house. By modern I don't mean a cube of glass, concrete and steel; it was traditionally shaped, on two floors, with pale blue timber cladding, a veranda, a slate roof. They wanted the appearance of tradition but all the advantages of modernity. Our farmhouse, despite its many failings, was more appealing, a genuine representative of Swedish architectural heritage rather than an imitation.

When I knocked on the door there was no reply, but their gleaming silver Saab – and Saab's not even a Swedish company any more – was in the drive. They were at home, most probably out on the land. In search of them I set off, walking through their fields, absorbing the sheer enormity of their property, an agricultural kingdom – perhaps fifty times the size of our little farm. Nearing the river, I came across a gentle slope covered in weeds, a bump in the landscape. Except it was man-made. Under the mound was the roof of a shelter not dissimilar to the bomb shelters constructed in London during the war or tornado shelters built in America. There was a steel door made from the same material as the roof of the pig barn. The padlock was hanging open. Taking a chance, I knocked and heard a commotion inside. Seconds later the door was pulled open. That was the first time I came face to face with Håkan Greggson.

. . .

FROM HER JOURNAL MY MUM produced a newspaper clipping. She held it up for inspection, her cracked nail slicing across the head of Håkan Greggson. I'd seen him before, in the photograph my mum had emailed – the tall stranger in conversation with my dad.

The clipping is from the front page of *Hallands Nyheter*. The majority of people in the region subscribe. When we refused, because we couldn't afford the cost, there was malicious chitchat about why we'd snubbed a local institution. There was no option but to subscribe. Chris was furious. I explained to him that you can't put a price on fitting in. Anyway, I'm showing this to you because you need to understand the power of the man I'm up against.

Håkan's in the centre.

To his right is the tipped-to-be leader of the Christian Democrats, Marie Eklund. A stern woman, one day she's going to be a great politician, by 'great' I mean success-ful rather than decent. She failed me. I went to her in person, with my allegations, at the height of the crisis. Her office refused to grant me an audience. She wouldn't even hear me speak.

On Håkan's left is the mayor of Falkenberg, the sea-side town nearest our farm. Kristofer Dalgaard. His friendliness is so excessive you can't help but question it. He laughs too loudly at your jokes. He's too interested in your opinions. Unlike Marie Eklund, he doesn't have any ambition except to stay exactly where he is, but maintaining the status quo can be as powerful a motivation as wanting to climb upwards.

And finally there's Håkan. He's handsome. I don't deny it. He's even more impressive when you meet him in person. Tall with broad shoulders, physically he's immensely powerful. His skin is tough and tanned. There's nothing soft about his body – nothing weak. He's rich enough to employ an army of people while he could act like a decadent emperor, issuing orders from his veranda. That's not his way. He wakes at dawn and doesn't finish work until the evening. When you're in his presence it's hard to imagine him ever being vulnerable. When he grabs you his grip is unbreakable. Though fifty years old, he has the vigour of a young man, with the cunning of an older man – a dangerous combination. I found him intimidating, even on that first day.

As he emerged from the gloom of his underground lair, I hastily launched into my introduction. I said something like – 'Hello, my name is Tilde, it's wonderful to meet you, I've moved into the farm down the road' – and yes, I was nervous. I spoke too much, and too quickly. In the middle of my good-natured babble I remembered the flag tied in my hair. I thought: how ridiculous! I blushed like a schoolgirl and tripped over my words. And do you know what he did? Think of the cruellest response.

• • •

M Y MUM HAD SO FAR ASKED several rhetorical questions. On
this occasion she was waiting for a reply. It was another
test. Could I imagine cruelty? Several possibilities occurred to me,
but they were so random and groundless that I decided to say:
  'I don't know.'

    Håkan answered in English. I was humiliated. Perhaps
    my Swedish was a little old-fashioned. But we were
    both Swedes. Why were we talking to each other in a for-
    eign tongue? I attempted to continue the conversation
    in Swedish but he refused to switch. I was confused, not
    wishing to seem rude. Remember, at this stage I wanted
    to be this man's friend. In the end, I replied in English.
    As soon as I did he smiled as if he'd won a victory. He
    started speaking in Swedish and never spoke to me in
    English again in all the time that I was in Sweden.

    As though this insult hadn't taken place, he showed me
    inside the shelter. It was a workshop. There were wood
    shavings on the floor, sharp tools on the walls. On almost
    every surface there were trolls carved out of wood, hundreds
    of them. Some were painted. Others were half-finished – a
    long nose poking out of a log, waiting for a face to be carved.
    Håkan claimed that he didn't sell any of them. They were
    given away as presents. He bragged that every house within
    twenty miles had at least one of his trolls, with some of his
    closest friends owning an entire troll family. You can see
    what he's doing? He uses those wooden trolls as medals,

awarding them to his trusted allies. When you cycle past anyone's farm, there are trolls in the window, lined up, one, two, three, four – father, mother, daughter, son, a complete set, a complete troll family, the highest honour Håkan could bestow, displayed as a statement of allegiance.

I wasn't given a troll. Instead, he handed me the knife and welcomed me to Sweden. I didn't pay much attention to the gift because I thought it inappropriate that I was being welcomed to my own country. I wasn't a guest. Irritated by his tone, I didn't notice the engravings on the handle, nor did I consider why he'd given me a knife rather than a troll figure. Now it's obvious – he didn't want me to have a troll displayed in our window in case people mistook it for a sign that we were friends.

As he showed me out, I caught sight of a second door, at the back of the shelter. A heavy-duty padlock hung from the lock. It might seem an irrelevant observation, but that second room will become important later. Hold it in your mind and ask yourself why it needed a second lock when there was already a lock on the front door.

Håkan proceeded to walk me back to the drive. He didn't invite me inside his house. He didn't offer coffee. He was escorting me off the premises. I was forced to raise the issue of renting our fields while we were walking, mentioning my idea about how we'd accept meat in exchange for the land. He had a different idea.

'How about I buy your whole farm, Tilde?'

I didn't laugh because he didn't seem to be making a joke. He was serious. Except it didn't make any sense. Why hadn't he simply bought the farm from Cecilia? I put this to him directly. He explained that he'd tried, claiming he'd offered twice as much as we'd paid and he would've offered three times as much, but Cecilia flatly turned him down. I asked why. He said none of their disagreements would interest me. However, he was happy to make me the same offer, the entire farm for three times the price we paid for it. We'd have trebled our money in the space of a few months. Before I could reply he added that life can be hard on a farm, instructing me to discuss it with my husband as though I were merely an envoy.

Let me be clear.

Before that conversation there'd been hardship and difficulties but no mystery. Now a question had been forced upon me, a question that kept me awake at night. Why had Cecilia sold the farm to a couple of outsiders with no personal connection to this region when the largest landowner in the region, a stalwart of the community and her neighbour for many years, coveted the property and was willing to pay much more?

∙ ∙ ∙

I SAW NO OBSTACLE STANDING between my mum and the truth: 'Why not ring Cecilia and ask her?'

That's exactly what I did. I hurried back to the farm and rang the nursing home – Cecilia had left a contact address and telephone number for a care home in Gothenburg. But if you thought a simple question would resolve the mystery, you're wrong. Cecilia was expecting the call. She asked me outright about Håkan. I explained that he'd offered to buy the farm. She became upset. She claimed to have sold us the farm because she wanted it to become our home. If I sold it for a quick profit it would be a betrayal of her trust. Now it became clear! That's why she instructed her agents to find buyers from further afield. That's why she used agents from Gothenburg, over an hour's drive away – she didn't trust any of the local agencies. She'd insisted on an interview as a vetting process to make sure we were unlikely to sell, trapped by our circumstances. I asked her why she didn't want Håkan to own the farm. I remember the following exchange exactly. She begged me:

'Tilde, please, that man must never own my farm.'

'But why?' I said.

She wouldn't elaborate. At the end of the conversation, I rang Håkan on the number he'd given me. While the phone was ringing I planned to speak to him calmly and politely. But as soon as I heard his voice I categorically declared:

'Our farm is not for sale!'

I hadn't even discussed the matter with Chris.

When Chris entered the kitchen he picked up Håkan's disgusting wooden knife. He looked at the naked woman. He looked at the sex-hungry troll. And he chuckled. I was glad I hadn't told him about the offer. I didn't trust his state of mind. Chris would've sold the farm.

Three days later the water in our taps turned brown, spotted with sediment, like dirty puddle water. These farms are so remote they're not on a mains system. They draw their water from individual wells. There was no option but to hire a specialist firm to dig a new well, wiping out half of our nine-thousand-pound reserve fund. While Chris despaired at our bad luck I didn't believe it was luck, the timing was too neat, the sequence too suspicious. I said nothing at the time. I didn't want to panic him. I didn't have any proof. There was no getting around the fact that our money might not last until the winter. We needed to accelerate our plans to make the farm pay if we were going to survive.

• • •

USING BOTH HANDS MY MUM pulled a rusted steel box from the satchel. The box was the size of a biscuit tin and very old. It was by far the largest item in the satchel.

When the contractors arrived to dig the well I found this buried in the soil, several metres below the surface. Chris and I were observing the work as though we were at a funeral, solemnly standing at the edge of the hole, saying farewell to half our money. As they dug deeper I caught a glimmer of light. I shouted for them to stop work, waving my arms. The contractors saw the commotion, shut down the drill, and before Chris could grab me I clambered down the hole. It was stupid. I could've been killed. I just had to save whatever was down there. When I emerged from the hole, clasping this box, everyone was yelling at me. No one cared about the box. All I could do was apologise and withdraw to the house, where I examined my discovery in private.

Lift the lid—
Take a look through them—
That's not what I discovered that day. Let me explain. The box did contain papers. It contained those same papers, but that writing wasn't on them. As you can see, the metal's cracked with rust in several places. The box had failed to keep out the moisture so the original ink on the pages had long since disappeared. You couldn't make out more than a few words. They were probably legal

documents. I should've thrown them on the fire. In my mind they were part of the farm's history. It felt wrong to destroy them, so I put them back in this box and left them under the sink. My next comment is very important: I thought no more about them.

I want to say that again because I can't tell whether you registered the point—

•   •   •

IN THE SPIRIT OF COLLABORATION, I interjected:
'You thought no more about them.'
She nodded appreciatively.

'When I returned outside, Håkan was standing where I'd been standing. It was his first time on our farm since we'd arrived—'

'Except for when he sabotaged the well, you mean?'

My mum acknowledged the seriousness with which I was treating her account rather than interpreting my question as pernickety scepticism.

I didn't witness that. So it was the first time I'd seen him on our land with my own eyes. But yes, you're right, he might have carried out the sabotage himself, or hired someone to do it for him. Anyway, that day his posture communicated a powerful sense of ownership as if this was already his property. Chris was by his side. The two men had never met. As I approached, hoping to witness caution and mistrust, I saw neither. I'd told Chris how much this man had upset me. But he was too excited by the prospect of an English-speaking friend to comprehend the truth – this man wanted us to fail. I heard Chris happily answering questions about our plans. Håkan was spying! They didn't even notice I was standing beside them. No, that's not true, Håkan noticed me.

Eventually Håkan turned around, pretending to see me for the first time. Making a show of being friendly, he invited us to the first of his summer barbecues, taking place by his stretch of the river. This year he wanted to throw the party to celebrate our arrival. It was absurd! After his having shunned us for weeks and sabotaged our well, we'd now be the guests of honour. Chris accepted the invitation at face value. He took Håkan's hand and shook it, stating how much he was looking forward to the party.

As Håkan left our farm, he asked me to walk with him in order that we might go over the specifics of the invitation. He explained that it was traditional for each guest to bring a dish of food. I knew the tradition very well and said so, asking what he wanted me to bring. He made a play of toying with possibilities before suggesting a freshly made potato salad, explaining that it was always very popular. I agreed, asking what time he wanted us there, and he said the food would be served from three. I thanked him again for the kind offer and he set off up the road. After a few steps he glanced back and did this—

• • •

M Y MUM HELD A finger to her lips as though she were a librar-
ian silencing a noisy reader. It was the gesture she'd made
earlier. Now she was claiming Håkan had done the same. Curious
at the coincidence, I asked:

'He was teasing you?'

Mocking me! The conversation had been a charade.
The invitation wasn't an act of kindness. It was a trap.
And on the day of the party the trap was sprung. We
set off just before three, following the river upstream,
a prettier route than walking along the road, and I was
sure we'd be among the first guests since we were exactly
on time. Except we weren't the first, the party was
in full swing. There were at least fifty people and they
hadn't just arrived. The barbecue was lit. The food was
cooking. Standing on the threshold of the festivities,
holding a tub of home-made potato salad – we looked
idiotic. No one greeted us for a few minutes until Håkan
escorted us through the assembled crowd to the table,
where we deposited our food. Late and lumbering
around with a potato salad was hardly the first impression
I'd wanted to make, so I asked Håkan if I'd made
a mistake with the time, a polite way of saying that he
must have made a mistake. He said the mistake was
mine, the party started at one. He then added that there
was no need to worry, he wasn't insulted – I must have
remembered him saying the food would be cooked from
three.

You might dismiss this as a trivial muddle. You'd be wrong. It was an act of deliberate sabotage. Am I someone who'd care if I mixed up the times? No, I would've apologised and that would've been the end of it. There was no mix-up because he only gave me one time. Håkan wanted us to arrive late and feel out of place. He succeeded. For the duration of the party I was on edge. I couldn't settle into any conversation, and instead of calming down with a drink, alcohol disturbed me further. I kept repeating to people that I was born in Sweden, held a Swedish passport, but I never became anything more than the flustered English woman who'd arrived late carrying a potato salad. Surely you can see the stagecraft in this? Håkan asked me to make the potato salad. At the time I thought nothing of the request. But he couldn't have asked me to make a less ambitious dish – a dish that no one could compliment without sounding ridiculous. I couldn't even use home-grown potatoes because our crop wasn't ready. Håkan's wife was lavishly praising other people's food, cuts of salmon, spectacular layered desserts, food that you could be proud of. She said nothing about the potato salad because there was nothing to say. It looked little different from the mass-produced version you can purchase in the supermarkets—

• • •

I REMARKED:

'This is the first time you've mentioned Håkan's wife.'

That's a revealing omission. It wasn't intentional but it's appropriate. Why? She's no more than a moon orbiting her husband. Håkan's point of view is her point of view. Her importance isn't how she acted: it's how she refused to act. She's a woman who'd scratch out her own eyes rather than open them to the reality that this community was involved in a conspiracy. I encountered her on many occasions. All I can picture is her stoutness – a solid mass, no lightness in her step, no dance, no play, no fun, no mischief. They were rich yet she worked relentlessly. As a result she was physically powerful, as good in the fields as any man. It's strange for a woman to be so strong and yet so meek, so capable and incapable. Her name was Elise. We weren't friends: that much you can tell. But it's hard to feel the sting of her dislike since she hadn't made the decision. Her opinions were shaped entirely by Håkan. If he'd signalled his approval, the very next day she'd have invited me round for coffee, allowing me entry to her circle of friends. Subsequently if Håkan had signalled his disapproval of me, the invitations would've stopped, the circle would've closed ranks. Her behaviour was consistent only with her fanatical belief that Håkan was right about everything. When our paths crossed she'd offer bland statements about the crops, or the weather, before departing with some remark about how exceptionally busy she was. She was always busy, never on the veranda with a novel, never swimming in the river. Even her parties were another way of keeping busy. Her conversation was a form of work – scrupulously asking the right questions without any genuine curiosity. She was a woman without pleasure. At times I felt sorry for her. On most occasions I wanted to shake her by the shoulders and shout:

'Open your fucking eyes!'

*　*　*

M Y MUM RARELY SWORE. If she dropped a plate, or cut herself, she might swear as an exclamation, but never for emphasis. She was proud of her English, largely self-taught, aided by countless novels borrowed from local libraries. In this case, her swearing seemed to capture a burst of anger, a flash of intense emotion breaking through her measured account. Trying to compensate, she hastily retreated into imitation legalistic sentences as if they were trenches dug to protect her against allegations of madness.

I don't believe, or have evidence, that Elise was directly involved with the crimes that took place. However, it is my contention that she knew. Work was her distraction, keeping her mind and body so busy that she didn't have the energy to piece the clues together. Imagine an ocean swimmer who doesn't dare take their eyes off the sunny horizon because beneath them is the deepest darkest abyss, cold currents swirling around their ankles. She chose to live a lie, the choice of wilful blindness. That was not for me. I'll not end up like her – I'll make the discoveries she was incapable of.

I hardly spoke to Elise at the party. She'd glance at me from time to time but made no effort to share her friends. As the party was drawing to a close, I had to either accept that my introduction to society had been a failure, or fight back. I chose to fight. My plan was to tell a gripping story. I settled upon the incident with the elk. It struck me as a shrewd choice since the story was local and I'd interpreted the incident as meaning that our time on the farm would be blessed and maybe other people would interpret it similarly. I tested the story on a small group, including the jovial mayor. They said it was remarkable. Pleased with the reception, I pondered which group of people to address next. Before I could decide, Håkan stepped towards me, asking that I repeat the story for everyone to hear. Some spy, probably the two-faced mayor, must have relayed the story's positive effect on my standing. Håkan gestured for silence, placing me centre stage. I'm not given to public speaking. I'm shy in front of crowds. However, the stakes were high. If I performed well my clumsy entrance would be forgotten. This story had the potential to define me in their eyes. I breathed deeply. I set the scene. Perhaps I became overexcited, there were details I could've omitted, such as the fact that I had stripped naked, an image I didn't need to share with everyone, and the fact that I was sure there was a dangerous voyeur in the trees – which made me seem paranoid. By and large my audience was captivated, no one yawned or checked their phones. At the end of the story, instead of applause, Håkan declared that he'd lived in this area his entire life and he'd never seen an elk in the river. I must have been mistaken. This man had encouraged me to tell the story aloud for the sole purpose of publicly contradicting me. I don't know how likely it is to see an elk in the river. Maybe it happens only once every ten years, maybe once every hundred years. All I know is this – it happened to me.

As soon as Håkan uttered his statement of disbelief the party sided with him. The mayor who'd only minutes ago told me how remarkable the incident was now confirmed that elks wouldn't come this far. There were theories explaining my mistake, statements about the lack of light, the trickery of shadows, and other implausible notions as to how a woman can imagine a giant elk swimming beside her when, in fact, there's nothing other than driftwood. Since he was standing on the outer fringes of the party, I wasn't sure how much Chris understood, because the conversation had been in Swedish. I turned to him for support. Rather than declaring that I wasn't a liar, he hissed at me:

'Shut up about that elk!'

The fight went out of me.

Gloating over his victory, Håkan placed a conciliatory arm around my shoulder. He promised to guide me through the forests where we could see an elk for real. I wanted to ask why he was being so horrible. He'd won a petty battle. But he was mistaken if he thought I could be bullied off my land. Sly nastiness would never win him the farm.

I was sad that day, sad that the party hadn't been a success, sad that I didn't have a new friend's phone number to call, sad that I hadn't received a single invitation to take coffee at another person's house. I wanted to go home and was about to tell Chris when I saw a young woman approaching the party. She was walking down from Håkan's farm dressed in casual baggy clothes. Without a doubt she was one of the most beautiful women I've ever seen, on a par with the models who grace glossy magazines, advertising perfume or designer clothes. Seeing her walk towards us, I immediately forgot about Håkan. It occurred to me that I'd been staring at this girl and it would be polite to disguise my interest. When I checked, everyone else was staring too, every man and woman turned towards her as if she were the entertainment for the evening. I became uncomfortable, as though I were participating in something disturbing. No one was behaving improperly, but there were thoughts in that crowd that shouldn't have been there.

The girl was young, on the cusp of adulthood – sixteen years old, I discovered later. You're correct if you presumed everyone at that barbecue was white. But this girl was black and I was curious, eager to observe who she was going to speak to, but she passed through the party without saying a word to anyone, not taking anything to eat or drink, continuing to the river. On the wooden pontoon she began to undress, her hooded top unzipped and dropped to the floor, tracksuit bottoms removed, flip-flops kicked off. Underneath those baggy clothes she was wearing no more than a bikini, more suitable for pearl diving than the freezing waters of Elk River. With her back to us she gracefully

dived into the river, disappearing under a froth of bub-
bles. She surfaced a few metres away and began to swim,
either indifferent to her audience or acutely aware of it.

Håkan couldn't conceal his fury. His reaction scared
me. His arm was still coiled around my shoulder. His
muscles tensed. He removed his arm, since it was giving
away his true feelings, sinking his hands into his pockets.
I asked after the identity of this young woman and
Håkan told me her name was Mia.

'She's my daughter.'

Mia was treading water, her fingertips breaking the
surface, examining us. Her eyes came to rest directly on
Håkan and myself. Under her gaze I felt a desire to call
out and explain that I was not with him, I was not his
friend. I was on my own – just like her.

On the flight to London it occurred to me that you
might decide I nurture a prejudice against adoption.
That's not true. However, Håkan and Mia felt wrong to
me. My feelings have nothing to do with race, please
believe that. My thoughts could never be so ugly. My
heart told me something was wrong. It didn't feel true
that they were father and daughter, that they lived in the
same house, ate at the same table, that he comforted her
in times of trouble and she sought his words of wisdom.
I admit that the revelation forced me to change the way I
saw Håkan. I'd pegged him as a primitive xenophobe. I

was wrong. Clearly his character was more nuanced. His sense of Swedish identity didn't depend on simplistic markers such as blonde hair and blue eyes. It depended on patronage. To Håkan, I'd surrendered my nationality by leaving my country and taking up the patronage of an English husband. Mia had been naturalised by Håkan's selection of her. Ownership is everything to that man. My instinct, even on that first day, was that she was in danger of the most serious kind.

•   •   •

A YOUNG WOMAN SWIMMING in the river on a summer's day hardly sounded like danger. I ventured:

'How was the girl in danger?'

This question irritated my mum.

You can't have been listening properly. I told you that Mia was being regarded with undisguised desire. Perhaps you've never appreciated this truth, but it's dangerous to be desired, to be the thought that distracts a person, the preoccupation that excites them. Nothing is more dangerous. You doubt that fact? Consider how Mia behaved. She climbed out of the river, not making eye contact with anyone at the party even though she was being watched. These are not natural actions. She dressed without drying, damp patches forming all over her clothes, and then walked back through the crowd, head aloft – not touching any of the food or drink, not saying a word, returning to the farmhouse. I refuse to listen to anyone who tells me that it meant nothing. How can I be so sure? I saw her again a week later when I was tending the vegetable garden. I don't know where Chris was that day. His dedication to the farm came in bursts. Sometimes he'd work from morning to night, at other times he'd disappear for many hours. Anyway, he wasn't by my side when I heard a commotion, looked up, and saw Mia cycling down the road. Her movements were erratic, almost out of control, pedalling at alarming speed as though she were being chased. As she passed the gate, I caught sight of her face. She'd been crying. I dropped my tools, running to the road, fearing that she was going to crash. Only by the grace of God did she remain on the bicycle, taking a hard left and disappearing from view.

I could hardly continue working as though nothing had happened, so I abandoned the vegetable garden and hurried to the barn, retrieving my bicycle and setting off in pursuit. I guessed that she was heading into town along the secluded cycle path that follows Elk River downstream to Falkenberg. It's inconvenient that you never visited, because this isn't the time for a description of Falkenberg, a pretty seaside town, when the real issue is Mia's state of mind and I'm trying to establish the presence of danger rather than describe quaint wooden houses painted pale yellow and old stone bridges. Suffice to say, before the river empties into the sea, the water widens, and on its banks are the town's most prestigious hotels, restaurants and shops. That's where Mia dismounted her bicycle, walking through the immaculate public gardens, deep in thought. I followed her onto the main shopping promenade, where I staged an accidental meeting. The combined effect of my sudden arrival with my dirty clothes, muddied from the vegetable garden, can't have been impressive. I didn't believe Mia would offer me more than a polite hello. So be it: I'd check that she was okay and then return home. I remember she was wearing bright pink flip-flops. She looked so fun and beautiful it was hard to believe that she'd been in tears. She didn't brush past me. She knew my name and knew I was from London. Håkan must have spoken about me. Some children will always take their parents' point of view. But not Mia, there was no hostility from her. Feeling encouraged, I invited her for coffee at the Ritz café located on the promenade. Despite the name, it was reasonably priced and there was a quiet back room where we could talk. To my surprise she agreed.

The café is self-service and I selected a slice of Princess Torta, with a thick layer of cream under a thin green sheet of marzipan. I took two forks so we could share, a pot of coffee and, for Mia, a diet cola. At the till I realised that I'd been in such a rush leaving the farm I hadn't brought any money with me. I was forced to ask the woman at the counter if I could pay another time. The café proprietor pointed out that she wasn't sure who I was, forcing Mia to vouch for me. As Håkan's daughter her words carried weight, and the woman waved us through, with our cake and coffee and cola on credit. I apologetically declared that I'd come back in the evening, that same day, since I didn't want to leave my debts for any longer than need be, particularly since the reason we came to Sweden was to never be in debt again.

While sharing the cake, I spoke a great deal. Mia was engaged when I was talking about my life but cautious when speaking about her life in Sweden. That was unusual, I thought; normally teenagers prefer to talk about themselves. I detected no brash confidence despite her exceptional beauty. Towards the end of the conversation she asked whether I'd introduced myself to all my neighbours, including Ulf, the hermit in the field. I'd never heard of Ulf. Mia explained that he'd once been a farmer but no more. Now he never left the premises of his property. His land was managed by Håkan. Once a week Håkan brought him everything he required to survive. With that final piece of information she said goodbye, standing up, graciously thanking me for the cake and cola.

As Mia was leaving I noticed the woman at the counter watching us. Clasped to her ear was a phone. I'm quite sure that she was speaking to Håkan, telling him that I'd just had coffee with his daughter. You can always tell from a person's eyes whether they've been talking about you.

●　　●　　●

I ASKED:
'Can you always tell?'
My mum's response was emphatic:
'Yes.'
Like a speeding car that had shot over a bump, wheels only briefly leaving the road, she returned to her account without the slightest elaboration.

I played Mia's last words over in my mind, and it struck me as an unusual way to finish a conversation. The reference to the hermit was surely a cryptic instruction that I should pay this man a visit. The more I thought about it, the more certain it seemed to me that this had been Mia's intention. I wouldn't wait. I'd visit him right away. So instead of returning home, I cycled up the road past my farm, past Håkan's farm, searching for the hermit's farmhouse. Eventually I saw the old house, stranded in the middle of the fields like a stray animal. It was hard to believe that anyone lived there since it was so run-down and neglected. The driveway was entirely unlike the perfectly maintained entrance to Håkan's farm. There were waist-high weeds between loose stones and the fields on either side were closing in, the countryside swallowing the path. Abandoned farm equipment dotted the approach, eerie and sad. There was the footprint of a barn, recently torn down.

I dismounted my bike. With each footstep I told myself

there was no need to check if Håkan was watching. I was almost at the farmhouse when my willpower faltered. I turned, just to reassure myself. But there he was, his giant tractor on the horizon black against the grey sky. Though I couldn't distinguish his face from this distance, there was no doubt in my mind that it was Håkan – imperious, atop his tractor throne. Part of me wanted to run and I hated him for making me feel so cowardly. Refusing to give in to fear, I knocked on the hermit's door. I didn't know what to expect, perhaps a glimpse of some gloomy interior with cobwebs and dead flies. I didn't expect a gentle giant of a man framed by a tidy hallway. His name was Ulf Lund, a man with Håkan's strength and size but touched with sadness, his voice so soft I had to strain to hear him. I introduced myself, explaining that I was new to the area, hoping we could be friends. To my surprise he welcomed me inside.

Walking through to the kitchen, I noticed that he seemed to prefer candlelight to electric light. There was a churchlike solemnity about his home. He offered coffee and took a cinnamon bun from the freezer, placing it in the oven and apologising for the fact that it would take a little time to defrost. He seemed content to sit opposite me in silence while the lonely bun warmed in the oven. I summoned the courage and asked whether he was married, fully aware that this man lived alone. He said that his wife had died. He wouldn't say how. He wouldn't even tell me her name, serving instead the strongest coffee I've ever tasted, so bitter I was forced to sweeten it. His pot of loose brown sugar had hardened. I cracked my spoon against the crust, realising that no one visited him any more. He duly presented me with the bun on a plate and I thanked him profusely even though the centre hadn't defrosted entirely, smiling as I swallowed a ball of cold sweet-spiced dough.

Afterwards, as I sat in the hallway, slowly putting on my shoes, examining my surroundings, two observations struck me. There were no trolls, none of the figures carved by Håkan. Instead, the walls were covered with framed quotes from the Bible, quotes stitched into fabric, each decorated with biblical scenes, stitched pharaohs and prophets, the Garden of Eden in coloured thread, the parting of the Red Sea in coloured thread, a burning bush, and so on. I asked if he'd done these. Ulf shook his head: it was the handiwork of his wife. There must have been over a hundred from the floor all the way up to the ceiling, including this one—

• • •

M Y MUM PULLED FROM THE SATCHEL a hand-stitched biblical quote, rolled up and bound with coarse string. She unfolded it in front of me, enabling me to study the text stitched in fine black thread. The edges were charred, some of the thread damaged by fire.

Burnt because only a few days ago Chris threw it into the iron stove, screaming at me that it meant nothing and—

'Let it fucking burn.'

My response was to grab a pair of tongs, snatch it from the flames half ablaze, while Chris lunged at me, trying to take it again, forcing me to retreat into the living room, brandishing the burning material from side to side as if I were staving off an attacking wolf. That was the first time he called me crazy, to my face. I'm sure he'd been saying it behind my back. But it's not crazy to save an article of evidence, particularly when it's proof that there was something rotten at the heart of this community, and so no, I would not 'let it fucking burn'.

• • •

MY MUM WAS KEEN TO ATTRIBUTE this outburst to my dad. She'd registered my reaction to her exclamation – 'Open your fucking eyes!' – carefully logging my surprise. I was reminded of her meticulous bookkeeping ledger, black ink on one side, red on the other. A mark had been made against her and she was evening the score. It was increasingly apparent that the way in which I listened to her story changed the story itself, and I reaffirmed my intention to present a neutral front, giving little away.

This biblical quote is different from the others that hung in the hallway. The fabric has no decoration, that's why my eye was drawn to it. While the others were surrounded by faintly comical biblical illustrations, this one was plain text. Ulf told me that his wife had been working on it at the time she died. There are several words missing, burnt to ash. Let me translate.

'For-my-struggle-is-against-flesh-and-blood-against-the-rulers-against-the-authorities-against-the-powers-of-this-dark-world-and-against-the-forces-of-evil-in-this-earthly-realm.'

The exact reference has been stitched. You can read it there – Ephesians chapter 6, verse 12. As a child I read the Bible every day. My parents were prominent figures in the local church, particularly my mother. I attended Sunday religious studies lessons. I enjoyed Bible classes. I was devout. That will come as news to you, since I now only attend church at Christmas and Easter, but church was a way of life in the country. On this occasion my knowledge let me down. I couldn't recall the Epistle to the Ephesians. I knew it was from the New Testament. The vast majority of the other stitched quotes on the wall were famous scenes from the Old Testament, and I was curious why his wife had changed tack, in her final days, choosing an obscure passage.

• • •

THE QUESTION FORMED IN MY HEAD of how this fabric quote – once framed and hanging on the wall – had come into my mum's possession. I couldn't believe the hermit had given away an item as precious as the stitching his wife had been working on when she died:

'Mum, did you steal this?'

Yes, I stole it, but not from Ulf, from someone who stole it from him, someone who understood its importance. I don't want to speak about that yet. You must let me keep to my chronology or we'll jump around and I'll end up telling you what happened in August before we've finished the month of May.

When I arrived back at the farm, the first thing I did was find my fifty-year-old Swedish Bible given to me as a gift by my father, inscribed to me in his beautiful old-fashioned handwriting – he always wrote with a fountain pen. I looked up Ephesians chapter 6, verse 12, which I've now memorised.

Listen again to her stitched version!

'For-my-struggle-is-against-flesh-and-blood-against-the-rulers-against-the-authorities-against-the-powers-of-this-dark-world-and-against-the-forces-of-evil-in-this-earthly-realm.'

Now listen to the correct biblical version. I'll emphasise

some of the words that are different, but feel free to make your own analysis.

'For-OUR-struggle-is-NOT-against-flesh-and-blood-but-against-the-rulers-against-the-authorities-against-the-powers-of-this-dark-world-and-against-the-spiritual-forces-of-evil-in-the-heavenly-NOT-earthly-realm.'

His wife changed the quote! She stitched her own version so that it read that our struggle was against the flesh and the blood, and she'd taken the forces of evil and located them not in heaven but on earth. On earth! What does this prove? It was a message, not a mistake. How could this poor woman ensure the message survived, that it wasn't destroyed after her death? She hung it on the wall – disguised among the other quotes, a message to those of us paying attention, a message, not a mistake, a message!

I was excited to share this discovery with Chris and I ran outside, calling for him. There was no reply. Unsure where he could be, I noticed spots of red on the gravel drive. Before I even crouched down I knew it was blood. The spots weren't dry. They were recent. Fearing Chris must be injured, I followed the trail to the outhouse. The drops continued under the door and I took hold of the handle, throwing the door open to reveal, hanging from a hook, a butchered pig, a whole animal sliced in half, opened up like a book, rocking backwards and forwards – a butterfly with

bloody carcass wings. I didn't scream. I grew up in the countryside and I've seen plenty of animals slaughtered. If I was
shaken and pale, that's not because I was shocked at the sight
of a dead animal but at the meaning behind this butchered
pig.

It was a threat!

I accept, on one level, that Håkan was merely fulfilling
his side of the agreement. In return for allowing him
to use our land I'd requested pork. Correct. But I'd expected
some sausages and rashers of bacon rather than
an entire pig. Yes, it was a good deal because there was
a lot of meat on this carcass, but why drop it off at that
time, why did it need to be delivered while I was talking to
the hermit? Doesn't it strike you as odd – the timing?
Look at the sequence of events: the sequence is
everything.

Firstly – Håkan received a call from the woman in the
coffee shop, informing him that I was in conversation
with his daughter.

Secondly – he saw me visiting the hermit in the field,
which he will have connected to Mia.

What does he do next?

Thirdly – he selects a butchered carcass, or butchers
one himself, freshly killed because it was dripping
blood, and comes round to our farm, leaving a blood trail
across our drive, hanging it up, not to fulfil a contract
but as a way of telling me to back off, to ask no more
questions, to mind my own business.

I should point out that Chris claims that the incident with the butchered pig didn't happen when I returned from visiting the hermit in the fields, it happened on an entirely different day, and in my mind I'd combined two separate events, connecting memories that had no connection. He wants to cloud this provocative sequence precisely because the sequence itself is so revealing.

Håkan's threat had the opposite effect to the one intended. It made me more determined to find out what was going on. I was sure that Mia wanted to talk. I didn't know what she wanted to talk about. I couldn't even guess. But I needed to speak to her again, sooner rather than later. I was on the lookout for opportunities to do so, but in the end Mia found me.

• • •

A TTACHED BY A PAPER CLIP to a page in her journal was a flyer for a barn dance. My mum handed it to me.

These dances took place at monthly intervals in a community barn, the equivalent of a town hall located a short walk up the road. They're aimed at men and women of a certain age, people who couldn't care less about what might be considered cool. The tickets are expensive, one hundred and fifty krona per person, roughly fifteen pounds. Because we were so near the venue and could hear the music, we were offered free tickets as a form of compensation. Chris and I decided to give it a try. After the failure of the barbecue we were beginning to miss the social dynamic of a city. The barbecue hadn't created a network of friends. I hadn't received any follow-up invitations. There wasn't a single person I could call upon. But there was another reason Chris and I decided to go. Before we left for Sweden we hadn't been intimate for several years.

•   •   •

I REMAINED RIGIDLY IMPASSIVE, betraying my discomfort as surely as if I'd opened my mouth in shock. It wasn't the subject of sex – it was my mum's unstinting honesty. I couldn't match it, not yet, not right now. Without the correct information, my mum misconstrued my discomfort as a merely juvenile response.

This might be embarrassing for you, but to understand what took place in Sweden you need to know every detail, even the very difficult ones, particularly the very difficult ones. After the collapse of our finances I lost interest in sex. So much of sex is about feeling good, not just about each other, but about your life in general. Many couples struggle to maintain sexual relations over a long marriage. Chris and I had been lucky. He was a handsome dark-haired young British man who hated authority and I was a pretty young blonde Swedish woman who'd never met someone so anarchic. We were lost souls who'd found a home in each other's company. Our sex became a celebration that we were a team, the two of us against everyone else. As long as we had each other we didn't need anybody else.

It went wrong when we bought those flats. Chris trusted me, he wanted to retire – he'd worked hard all his life, he was ready to take it easy. He started fishing more, he spent hours planning holidays abroad, reading travel books, wanting to visit the places we'd never seen. He never had any affinity with the banks or with estate agents and gladly accepted my decisions. When the market crashed he sat, helpless and silent, as I tried to unravel our investments. We weren't a team any more. I was alone. He was alone. I began to go to bed early in order to wake early. He went to bed late and woke late. Our lives fell out of step. Part of our ambition for Sweden was to recover our rhythm, our camaraderie as well as our passion, to rediscover sex as though it were an archaeological treasure buried under the dust and rubble of four awful years.

On the ferry ride to Sweden, under the stars, Chris and I kissed, not a kiss on the cheek, not the nervous kiss of young lovers, but the kiss of overly familiar life-partners afraid they could never be as passionate as they once were. We didn't just kiss: we had sex, in a public place, on the top deck, in a cold secluded spot behind a lifeboat, on a ferry in the middle of the English Channel. I was apprehensive, we could've been caught, but when Chris made his advances I could see him expecting me to say no, to make some excuse, to worry, so I went along with it, more than anything as a symbol of change, to let him know that things were going to be different for us – we'd be an unbreakable team once more.

Afterwards, standing on the bow of the boat, waiting for sunrise and the first sight of land, I genuinely believed this was our time – our biggest adventure but also, realistically, our last adventure together. And this one was going to turn out great because we were due our share of contentment. Everyone's owed a slice of happiness, that's sentimental, happiness isn't a human right, but it should be.

With the stress of the farm, the contamination of the well, the problems with Håkan, there were a number of distractions, but there'd always been distractions. Chris and I made a pact that we'd be disciplined, we'd schedule sex – we'd make appointments. There'd be no excuses. We'd use events such as this barn dance to force us into the mood.

That night I wore a faded pink dress that must have been thirty years old, saved from a time when Chris and I used to dance in London clubs. Chris wore a bright silk shirt, it didn't date back as far as my dress, but dressing him in anything that wasn't jeans and a jumper was a positive sign. I didn't have any perfume and we couldn't afford to buy more, so I made my own by crushing pine needles from the forests, which give out an intense oil, dabbing it behind my ears.

We left the farm hand in hand, walking up the road, through the dark countryside, following the sound of the music. We arrived late, unable to see into the barn because it didn't have a single window. A string of dim orange bulbs spotted with giant moths hung above the door, marking the entrance, a huge sliding door made out of heavy timbers. Chris was forced to grip it with both hands, heaving it back, and we stood there like travellers from an ancient time arriving at a bustling country inn, seeking refuge from a storm.

Inside it smelled of good times: alcohol and sweat. There were so many people dancing that the whole floor trembled and glasses on the tables rattled. No one stopped to stare at us: they were too busy dancing. The band was set up on the stage, five men in cheap black suits with skinny black ties and Ray-Ban sunglasses, a Blues Brothers tribute band. However foolish they might have looked to unkind eyes, they could really sing and they were determined that we should have a good time. Those who wanted to sit out the music were at the back, at tables, feasting on the food they'd brought, but mostly they were drinking. There was no paying bar, the venue didn't have a licence to serve alcohol, you were supposed to bring your own. This came as a surprise to Chris and me since we hadn't brought anything and we were looking forward to a drink. It didn't matter. Within minutes we were offered plenty by the other guests, schnapps poured from a giant Thermos mixed with strong black coffee, served with a wink and a nudge, as though we were in a Prohibition dive and, my God, it was strong, caffeine and sugar and alcohol, and soon I was drunk.

Håkan didn't own the barn, or have anything to do with the organisation of this event. I'd made sure of that earlier in the week. After kindly thanking him for his delivery of the pork, giving him no indication that his intimidation had been a success, I'd asked whether he liked to dance. He'd scoffed and said never. I could relax. He wouldn't show. After several cups of cloudberry liquor and coffee, my laughter became louder until I didn't even know why I was laughing any more. Everyone seemed to be laughing. The crowd was there for one reason only – to have fun. They were from all over the region. Unlike the petty local politics of the barbecue, this random group readily accepted anyone of the same mind, anyone who wanted to dance. No one was an outsider here.

With a couple of drinks in our bellies Chris and I joined the dance floor. Whenever the music stopped my thoughts were in a wonderful whirr and everyone around me was in a similar state, simultaneously catching their breath and embracing whoever they happened to be standing beside. On the dance floor everyone had the right to kiss anyone. That's when I saw Mia at the door. I don't know how long she'd been in the barn. She was standing against the back wall, wearing rough-cut denim shorts and a white shirt. She was the only young woman there, the only woman under the age of twenty. She was alone. I couldn't see Håkan, or his wife. Despite our long conversation, I felt curiously shy. In the end she walked towards us, tapping Chris on the shoulder, asking if she could have the next dance. Obviously I thought she meant could she dance with Chris, the pair of them, and so I smiled and told him to go ahead. But Mia shook her head, saying she wanted to dance with me! Chris laughed and said that was an excellent idea – he was going outside to smoke.

The band began to play. The song was fast, the fastest they'd played so far, and we were dancing – Mia and me. I was drunk, wondering if Mia had come to this dance to talk to me. To test the theory I asked whether she attended these events often, and she shook her head and said this was the first she'd ever been to. At that point I asked if she was okay. Her poise and confidence fell away. She seemed young and lost. I felt her fingers press against my back – like this—

•   •   •

PULLING ME UP FROM THE CHAIR, my mum positioned me in the middle of the living-room floor as though we were dance partners. She placed my hands on her back, re-creating the scene.

We continued to dance but she didn't want to talk any more. When the music finished Mia let go. She turned to the band and whistled, clapping loudly, enthusiastically showing her appreciation, pausing only to brush her hair behind her ear.

People were watching us.

Without a word to Mia, I returned to the tables at the back of the barn, leaving her whistling and applauding. Chris was holding a full glass of schnapps to his lips, holding it there, pressed against his bottom lip, but not drinking. He looked at me as if I'd behaved inappropriately, and I couldn't shake the feeling that I had somehow behaved inappropriately. I poured myself a glass, raised a toast, finished it in one, and turned around. The huge barn doors were wide open. Moths were fluttering for the light. And Mia was gone.

•   •   •

M Y MUM BROKE FROM THE DANCE STANCE. Briefly she appeared to have forgotten about me. For the first time her flow faltered, and only when I rested my hand on her shoulder did she start again, slowly at first, her tempo building, recovering her lost momentum.

Chris and I danced a few more numbers. For me, it was no longer with the same joy. My heart wasn't in it. The drink didn't make me happy. It made me tired. Before long Chris and I walked back to the farm. As for the sex, I tried. I hoped to be everything he wanted. But it had never felt like work before. Chris told me that I should have a smoke, to help me unwind. He proceeded to roll a joint. I wasn't opposed to the idea. I hadn't smoked the drug for many years. Maybe it would help. Anyway, this was a night of fun. So I waited for him to finish and took a drag, counting down the seconds until my head turned light. When it happened, I stood up, the sheet slipping off me, standing naked, blowing smoke in an imitation of a sultry seductive figure. Chris lay on his side, watching, telling me to finish the whole joint, wanting to see what I'd do next. I tried to imagine what else I could do, what was sexy – I'd known once, instinctively known without having to think – and then it occurred to me that Chris had brought only a little weed with him from London. That small amount was surely gone: we were a month at the farm. I wondered where he could have found this weed and how he could have paid for it. I asked him, not

angry, not accusingly, but curious, where did the weed come from? He took the joint from me. His reply was barely audible, his lips hidden by smoke. All I heard was:
'Håkan.'

As Chris gestured for me to return to bed, this fact split into two, the fact that Håkan had given him the weed meant that Chris and Håkan must have met without my knowing. These two facts then split, now four. They must be friendly enough to discuss the availability of weed and they must have been intimate enough for Chris to discuss our finances since he didn't have the money for drugs and couldn't access the little money we had without me knowing. It follows that he must have explained our predicament to Håkan, the man strategising to steal our farm. I was certain that Håkan had made Chris a gift of the drug not out of generosity but as a reward for his indiscretion. These disturbing facts began to multiply, out of control, budding and splitting, filling my mind until I couldn't stay in the room any more, not with the smell of Håkan's stinking weed burning in our home – in our farm!

I hastily threw on some clothes and ran out with Chris standing naked on the steps, bellowing to me:
'Come back!'
I didn't stop, I ran, as fast as I could, past the deserted barn where we'd danced earlier, past Håkan's farm, past the hermit in the field, reaching the foot of the hill around which all of our farms were arranged.

The slopes were wild meadow: the top was dense forest. By the time I reached the tree line I was dripping in sweat and collapsed into the long grass, catching my breath, staring out over the landscape. I lay there until I began to shiver. That was when I saw headlights on the road, not one set of lights, but two, not two, now three, not three, but four sets of headlights. At first I thought it was the drug playing tricks on my eyes, so I counted again, four cars travelling one after the other, creeping slowly through the countryside, in convoy, in the dead of night, in a part of the world that might normally only see four cars pass by in a single day. Snaking round the narrow country roads, they moved as if joined together, a nocturnal monster searching for prey. Reaching Håkan's drive they turned, all four cars parking in his drive. The headlights were switched off. The world was dark again. Then, one by one, the beams from four torches flickered over the fields, and finally a fifth beam emerged from the house, joining this gang, taking the lead. I couldn't see the people, just their lights, and watched them walk towards the river in single file, except they never reached the river. Instead, they disappeared into the underground cellar, the wood-carving shed – five sets of lights turning off the path, disappearing into that underground cellar in the dead of night, a cellar filled with trolls and knives and an unexplained padlocked door—

· · ·

M Y PHONE RANG. Though I'd switched it to silent, the image of my dad appeared on the screen. It was the first time he'd rung since I abruptly cut him off. Leaving the phone on the table, I said to my mum:

'If you want, I'll ignore it.'

Answer it. Take the call. I already know what he's going to say – he's changed his mind. He no longer intends to remain in Sweden. His bags are packed. He's ready to drive to the airport. Or he's there already, ticket in hand.

• • •

IT STRUCK ME AS MUCH MORE likely that my dad was ringing to check how we were. In the circumstances he'd shown considerable patience. More to the point, it had been his idea to remain in Sweden, providing me with the space to talk to Mum. A flight to London would be a provocation. I understood that now. He'd admitted as much. He couldn't help her. She'd run from him. If he came to my apartment, she'd try to escape.

In the end I spent so long weighing up the situation that I missed his call. My mum gestured at the phone:

> Call him back. Let him prove he's a liar. He'll claim to be concerned with how you're holding up under the strain of listening to my sinister allegations. He'll offer comforting certainty, there's been no crime and no conspiracy, there are no victims, and there will be no police investigation. All that needs to happen is for me to swallow pills until these allegations drop from my mind.

. . .

M Y DAD HAD LEFT A VOICEMAIL. Despite numerous missed calls he'd never left one before. Wary of hiding anything from my mum, I said:

'He's left a message.'

'Listen to it.'

'Daniel, it's Dad, I don't know what's happening – I can't stay here, doing nothing. I'm at Landvetter airport. My flight's in thirty minutes but it's not direct. I fly to Copenhagen first. I'm due to land at Heathrow at four this afternoon.

'Don't meet me. Don't mention this to your mum. I'll come to you. Just stay at home. Keep her there. Don't let her go . . .

'There's so much I should've told you already. The stuff she's been saying – if you listen to it long enough it starts to sound real, but it's not.

'Call me, but only if it doesn't unsettle her. She can't know that I'm on my way. Be careful. She can lose control. She can be violent.

'We'll make her better. I promise. We'll find the best doctors. I was slow off the mark. I couldn't talk properly with the Swedish doctors. It will be different in England. She'll be okay. Don't lose sight of that. I'll see you soon.

'I love you.'

•   •   •

I LOWERED THE PHONE. By my dad's own assessment, if he walked into the apartment, taking my mum by surprise, there was the possibility of a violent confrontation. My mum would turn against both of us.

My mum said:

'How long do we have?'

My dad had set in motion a ticking clock, upsetting the already fragile calm. I felt no inclination to follow his instructions. In order to preserve my privileged status as someone she trusted, I handed her the phone. She accepted it as if it were a precious gift, cupping it in her open palms. She didn't raise it to her ear, saying to me:

'This show of faith gives me hope. I know we haven't been close for many years. But we can be again.'

I thought upon my mum's assertion that we weren't close any more. We met up less frequently. We spoke less. We wrote less. Lying to her about my personal life had forced me to pull away, to limit the number of lies I'd need to tell. Every interaction carried the risk of discovery.

I was not close to my mum any more.

It was true.

How had I allowed that to happen? Not by design, or intention, not by a rupture or a row, but by careless small steps. And now, looking over my shoulder, certain my mum was no more than a few paces behind, I saw her far away.

As she played the voicemail I expected a powerful reaction, yet my mum's face remained blank. Finished with the message, she returned the phone, for once unaware of my feelings, distracted by the news.

She took a deep breath, picked up the troll knife and slid it into her pocket, arming herself against my dad's arrival.

A man prepared to pay for his freedom with the life of his wife – what is that, not a man but a monster. Why give me a warning? Why not sneak over? I'll tell you why. He wants me to lose control, to rant and rave. That's why he left you the message. Ignore what he said about the need for secrecy. That's a lie. He intended for me to listen to it. He wants me to know that he's coming!

* * *

E VEN THOUGH IT WAS MADE of wood and blunt, I hated the knife being in her pocket.

'Mum, please give me the knife.'

'You're still seeing him as your father. But he's hurt me. He'll hurt me again. I have a right to defend myself.'

'Mum, I won't listen to another word until you put the knife on the table.'

She slowly removed the knife from her jeans, offering it to me by the handle and saying:

'You've been wrong about him so far.'

Using a pen from her satchel, she jotted down a series of numbers in the back of her journal.

We have three hours at the most until he arrives. I've based my calculations on him catching a direct flight. He claimed to be catching a flight via Copenhagen, but that's a lie so that he can arrive early and catch us off guard. Time is against us! We can't afford to waste a single second. However, there's another lie to correct. The Swedish doctors spoke excellent English. It isn't true that they couldn't understand Chris – they understood him perfectly, they understood every weasel word. The point is that they didn't believe him. Ring the doctors right now and marvel at their fluent English, speak to them in complex sentences, count how many words they don't understand. The total will be zero, or close to it. Ring them at any stage, when your confidence in me wavers, and they'll confirm my account. The professionals judged me fit to release and agreed to my request that Chris be told nothing, allowing me the brief window of time to make my escape to the airport.

As for the middle of the message, when Chris's voice falters – that wasn't the sound of love, or compassion, tears weren't welling in his eyes. If it was real, it was the sound of a man on the brink, worn down by his scramble to cover up his crimes. It's his state of mind we should question, torn between self-preservation and guilt. He's a man with his back against a wall, the most dangerous kind of animal. We're all capable of sinking to levels of intrigue that were once seemingly beyond our reach. Chris has gone so far as to use my childhood against me, secrets told to him in confidence, whispered at night after we'd made love, intimacies of the kind you'd only ever share with a person you trusted as your soulmate.

● ● ●

THIS DESCRIPTION OF MY DAD didn't ring true. He hated indiscretion. He wouldn't gossip about his worst enemy, let alone manipulate a secret told to him by my mum. I said:

'But Dad just isn't like that.'

My mum nodded:

'I agree. Which is why I trusted him completely. He isn't like that, as you put it. Except when he's desperate. We're all different people when we're desperate.'

I wasn't satisfied. The argument could be applied to any characteristic that didn't seem plausible. Uncomfortable, I asked:

'What were these secrets?'

My mum pulled from the satchel an official-looking manila file. There was a white sticker on the front with my mum's name, the date, and the address of the Swedish asylum.

In order to convince an honest doctor that a person is insane, one of the first lines of investigation is the subject's family. In my case there's no history of mental health problems. However, many went unrecorded, so my conspirators aren't beaten yet. They have another option. They turn their eye to my childhood, offering up an undiagnosed trauma, implying that my insanity predates any allegations against them. Such an approach requires one of the villains to be close to me, someone with intimate information, such as my husband. It becomes essential, if they're to preserve their liberty, for Chris to betray me. Now you have some sense of the pressure he was under? It was an unnatural decision for him, but by that stage he was too far down the road to pull back.

During my period of incarceration in the asylum I was confronted by the doctors in a cell, two men who sat down opposite me at a table bolted to the floor armed with Chris's account of my childhood, not a general account, but more specifically an incident that took place in the summer of 1963. I won't call it fiction, it was something else, not manufacturing a story from scratch, no – subtler – an adaptation of the truth, ensuring their account cannot be categorically disproved. The doctors presented me with this cruelly crafted account as though it were fact and asked for my response. Fearing permanent imprisonment in that asylum, realising the importance of my reply, I asked for a pencil and pad of paper. You have to understand I was in a state of shock to find myself locked up. There was madness around me, genuine madness. I was terrified. I didn't know if I'd ever leave. These doctors were judge and jury over my life. I doubted my ability to speak clearly. I was becoming confused between English and Swedish. Rather than rambling, I proposed an alternative. I'd write down exactly what happened in 1963, not speaking but writing, and they could judge from the careful document whether the childhood incident was relevant.

You're holding the testimony I wrote for them that

night. The doctors returned it at my request when I left the asylum. I believe they kept a photocopy in their files should you need to cross-check, or perhaps this is a copy—

Yes, I hadn't noticed before, but this is a copy, they kept the original.

You and I haven't spoken about my childhood in any depth. You've never met your grandfather. Your grandmother is now dead. In a sense she was never alive to you. From this you might deduce that my childhood wasn't a happy one. Well, that isn't true – there was happiness, a great deal of happiness, many years of happiness. At heart I'm a country child with simple tastes and a love of the outdoors. It wasn't a life of misery.

In the summer of 1963 an event changed my life, broke my life and made me a stranger in my own family. Now that event is being misrepresented in order that my enemies might institutionalise me. To protect myself I have no choice but to lay out my past before you. My enemies have created a malicious version of events so disturbing that if you hear what they say it will change the way you look at me. And when you have a child of your own you'll never trust me to be alone with them.

•   •   •

I SIMPLY COULDN'T IMAGINE an event so terrible it would change my entire understanding of my mum, let alone one that made me doubt her suitability to look after a child. However, I was forced to accept that I knew very little about my mum's upbringing. I couldn't remember any specific mention of the summer of 1963. Anxious, I opened the file. Inside there was a cover letter written by my mum before the main body of the text:

'You want me to read this now?'

My mum nodded:

'It's time.'

·   ·   ·

Dear Doctors,

You might be curious as to why I'm writing using English rather than Swedish. Over the course of my life abroad my written English has improved while my written Swedish has been neglected. I left the Swedish educational system at the age of sixteen and have hardly used my mother tongue during my time in London. In contrast, I've worked hard to improve my English, bettering myself with the assistance of noble literature. Using English is not a statement against Sweden. It does not express ill feelings towards my homeland.

I'd like to state for the record that I feel no personal desire to discuss my childhood. It's been introduced as a cynical diversion from the real crimes that have taken place. There's no connection between the past and the present, but I accept that my denial will make you think that there is.

My enemies have described an event that took place in the summer of 1963. Their hope is to trap me in this asylum until I retract my allegations against them or until my allegations are of no consequence because my credibility has been undermined. I accept that elements of their story are true. I cannot claim it's all lies. Were you to carry out an investigation into their version you'd find the broad details correct such as the location, names, and dates. However, just as I would not claim to be friends with someone who brushed past me on a crowded train merely because our shoulders touched, their story cannot claim to be the truth merely because there's fleeting contact with real events.

What you're about to read is the true account of what happened. Yet these are memories from over fifty years ago and I cannot remember word for word what was said at the time. Therefore you might conclude that any dialogue is being made up and consequently you'll doubt the entire content of my statement. I agree, in advance, that the dialogue serves only to capture a rough spirit of the conversation since the exact words have been lost forever, and so have some of the people speaking them.

Yours sincerely,
Tilde

* * *

The Truth about the Farm

Our farm was no different from thousands of others in Sweden. It was remote and beautiful. The nearest town was twenty kilometres away. As a child the sound of a passing car was unusual enough to bring me outside. We didn't own a television. We didn't travel. The forests, lakes and fields were the only landscape I knew.

The Truth about Me

My mother nearly died during my birth. Complications left her incapable of having any more children. For this reason I have no brothers or sisters. My friends were widely scattered. I accept that sometimes I was lonely.

The Truth about My Parents

My father was strict but he never hit my mother and he never hit me. He was a good man. He worked for the local government. My father was born in the area. He built the farm with his own hands when he was just twenty-five. He's lived there ever since. His hobby was beekeeping. He maintained wild meadows for his hives. His unusual mix of flowers created a white honey that won many prizes. Our living-room walls were covered with national beekeeping awards and framed clippings of the articles written about his honey. My mother helped with the work but her name wasn't on the honey labels. Both my parents were important members of the community. My mother worked a great deal with the church. In short, my upbringing was comfortable and traditional. There was always food on the table. I had no cause to complain. This brings us to the summer of 1963.

The Truth about the Summer of 1963

I was fifteen years old. School had finished. Long summer holidays lay ahead of me. I had no plans beyond the usual entertainments and chores, helping on the farm, cycling to the lake, swimming, picking fruit, and exploring. Everything changed one day when my father told me that a new family had moved into the area. They'd taken possession of a nearby farm. It was an unusual family because it was made up of a father and a daughter but no mother. They'd left Stockholm to start a life in the country. The girl was my age. After hearing the news I was too excited to sleep and lay awake contemplating the prospect of a friend close by. I was nervous because she might not want to be my friend.

The Truth about Freja

In pursuit of her friendship I spent as much time as possible in the vicinity of the new girl's farm. Too shy to knock on their door, I resorted to indirect methods that might seem odd, but I'd led a sheltered life and was socially inexperienced. In between our two farms was a clump of trees too small to be called a forest. It was an area of wild land impossible to sow or harvest because of several large boulders. I went there every day. I'd sit at the top of a tree, facing the new girl's farm. Each day I waited many hours, scratching shapes into the trunk. After a week or so I began to doubt that this new girl wanted to be my friend.

One day I saw the father walking through the fields. He stopped at the bottom of my tree and called up:
    'Hello up there.'
    I replied:
    'Hello down there.'
    They were our first words:

'Hej där uppa!'

'Hej där nerra!'

'Why don't you come down and meet Freja?'

That was the first time I heard her name.

I climbed down the tree and walked with him to their farm. Freja was waiting. The father introduced us. He explained how much he hoped we could become friends because Freja was new to the area. Though Freja was the same age as me she was much prettier. Her breasts were already large and she styled her hair fashionably. She was the kind of girl every boy paid attention to. She was less of a child and more of an adult whereas I was still a child. I suggested building a shelter in the woods, unsure whether she'd scrunch up her face in disgust at the idea, because she was from the city and I didn't know any grown-up girls from the city. Maybe they didn't like building tree shelters. She said okay. So we ran to the clump of trees. I showed her how to create a roof by bending saplings and tying them together. If this sounds like a tomboy task for two fifteen-year-old girls, then maybe it was. But physical activity was natural to me. It was all I knew by way of diversions. Freja was more sophisticated. She knew about sex.

By midsummer Freja had become the friend I'd always desired. I imagined saying to her by the end of the holidays that she was the sister I'd never had and that we would be best friends for the rest of our lives.

The Truth about the Troll

I arrived in the forest one morning and found Freja sitting on the ground. Her arms were clasped around her knees. She looked up at me and said:

'I've seen a troll.'

I was unsure if this was a scary story or if she was being serious. We'd often tell each other scary stories. I'd tell her stories about trolls. So I asked her:

'Did you see the troll in the forest?'

She said:

'I saw it on my farm.'

It was my duty to believe my friend when she told me something was true. I took hold of her hand. She was shaking.

'When did you see it?'

'Yesterday, after we'd been playing in the fields. I went home but I was too dirty to come inside the house, so I used the outside hose to wash the mud from my legs. That's when I saw the troll, at the back of the garden, behind the red-currant bushes.'

'What did the troll look like?'

'It had pale skin rough like leather. Its head was huge. And instead of two eyes it had one enormous black eye that didn't blink. The troll just stared at me and wouldn't look away. I wanted to call out to my dad but I was afraid he wouldn't believe me. So I dropped the hose and ran inside.'

Freja didn't play that day. We sat together, holding hands, until she stopped shaking. After hugging Freja goodbye that evening I watched her return home through the fields.

The next day Freja was so happy she kissed and hugged me and said that the troll hadn't come back, and she apologised for alarming me, it must have been her imagination playing tricks.

But the troll did come back and Freja was never the same again. She never felt safe. She was always afraid. She became another person. She was sadder and quieter. Often she didn't want to play. She was scared of returning home each evening. She was scared of her farm.

The Truth about Mirrors

Some weeks after she'd first seen the troll I found Freja in the forest holding a mirror. She was certain that the one-eyed troll was using mirrors to spy on her. That morning she'd woken up and turned all the mirrors around so they faced against the wall, every single mirror in the house, except for the one in her bedroom. She suggested we smash it and bury the shards in the soil. I agreed. She hit it with a heavy stick and when it smashed she started crying. Freja returned home that evening to find all the mirrors turned the correct way round. Her father wouldn't tolerate such peculiar behaviour.

The Truth about the Lake

My plan was simple. Freja had only ever seen the troll on her farm. What if the two of us ran off to the forests far away? We could easily survive for a few days if we saved up enough food. If we didn't see the troll then we could be sure that the solution would be to leave her farm. Freja agreed to my plan and we met on the road at six in the morning and started cycling. We couldn't stay in the nearby clump of trees because we'd quickly be discovered. We needed to reach the forests that surrounded the great lake. These were forests so big you could disappear and never be found again. My parents were accustomed to me being outside for the entire day. They'd only start to worry when I didn't show up for dinner.

A rainstorm started at midday. The downpour was heavy. You had to shout to be heard. Quickly Freja was too exhausted to go any further. Dripping wet, we dragged our bikes off the road. Once in the forest we camouflaged them under leaves and twigs. I created a shelter under the trunk of a fallen tree. We ate sugar-iced cinnamon buns and drank redcurrant juice. The food I'd calculated would last for three days was almost finished after a single meal. Every couple of minutes I asked Freja:

'Can you see the troll?'

She'd look around, then shake her head. Even though we were wet and tired we were also happy, wrapped up in our rain jackets. I waited until Freja fell asleep before I allowed myself to shut my eyes.

When I woke up Freja was gone and the forests were dark. I shouted her name. There was no response. The troll had come for Freja. I began to cry. Then I became scared because the troll might come for me. I ran as fast as I could until I reached the great lake and could go no further. I was trapped against the water's edge, certain the troll was only a few metres behind. I took off my jacket and swam. I'd never read a story where a troll enjoyed swimming. They were dense, heavy creatures and I was a strong swimmer for my age.

That night I swam too far. When I eventually stopped swimming I was the furthest I've ever been from the shore. The giant pine trees on the sides of the lake were so far away they were just specks. At least I was alone. At first this thought gave me comfort. The troll wasn't after me. I was safe. Then the thought made me sad. I remembered I'd lost my friend. Freja was gone and when I returned to the shore I'd be alone again. My legs felt heavy. I was so tired. My chin dipped below the water, then my nose, then my eyes, and finally my whole head. I was drowning. I didn't make the decision to die. But I didn't have the energy to swim.

I sank below the surface. I should have died that night. I was lucky. Even though I was many hundreds of metres away from the shore, by chance that area of water was shallow. I rested for a moment underwater on the silt bottom of the lake, then pushed up and broke the surface. I gasped, took a deep breath before *sinking back down to the bank. I rested for a little while then pushed up, breaking the surface, taking a breath. I repeated this process over and over, moving closer to the shore. With this strange method I managed to return to dry land, where I lay flat on my back for some time looking up at the stars.*

When my strength returned I walked through the forests. Eventually I found the road but couldn't find the hidden bicycles. Dripping wet, I began the walk home. Up ahead were the bright lights of a car. It was a local farmer. He was looking for me. My parents were looking for me. Everyone was looking for me, including the police.

The Lie

When I arrived back at the farm I kept saying the same thing:
    'Freja's dead!'
    I explained about the troll. I didn't care if they found these stories fanciful. She was gone. That was all the proof they needed. I wouldn't stop talking about the troll until they drove me to Freja's farm. Finally my father agreed to investigate. He didn't know how else to calm me down. He took me to their farm. Freja was at home. She was wearing pyjamas. Her hair was brushed. She was clean. She was beautiful. It was as if she'd never run away. I said to Freja:
    'Tell them about the troll.'
    Freja told them:
    'There is no troll. I never ran away. And I'm not this girl's friend.'

• • •

Dear Doctors,

I've been writing all night, the process has not been easy and I'm exhausted. We're due to meet again soon. I'm running out of time and would like to sleep before we discuss these pages, so I'm going to reduce the following events to a series of quick points.

After Freja's lie I was sick for many weeks. I spent the remainder of that summer in bed. When I eventually recovered, my parents no longer allowed me to leave the farm by myself. My mum said prayers for me every night. She'd kneel by my bed and pray, sometimes for a whole hour. At school, children kept their distance from me.

The next summer, on one of the first hot days of the year, Freja drowned in the lake, not far from the place where we'd sheltered together under the trunk of a tree. The fact that I'd also been swimming in the lake that same day meant that there were rumours I'd been involved. Children at school claimed I'd killed her. They thought it was suspicious that I didn't have an alibi. These stories spread from farm to farm.

To this day I'm not sure if my parents believed I was innocent. They too wondered if maybe I'd chanced across Freja in the lake that hot summer's day, maybe we'd argued, and in the middle of that argument she'd called me a freak and maybe I'd been so angry I'd pushed her head under-water and held her there, held her and held her and held her until she couldn't lie about me any more.

The days that followed were the worst days of my life. I sat at the top of the tall tree, staring at Freja's farm, and considered whether to jump. I counted all the branches I'd crash through. I imagined myself broken at the bottom of the tree. I stared at the ground and kept saying:

Hello down there.

Hello down there.

Hello down there.

But if I killed myself everyone would be sure that I'd murdered Freja.

When I turned sixteen, on the day of my birthday, at five in the morning, I left the farm. I left my parents. I left that area of Sweden forever. I couldn't live in a place where no one believed me. I couldn't live in a place where everyone thought I was guilty of a crime. I took with me the small amount of money I'd saved up and cycled as fast as I could to the bus stop. I tossed the bike into the fields and caught a bus to the city and never went back.

Yours sincerely,
Tilde

• • •

EVEN THOUGH I'D FINISHED, I held on to the pages, pretending to read, needing more time to collect my thoughts. At no stage in my life had I caught a glimpse of my mum as the lonely young girl depicted in this account, seeking the love of just a single friend. My failure of curiosity was so complete, a question presented itself to me:

Do I even know my parents?

My fondness for them had drifted into a form of neglect. An excuse might be that Mum and Dad had never volunteered any difficult information. They'd wanted to move on from the past and carve out happier identities. Maybe I'd justified my actions by arguing that it wasn't my place to rake over painful memories. But I was their son, their only child – the only person who could've asked. I'd mistaken familiarity for insight and equated hours spent together as a measure of understanding. Worse still, I'd accepted comfort without query, wallowed in contentedness without ever investigating what lay beneath my parents' desire to create such a different home life from their own.

My mum was smart to my tricks, aware that I'd finished reading. She placed a hand on my chin, slowly raising my eyes to meet hers. I saw determination. This wasn't the lost young girl I'd just read about.

> You have a question for me, a hard question for a son to ask his mother. But I won't answer it unless you ask it yourself. You must say the words. You must have the courage to look me in the eyes and ask if I murdered Freja.

• • •

M Y MUM WAS RIGHT. I wanted to ask the question. Reading the
pages, I'd wondered about the events of that day in the lake.
It wasn't difficult to picture an accidental confrontation – my mum
physically powerful from years of working on the farm, city-born
Freja beautiful and weaker. Their paths had crossed. My mum had
lost her temper, furious after months of isolation and misery, shaking her former friend, holding her head underwater, overcome with
the humiliation of her disgrace. Gaining control of her emotions,
ashamed of her actions, my mum would've retreated to the shore,
only to glance back and see that Freja hadn't surfaced – unconscious
underwater. Frantic, my mum would've returned, trying to save her,
but to no avail. Then she'd panicked, fleeing the scene, leaving the
body of her friend adrift in the lake:

'Did you have anything to do with Freja's death?'

My mum shook her head:

'Ask the question. Did I murder Freja? Ask it!'

She began repeating over and over:

'Did I murder Freja? Did I murder Freja? Did I murder Freja?'

She was goading me, rapping her knuckles against the table each
time she said the name. It was disturbing. I couldn't bear it any more.
Before she hit the table again, I caught her fist, the energy of the
blow transferring into my arm, and asked:

'Did you murder her?'

No, I didn't.

Go to any school, I challenge you, anywhere in the world,
and you'll find an unhappy child. About that unhappy child
there will be malicious gossip. This gossip will consist

mostly of lies. Though they're lies it doesn't matter, because when you live in a community that believes those lies, repeats those lies, the lies become real – real to you, real to others. You can't escape them, because it's not a matter of evidence, it's nastiness, and nastiness doesn't need any evidence. The only escape is to disappear inside your head, to live among your thoughts and fantasies, but this only works for so long. The world can't be shut out forever. When it begins to break through, then you must escape for real – you pack your bags and run.

As I look back on it, Freja was troubled. Her mother was dead. Her life had been turned upside down. After she betrayed me as a friend, she became sexually involved with a young man, a hired labourer on one of the larger farms. There were rumours that she was pregnant. She didn't attend school for a time. The stench of scandal. Don't ask me what's true. I don't know. I didn't care what people said about her. I wept when Freja died. No one wept more than me. I wept, even though she'd betrayed me, even though she'd turned her back on me, I wept. I could weep again, even today, I loved her so much.

Now that you've heard the truth about the summer of 1963 you must accept that those events have nothing to do with the crimes that took place this summer. There's no connection. We're talking about different people in a different place at a different time.

•   •   •

FRUSTRATED WITH THE CRYPTIC REFERENCE to 'crimes', and feeling emboldened, I challenged the word directly:

'Is Mia dead?'

My mum was startled. So far she'd exercised control over the flow of information. I'd been docile and obliging. No more: I wanted a summary of what we were discussing before we went any further. I'd allowed her to be coy and evasive for too long. My mum said:

'What did you think this was about?'

'I don't know, Mum. You keep talking about crimes and conspiracies but you won't say what they are.'

'Chronology is sanity.'

She said this as though it were well-known and widely accepted wisdom.

'What does that even mean?'

'When you jump around, backwards and forwards, people begin to question your mind. It happened to me! The safest way is to start at the beginning and move to the end. Follow the chain of events. Chronology is sanity.'

My mum was describing sanity as though it were the same as an old-fashioned police test for a drunk driver, asking the suspect to walk in a straight line.

'I understand, Mum. You can tell me what happened your way. But first I need to know what we're talking about. Give it to me in one sentence. Then I'll listen to the details.'

'You won't believe me.'

I was taking a risk being so direct. I wasn't sure if my mum might leave if I pushed her too hard. With a degree of trepidation, I said:

'If you tell me, right now, I promise not to make any judgments until I've heard the whole story.'

It's obvious that you still believe nothing really happened in Sweden. I told you at the beginning, this is about a crime. There's been a victim. There have been many victims. You need more information? Yes, Mia's dead. A young girl I grew to love is dead. She is dead.

Now ask yourself a few questions. What wild theories have I ever believed in before? Do I search for conspiracies in every news story? Have I ever falsely accused anyone of a crime? I'm running out of time. I must go to the police today. If I go by myself to a police station the officers will contact Chris. He'll tell them the story of my sickness and he'll tell it well. These police officers will almost certainly be men, men just like Chris. They'll believe him. I've seen it happen. I need an ally, preferably a member of my family, by my side, someone to support me, and there's no one left except you. I'm sorry this falls on your shoulders.

You asked me directly. I answered. Now I'm asking you directly. Is this too much for you? Because if you're stalling for time until your father arrives, if your tactic is to keep me talking while you don't listen to a word, trapping me here under false pretences so that the two of you can drive me to an asylum, then let me warn you, I'd consider that a betrayal so grave our relationship would never recover. You would no longer be my son.

•   •   •

THE IMPLICATION HAD ALWAYS BEEN that if I didn't believe her then our relationship would suffer. My mum saw the situation in starker terms. To be her son I must believe her. Had the situation been less extraordinary the threat would've seemed overstated. Except my mum had never said words like this. Their newness made them real. It was a notion I'd never considered – my mum not loving me. I thought upon the way she'd left her farm as a child, running away from her parents with no letter, no phone call, disappearing without a trace. She'd cut close ties before. She could do it again. However, she was flatly contradicting her instructions not to allow emotion to influence me. Our relationship was being pulled into play. I couldn't promise to believe my mum merely to pacify her.

'You asked me to be objective.'

I added quickly:

'I can repeat the promise I've already made: to keep an open mind. Right now, sitting here, I don't know what's true. I do know, Mum, no matter what happens in the next few hours, no matter what you tell me, I'll always be your son. And I'll always love you.'

My mum's hostility broke apart. I wasn't sure if she was moved by my petition of love, or by an acknowledgment that she'd made a tactical mistake. Sounding disappointed with herself, she repeated my words:

'An open mind, that's all I ask for.'

Not quite, I thought to myself, as her focus returned to the journal.

Earlier we spoke about the previous owner, elderly Cecilia, and the mystery of why she sold us the farm.

The mystery goes deeper. She left behind a boat moored to the wooden pontoon, an expensive rowboat with an electric motor. Both were new. Ask yourself why frail Cecilia would spend so much money on a boat when she was planning to sell her farm and move into the city?

There are lots of subjects I don't know anything about. Until my recent time in Sweden I can't have spent a single second thinking about motorboat engines. As soon as I became aware that the boat was a vital clue I set about educating myself. It was a revelation to me that the shell of a boat was purchased without an engine – the engine is an additional expense. What's more, the so-called E-Thrust Electric Motor Cecilia selected isn't the cheapest, not by far. It's priced at three hundred euros. My research has uncovered that it's possible to buy cheaper engines that would've been compatible with the boat. The next question is, why did she leave us this particular electric motor?

I want you to look at the specifications for the engine. Among the list is the answer – the reason she picked that engine and left it behind. See if you can find it.

* * *

F ROM HER JOURNAL MY MUM handed me a printout from the Internet.

E-THRUST 55lb Electrical Engines

First time available in Europe!

Based on *superior* US design and technology, these engines represent outstanding power and performance – year after year.

- Peak Thrust: 55lb
- Power Input: 12v (Battery not included)
- LCD Monitor 7 settings
- 360 degree steering
- Stainless Steel
- Length 133cm/52"
- Width 12cm/4.7"
- Depth 44cm/17.3"
- Weight: 9.7kg/21lb
- Telescopic Speed Control: 5/2 (forward/reverse)
- Propeller: 3-Blade Montage
- Instruction Manual: Yes. Instruction Language: English/German/French
- Recommended Boat Size: Max. 1750kg/3850lb
- CE approved: Yes

• • •

I RETURNED THE PAGE AND ADMITTED:
'I don't know.'

Easy to miss in that list, hardly worthy of a second thought – it's the third feature, the LCD monitor with seven settings.

Let me explain.

We'd been on the farm for almost two months and Chris hadn't gone out on the river once. Not even for five minutes. In order to sell holidays we needed evidence that Elk River was good to fish. But Chris's rods were sitting in the barn. What was I asking him to do? Not some chore he despised. He loved to fish. He'd helped choose the farm based upon the river. He'd inspected it. I'd regularly say to him: please fish the river. He'd shrug, roll a cigarette, and say maybe tomorrow. Then, after weeks of ignoring my requests, Chris declared that he was going out on the river with Håkan. By this stage the two men had become friends, often spending time in each other's company. I didn't complain. The friendship was good for him. Chris's mood had improved since those dark cold April mornings when he wouldn't get out of bed or budge from in front of the stove. Privately, I was jealous, not of his relationship with Håkan whom I mistrusted and disliked, but of the way in which a group of friends had been opened to him, including the two-faced mayor, prominent businessmen, and members of the town council. Chris had been welcomed into the

very heart of the local community. I wondered whether
Håkan was being excessively kind to my husband in
order to torment me. But I'm not petty. I'm practical
and pragmatic. We needed good relations with the community, and if those relations were built around Chris,
rather than me, so be it. Of course, it stung that having
ignored my frequent requests to fish he responded so
eagerly to Håkan's suggestion. Even so, I made no snide
remarks. Instead, I expressed my gratitude that finally
he'd bring me a salmon to photograph.

After breakfast Chris collected the electric motor from
the barn. I remember that morning fondly. I wasn't suspicious. I wasn't paranoid. I made Chris sandwiches
using bread baked in our oven. I prepared a Thermos of
tea. I kissed him, wished him luck. Standing on the end
of our jetty I waved him goodbye, confident in his abilities
and full of hope for our river. I cried out for him
to bring me back a magnificent fish. And that's exactly
what he did.

• • •

MY MUM PULLED A PHOTOGRAPH from her journal, the fourth so far.

This was taken shortly after Chris and Håkan returned from their fishing trip, note the time and date stamp in the corner. What's to protest about? I asked Chris to bring back a magnificent salmon and he succeeded. The photograph is perfect promotional material for our guest lodges – two men proudly holding their catch. But something's very wrong with this photo.

Look closer.

Examine Chris's expression.

That's not pride or excitement. His lips are squeezed as though great pressure were required to hold the smile together.

Now study Håkan's expression.

Note the direction of his eyes – a sideways glance at Chris. There's calculation here. The photograph isn't celebratory. Why not? Where's the joy? Remember the stakes. Our money was set to run out by the end of the year and this fish should've been proof that we could earn more.

I can see you're thinking that I might have spoiled the evening by being needlessly suspicious and that these men are reacting to something inappropriate done by me. You're wrong. I congratulated them warmly. I even managed to be nice to Håkan, proposing that he come round when we cooked it. But I quickly became confused. The men were clutching an exceptional fish yet their reaction was muted. I made a motion to take the salmon from Chris and his instinct was to pull away. I explained we needed to wrap it and put it in the fridge. Only then did he allow me to hold the fish. Rebalancing the weighty fish, my finger slipped under the gill. Do you know what I discovered?

Ice!

I could feel it on the tip of my finger – a cold crystal, and then it was gone, melted with the heat of my touch, disappeared before I could make an examination. The evidence was gone, but I'd felt it, I was sure. This fish wasn't from the river. It had been bought.

I rushed inside, dropping the fish on the kitchen table. Alone, I checked both gills. There was no more ice but the flesh was freezing cold. I didn't put the salmon in the fridge. Instead, I crept back into the living room, taking a concealed position behind the curtains. Through the window I watched as Chris and Håkan spoke. Unable to lip-read, I can't tell you what they were saying, however, I can tell you that these were not two triumphant fishermen. Håkan put a hand on Chris's shoulder: Chris gave a slow nod. He turned to the house, forcing me to pull back sharply.

In the kitchen I pretended to be jolly and busy as Chris passed through. He didn't even glance at the salmon, his great prize. He took a shower and slipped into bed, saying he was tired. I couldn't sleep that night, nor could Chris, not immediately, even though he should've been exhausted. He lay there by my side, pretending to sleep. I wanted to crawl into his thoughts. What was keeping him awake? Why had they purchased such an expensive salmon as an alibi? I use the word 'alibi' deliberately – a salmon as an alibi. That was the purpose of the fish, to serve as an alibi, one that must have been paid for by Håkan, because a whole salmon would've been costly. Perhaps it would've been as much as five hundred krona, or fifty pounds. Our finances were too tight for Chris to spend so much money without me knowing. Håkan must have bought it and given it to Chris.

I couldn't investigate until I was certain Chris was asleep. I waited until two in the morning when his breathing finally changed and he fell asleep. He'd underestimated me, unaware that I'd felt the fragment of ice. I crept out of bed and tiptoed across the floor, putting on a coat and heading to the barn where the electric motor was stored. Standing in that barn, staring at the engine, my first thought was that maybe Chris had travelled no more than a few hundred metres upstream and disembarked at Håkan's jetty. The two men had then sneaked off somewhere else in his car. I began to examine the engine, doing no more than paw its exterior, pressing every switch until I saw the soft blue glow of the monitor.

As I flicked through the seven settings, it showed me the amount of power left in the battery represented as a percentage. The engine was fully charged before Chris and Håkan went out on the river. The battery was now at six per cent! Put another way, they'd used ninety-four per cent of the charge. My first theory was wrong. They'd travelled a great distance, expending almost the entire battery. They'd been on the river but they hadn't been fishing.

The fact of Cecilia's generosity returned to me. Why had she left me this boat? She wanted me to explore the river! The specific characteristics of this engine were part of Cecilia's design. Using the LCD monitor as a crude guide, I could re-create their journey by seeing how far I could travel using the same amount of power. I decided not to wait. I'd do it tonight, while Chris slept, before dawn. I'd take the boat upriver and find out where they'd been – it had to be now!

• • •

I RAISED MY HAND, INTERRUPTING to check that I'd understood correctly:

'You took the boat out in the middle of the night?'

The next day it might pour with rain, evidence might
be washed away – it had to be that same night and I
needed to do it without Chris and Håkan knowing.

It took over an hour to recharge the motor. I sat in the
barn, watching the numbers slowly count up. With the
batteries at one hundred per cent I set about transporting
the engine to the river, forced to use the wheelbarrow in
order to push it through the fields, trying not to make
a noise, scared it would topple over. If Chris were to
wake I'd have no explanation. Thankfully I reached the
jetty undetected and found the process of attaching the
engine to the boat easy. That must have been factored
into Cecilia's thinking when she selected it. I checked
my watch, estimating that Chris wouldn't be awake until
eight at the earliest. To play it safe, I calculated that there
were five hours to explore and return.

Adjusting the motor speed to the middle of the range, I
pulled away from the jetty. They hadn't travelled downstream – I knew that for certain. The river had been
dammed in order to power a quaint hydroelectric station,
designed to look like an ancient watermill. There was no way
for a boat to pass. They could only have travelled upstream.

147

My worry was how far. I secured my cheap plastic torch to the front of the boat, angling the beam at the water's surface, attracting a cloud of insects, concerned someone would see me, but I held my nerve, in that small boat in the middle of that dark river while the rest of the world slept, the only person awake and searching for the truth.

The river followed gentle curves between fields belonging to various farms, man-managed and uniformly dull. I couldn't see where Chris might have stopped, or for what reason, so I continued upstream, reaching the edge of the forests. It was like crossing the border into a different realm. The sounds changed. The feeling changed. From here on the river was completely enclosed. Whereas the farms had been silent, these forests were teeming with life, stirred into motion by my arrival. Bushes rustled. And creatures watched me.

Finally, with only forty per cent of the battery power remaining, I stopped the motor, allowing the boat to drift. Logically I'd reached the rough point of their final destination, because any further and there wouldn't be enough power to return to the farm. The reason I didn't stop at fifty per cent is because a return journey would require significantly less power since the boat would be travelling with the flow.

Holding the torch, I examined this place, the boat gently rocking under me. With the light I caught flashes

148

of luminous eyes that, in a blink, were gone. The night air was clear. There was no trace of fog or mist. When I looked up at the sky I saw a spread of stars and thought to myself, as many stars as there were possible answers. Chris and Håkan could've moored the boat to any of the trees and walked through the forest to reach their destination. There was no way for me to be sure. I sat down, bitterly frustrated, conceding that I'd have to return without an answer.

As I secured the torch back to the front of the boat, I noticed that directly ahead there was a branch in the middle of the river stretching out towards me. Curious, I peered into the darkness, discerning a tree growing out of an island – an island shaped like a teardrop. I motored forward, grabbing the branch and mooring the boat to the tip of Teardrop Island. There were marks around the trunk, rub lines where other boats had moored, too many to count, an entire portion of the trunk worn smooth by a long history of visits. On the muddy bank just above water level were partial sets of footprints, some old, some new – the sheer number and variety telling me that far more people had been on this island than merely Chris and Håkan. I was struck by the realisation that even though it was the middle of the night I might not be alone. I considered untying the boat and continuing my examination from relative safety, separated by a clear stretch of water. But I needed to see the island up close, not from a distance. I walked towards the cluster of trees situated at the rear of the island, the fat end of the teardrop. In between the trees there was a dark angular shape, a man-made shelter, a shack, a refuge constructed far away from the eyes of people, made from timber, not sticks from the forests, but planks secured with nails. The roof appeared water-tight. This was the work of men, not children. Moving around the side I saw that there was no door, just an open space and a ragged curtain. I pulled back the curtain and saw a rug, a sleeping bag unzipped, opened out like a blanket, a kerosene lamp with sooty glass. The dimensions of the space were impossible to ignore, not high enough to allow a person to stand up but wide enough to lie down. The smell was unmistakably of sex. There were cigarette butts in the mud. Some were branded. Some were hand-rolled. I picked one up and sniffed weed. With a twig I raked through the ashes of a thousand fires, finding at the side the melted remains of a condom – an obscene streak of plastic snot.

· · ·

I T WAS A DISTURBING LOCATION and I could feel my mum circling a disturbing allegation, hinting at it, without stating explicitly what she had in mind. But it wasn't my place to presume or fill in the gaps:

'What do you believe took place on that island?'

My mum stood up, opening the kitchen cupboards, searching until she found the sugar, scooping out a handful and carefully pouring it on the table, spreading it evenly in front of me. With her fingertip she drew the shape of a teardrop in the middle of the fine white granules.

> When it comes to sex do you know what people fan-
> tasise about more than anything else? A private space
> of their own, a space where they can do anything and
> the rest of the world will never know. No judgment, no
> obligations, no shame, no disapproval, and no repercus-
> sions. If you're rich, maybe it's a yacht far out at sea. If
> you're poor, maybe it's a basement where you stash your
> dirty magazines. If you live in the countryside, it's an
> island in the forest. I'm talking about fucking, not making
> love. Everyone wants to keep their fucking a secret.

● ● ●

A s if caught by a powerful reflex action, my hand shot out and swept aside the sugar island, brushing the shape away. Too late I understood how revealing my reaction had been. The sudden movement carried the implication of anger and took my mum by surprise. She pulled back, staring at me, interrogating my expression. She'd no doubt interpret my gesture as brazen contempt for her theory. In fact, it was a rather pitiful confirmation that she was right. I'd created my own version of that island. My mum was sitting in it – this apartment. There'd been many times when I'd wondered if it were possible to keep my sexuality a secret from my parents and also hold on to my relationship with Mark. He would never have accepted it, which is why the thought remained unspoken. Had it been possible, I might have spent the rest of my life living on an island of my own creation, growing ever more remote from my parents. With sugar-crusted fingertips, I apologised:

'I'm sorry. It's hard for me to accept. About Dad, I mean.'

My mum wasn't mollified, sensing something in my thoughts that she couldn't quite identify. I asked, apprehensive of what was coming next:

'You think Dad and Håkan went to this island?'

'I know they did.'

I hesitated, bracing myself for the reply:

'What did they do there?'

The question isn't what. The question is who – who else was being brought there? We know for certain that they didn't fish. I searched every part of the island but

152

couldn't find any clue. It was hard to leave without an answer, but checking my watch, I realised the danger I was in. The sun would be rising in a matter of minutes.

Luckily travelling downstream was much faster. Even so, it was morning. The sun was strengthening. Håkan and Elise would be awake. They were always up with the sunrise. I could only hope they weren't on the riverbank. I passed by Håkan's jetty, greatly relieved not to see him or his wife. Just when I believed myself to be in the clear the engine cut out. The battery was dead. I was adrift in the middle of the river.

Before you argue that the engine cutting out means that Chris and Håkan couldn't have reached Teardrop Island, factor into your calculations my inefficiency upriver. I frequently steered the boat from side to side, to see if there was somewhere they might have disembarked. Later, when I returned to Teardrop Island, I managed the round trip in a single charge of the electric motor. Anyway, that morning, with Chris waking soon, I was forced to row the remaining distance. I'd not rowed a boat for many years. The faster I tried to row the worse my rowing became. Reaching the jetty, my arms ached. I wanted to collapse and catch my breath but there was no time. It was almost eight in the morning. I detached the motor, heaving it out. As I pushed the wheelbarrow up the slope, towards the farm, my heart sank. Chris was already awake! He was smoking outside. He saw me. He waved. I stood, dumbly, then waved back, forcing myself to smile. The engine was in the wheelbarrow. I threw my coat over it, but perhaps he'd seen it already. I needed an excuse. It was plausible that I could've used the wheelbarrow for some other purpose and so continued towards the farm, glancing down at the wheelbarrow, seeing the engine poking out under my jacket. It wouldn't survive any kind of scrutiny, not even a quick glance, so I cut across the field and left the wheelbarrow behind the barn.

Arriving by Chris's side, I gave him a kiss – I forced myself to – and said good morning. I set about examining the vegetable garden, making up some story about working by the riverside and clearing the reeds. He said very little, finishing his cigarette before going inside for breakfast. I grabbed my chance, running back, pushing the wheelbarrow round, into the barn, and depositing the engine inside, plugging it into the charger. When I turned, Chris was at the door. He'd abandoned his breakfast. With no idea how much he'd seen, I told him he'd forgotten to plug it back in. He didn't reply. I picked up some washing and walked towards the house, glancing over my shoulder. Chris was at the barn door, staring at the engine.

• • •

MY PARENTS WERE BEHAVING like a couple that I simply didn't recognise. Their whole manner of interaction seemed to have changed over the summer. I asked:

'If he caught you, why didn't Dad confront you? Why didn't he ask what you were doing? I don't understand the silence.'

'What could he say? He caught me in the barn beside the motor. It was in his interest not to draw attention to the boat.'

My point was a wider one:

'It sounds like the two of you just stopped talking.'

I was about to push my question further when my mum raised her hand, silencing me and saying:

'You're asking about our relationship?'

'Forty years together can't fall apart in a few months.'

'It can take far less time than that. You crave security, Daniel. You always have. Let me tell you. There is none. A great friendship can be swept aside in an evening, a lover changed into an enemy with a single admission.'

It was, on one level, a warning – this would happen to us if I didn't believe her account. She said:

'Your father and I were both pretending. I was pretending to be ignorant of Teardrop Island. He was pretending not to have noticed how serious my investigation had become.'

My mum picked up her journal, looking for a specific entry:

'Let me give you an example.'

Glancing at the pages, I saw the notes were becoming considerably more detailed.

On 10 June I woke early, skipped breakfast, and cycled

to the station, catching the first train into the city of Gothenburg. I was going on a journey and I had no intention of telling Chris. Normally we'd discuss everything, but it was necessary to keep this a secret since my plan was to visit Cecilia and ask about Teardrop Island in person, not speak over a phone line, scared that Chris might hear, but to put to her these questions directly – why had she left me the boat, what were her suspicions, what was she not telling me?

Cecilia had moved into a care home in Gothenburg, a city with many difficult memories for me. I'd lived there for a few months as a teenager, scratching together enough money to buy a boat passage to Germany. During those months I'd worked as a waitress in a hotel café on Kungsportsavenyn – the main promenade. I pictured the police searching for me, having decided to charge me with Freja's murder. I lived like a fugitive. I cut my hair short, changed my clothes, and created a false name. I remember once serving a customer coffee on the terrace and seeing a pair of police officers on patrol. My arm trembled so much that I spilled coffee over the customer and was reprimanded by my manager, saved only because men liked to flirt with me and they'd leave large tips, which the manager always pocketed for himself.

Arriving in the city that morning, I decided to walk to the care home. It saved me some money, the sun was on my side, and I wanted to pass the café on

Kungsportsavenyn because I wasn't a scared young woman any more. The home was on the outskirts, across the bridge, a great distance from the centre. I walked all the way, wondering what Cecilia was going to say. The building was welcoming. There were well-tended gardens, an ornamental pond surrounded by benches where people sat and chatted. Inside, the communal areas were clean, the reception was tidy, and the woman at the desk friendly. When I introduced myself I asked if Cecilia had many visitors. The woman confided in me that she'd had none, not one, not a single visitor in her entire time at the home. I was angry at this news. We'd been made to swallow a story about community and togetherness. How could no one have visited this woman? It was a cruel exile. Håkan was punishing her for not selling him the farm. He'd decreed she should be left without the smallest gesture of kindness.

Cecilia was seated in her room, her knees up against the radiator, looking out into the garden. She wasn't reading or watching the television. She was just sitting there. She might have been like that for hours. There's something heartbreaking about a person indoors staring out into a sunny garden. As for the room, it was anonymous. With two hours' work it could be made ready for someone new. This wasn't a home. It was a place of transit – a waiting room between life and death. We couldn't speak here. I had to remind her of the outside world. We'd talk in the garden. As I crouched beside her, I was struck by the changes in her body. When we'd met on her farm she was physically frail but strong in spirit. Her eyes were bright and her mind was sharp. Now when she looked at me her eyes were watery as if her character had been diluted with a thousand parts of nothing. But she recognised me, which was a relief, and she agreed to sit with me by the pond.

A court might query the credibility of Cecilia's testimony. I accept that her level of awareness varied – at times she could engage directly, at other times her thoughts were elsewhere and questioning required patience. I allowed for diversions and tangents, coaxing her towards the mystery of why she'd sold me that farm. Without prompting, she asked if I'd discovered the truth about Anne-Marie, the wife of the hermit in the field. It was a subject I hadn't even mentioned! I summarised all that I knew – she'd been religious, she stitched biblical quotes, she'd died and her husband seemed devastated by the loss. Cecilia was greatly irritated with my ignorance, as though I'd failed her. She said: 'Anne-Marie killed herself.'

Caught by a wave of lucidity, Cecilia told me the story. Anne-Marie had been aged forty-nine with no medical history of depression. Cecilia loved her as a friend, a woman she'd known for many years. This good-natured friend had woken one morning, showered, changed into her work clothes, walked out of the farmhouse, into the pig barn, ready for a day's work. Either something awful was discovered or something awful took shape in her mind, because she tied a rope from the beams. She hanged herself at first light while her husband was sleeping. Ulf had come downstairs for breakfast, seen the open barn door, and was sure the pigs must have escaped. He'd rushed out of the house, across the yard, into the barn to save the pigs, only to discover all the animals in the far corner, bunched together. It was at this point, so the official version goes, that he turned around and saw his wife. There was no note, no explanation, no warning, and no financial worries.

According to Cecilia the response was typical of the community, swallowing bad news in the same way an ocean might swallow a sinking ship. They'd slaughtered the pigs as if they were witnesses to a crime. They'd dismantled the barn beam by beam. At Anne-Marie's funeral Cecilia had touched Håkan's arm and asked him why, not as an accusation but as a melancholy question that only God could answer. Håkan had angrily shaken her off, saying he had no idea. Maybe he didn't have any idea, but he also had few qualms about profiting from her death. Håkan expanded his kingdom, taking over Ulf's land. He'd presented it as an act of charity, helping a grief-stricken man.

Cecilia had been speaking for some time. Her lips were dry and cracked. Concerned that I was tiring her, I instructed her to remain on the bench while I fetched some refreshments. It was a decision I will always regret. I should never have interrupted her flow. When I returned with a coffee she was gone. The bench was empty. I saw a crowd forming around the pond. Cecilia was standing in the middle of the water. The level was up to her waist. She seemed quite calm. Her arms were crossed across her breasts. Her wet, white care-home dress had turned translucent, reminding me of a river baptism, waiting for the priest to lower her under the water. Instead, a male nurse rushed in, putting an arm around Cecilia and scooping her up. She can't have weighed very much. I followed them into the nursing home, where they hurried her off for a medical examination. Making the most of the distraction, I returned to her room, searching it from top to bottom, amazed at how few items she possessed. Her belongings must have been sold. In the drawers there were books, but only children's stories, no Bible and no novels that I could see. In her wardrobe I found this leather satchel. Cecilia was once a schoolteacher and I supposed she used it for carrying textbooks. I stole it because I needed a bag, not an impractical handbag, but a decent-sized bag that could accommodate my notes and any evidence—

•   •   •

MUM AND I STOOD UP at the same time, reacting to the noise of someone trying to enter the apartment. The front door had been opened. We heard it catch against the chain, loudly at first, then softly as a more cautious second attempt was made. I'd seen my mum take the security chain off at my request, but she must have reattached it when my back was turned, convinced that my dad would make an unannounced return. Downstairs a hand could be heard fumbling at the chain, reaching around the door, trying to unbolt it. My mum cried out:

'He's here!'

In a scramble she began packing up the evidence. Working fast, she returned each piece of evidence to its place in the satchel. She slotted the smaller items into the front pockets, the larger items, including the rusted steel box, into the rear, highly ordered with no wasted space. It was clear that she'd done this before, keeping her evidence mobile and ready to move at a moment's notice. My mum glanced at the access door to the roof garden:

'We need another way out!'

My dad had tricked us. He'd lied, flying direct, arriving sooner, catching us by surprise just as my mum had claimed – these were my initial thoughts, affected by the intensity of my mum's reaction. However, I discounted this explanation. My dad didn't have keys. The only person it could be was Mark.

With the satchel packed, my mum was ready to throw it over her shoulder. I put my hand on top of it, stopping her escape:

'It's not Dad.'

'It's him!'

'Mum, it's not. It's not him. Please, wait here.'

I snapped at her, unable to remain calm, gesturing for my mum to remain where she was, doubtful she'd obey. I hurried downstairs and into the hallway. Mark was no longer struggling with the door but wedging it open with his foot while holding his phone, about to ring me. I'd failed to keep him informed, completely caught up in my mum's account. I should've guessed his reaction – he'd already expressed his concern that I was on my own. In a hushed voice, I said:

'I'm sorry I didn't call, but this is a bad time.'

I hadn't intended to sound aggressive. It took Mark by surprise. I was panicking; after years of my carefully constructed deceit, the entire rotten structure was set to collapse before I'd had a chance to carefully stage-manage its demise. No longer in control, I waved him back, pushing the door shut, taking the chain off, opening it fully. Mark was about to speak when he paused, looking over my shoulder.

My mum was standing at the far end of the hallway, clasping her satchel. In the front pocket of her jeans I could see the outline of the wooden knife. The three of us stood motionless, with no one speaking. In the end, my mum took a small step closer, observing Mark's expensive suit and shoes, asking:

'Are you a doctor?'

Mark shook his head:

'No.'

Normally polite and chatty, Mark could offer no more than a monosyllabic response, unsure what I wanted him to say.

'Did Chris send you?'

'I live here.'

I added:

'This is Mark. It's his apartment.'

I realised, too late, what a meagre introduction it was after years of waiting to introduce him to my parents. My choice of words made him sound more like a landlord than a lover. My mum's attention had moved from his clothes to his face. She said:

'My name is Tilde. I'm Daniel's mum.'

Mark smiled, about to move forward, but he checked himself, sensing the precarious balance of emotions.

'It's good to meet you, Tilde.'

For some reason my mum didn't like the way he used her name. She took a small step back. Controlling her nervousness, she said:

'Would you like us to go somewhere else?'

'You're welcome to stay as long as you like.'

'Are you staying?'

Mark shook his head:

'No, give me a minute and I'll be gone.'

My mum stared at him. In any other circumstances it would've been impolite. Mark held her stare with a placid smile. My mum dropped her gaze to the floor, adding:

'I'll wait upstairs.'

Before leaving the hallway, my mum gave Mark a final look, ever so slightly tilting her head to the side, as if correcting her view of the world.

We waited in silence as my mum slowly climbed the stairs, listening to her heavy steps. Alone, I turned to Mark. The encounter I'd dreaded for so long had taken place in a way I could never have imagined – my mum had met my partner and yet, not really, they'd exchanged names and looks. I'd offered more deceit, unable to say the words, 'This is the man I live with,' opting instead for 'This man lives here.' It wasn't a lie but it was as weak as one. Mark was mournful about the exchange – he'd wanted so much more from the occasion. Speaking in a low voice, he brushed aside his own emotions and asked:

'How is she?'

'I don't know.'

I saw no point in summarising my conversation so far. He said:

'Dan, I needed to be sure you were okay.'

He would never have come here merely to be involved, or because he felt left out. He was here as a precaution against the possibility of disaster, hedging against the chance that I'd lost control of the situation. He and my mum would've agreed that I was untested in difficult waters. I nodded:

'You were right to come back. But I can manage.'

Mark was unconvinced:

'What's your plan?'

'I'm going to finish listening, then make a decision about whether she needs treatment. Or whether we need to talk to the police.'

'The police?'

'It's so hard to be sure.'

I added:

'My dad's flying over. He changed his mind. His plane lands very soon.'

'Will he come here?'

'Yes.'

'Are you sure you want me to leave?'

'She won't talk with you in the apartment. Not freely, not like she has been.'

Mark considered:

'All right. I'll go. But here's what I'll do. I'll sit in the coffee shop round the corner. I can read, do some work. I'm two minutes away. You call me when anything changes.'

Mark opened the door:

'Get this right.'

I expected to find my mum eavesdropping. But the hallway was empty. I returned upstairs to find her at the window where I joined her. She took hold of my hand, pronouncing his name as though trying the sound for the first time:

'Mark.'

And then, as though the idea had just popped into her head:

'Why don't you talk for a bit?'

Unsure of my emotions, I squeezed her hand. She understood, because she responded:

'I remember one holiday we spent on the south coast. You were very young. Six years old. The weather was hot. There was a blue sky. Driving to the beach at Littlehampton, we were certain it was going to be a perfect day. When we arrived, we discovered a bitter sea wind. Rather than give up, we took refuge in a sand dune, a sheltered dimple at the back of the beach. As long as the three of us remained completely flat we couldn't feel the wind. The sun was warm, and the sand too. We lay there for a long time, dozing, sunbathing. In the end I said, "We can't stay here forever," and you looked at me and asked, "Why not?"'

I said:

'Mum, we can talk about my life another time.'

My mum's voice was as sad as I'd heard it all day:

'Not another time, today. When I finish, once we've gone to the police, I want you to talk. I want to listen. We used to tell each other everything.'

'We will again.'

'You promise?'

'I promise.'

'We'll be close again?'

'We'll be close again.'

My mum asked:

'Ready to hear the rest?'

'I'm ready.'

We all make mistakes. Some we can forgive. Some we can't. I made one unforgivable lapse of judgment during this summer. For a brief moment I doubted my own conviction that Mia was in danger.

Once a week, I'd cycle down to the beach – not the tourist beach, a beach further north. It was rugged, with dunes and clumps of bracken backed by deep forests, not a holiday beach. No tourists ever came. I'd take my regular run along the sand. One evening I'd been running for about thirty minutes and I was about to turn back when I saw movement up ahead in the forest. It was bright white, like the sail of a small ship passing among the trunks of pine trees. Normally these beaches and forests were empty. Emerging from among the trees, Mia stepped out onto the beach, dressed like a bride with flowers in her hair and flowers in her hands. She was wearing a midsommar dress, ready to dance around the maypole. I hid behind a bracken bush to see what she was going to do next. She continued up the beach until she reached an abandoned lighthouse. She hung her flowers on the door and went inside.

It was as if I'd witnessed a ghost story except the girl was real and the footprints clear in the sand. Mia was waiting for someone. The flowers were a signal to an observer that she was inside the lighthouse. I was determined to see who was going to meet Mia. The longer I waited the more confused I became, and part of me wondered if the other person had seen me. Maybe they were hiding in the forest and wouldn't appear until I was gone. After almost an hour I questioned myself. Clearly Mia was not distressed. She'd walked to this lighthouse freely, out of her own volition. I was curious but I was also cold. Afraid I'd fall ill before the town's midsommar festival, I decided to leave.

I'll never forgive myself for that lapse in judgment. It's my belief that the man who eventually arrived was Mia's killer.

●   ●   ●

Although tempted to ask for more information, I sensed that my mum was no longer avoiding specifics but building towards an explanation of the events around and including Mia's murder. She hadn't sat down and showed no signs of being willing to do so. With the satchel still hanging around her shoulder, she opened the bag, pulling out a midsommar invitation.

Each year the town organises two separate midsommar celebrations, one for tourists holidaying in the area and a more prestigious celebration exclusively for residents. This is an open invitation to the first party, handed out on the beaches and at the hotels. Though it's decorated with images of young children dancing round the maypole, flowers in their golden hair, promising a festival pure of heart, it's a moneymaking exercise. The festivities are executed on the cheap. How do I know? I worked there. Mia stopped by the farm and told me about the opportunity of paid work. She must have known we were short of money. She was trying to help us. I contacted the organisers, and they gave me a job in the beer and schnapps tent.

On the day of the party I arrived at the fields, owned by Håkan, early in the morning, imagining a team of people motivated to host a great event. A responsibility was on our shoulders. This festival is about a love of our land, dating back to a celebration of harvests, expressing our deep affection for Sweden itself. What I witnessed that day was depressing. The white canvas tent where food was served was clammy and old. There were bins everywhere. There were hand-painted signs bossing people about. Don't do that. You must do this. A long line of plastic portable toilets was more prominent than the maypole itself. The price of a ticket was inclusive of food and non-alcoholic drink. When you consider it's only two hundred krona, or about twenty pounds, that seems reasonable. However, the food is prepared in bulk with a clear cost-cutting strategy. You recall how Håkan asked me to bring potato salad to his party. I saw first-hand how lowly the potato salad was considered, prepared in buckets, slopped out using giant ladles, a food fit for tourists. That's why Håkan had asked me to bring it to his party, tourist-grade food, because that's how he saw me, a tourist in Sweden.

In the alcohol tent we were serving beer and spirits with more staff than the entire food tent, where the queues would stretch out for hundreds of metres. That was a deliberate tactic to stop people coming back for second helpings. Needless to say, the men in particular quickly turned to the beer tent. We were full from the beginning. No matter what I thought of the setup, people were having fun. The weather was warm and the guests were inclined to have a good time.

During my lunch break, I ventured to the maypole to watch the midsommar performance. Students dressed in traditional costume were dancing. While I was watching, someone tapped me on the shoulder and I turned to see Mia, not dressed in white with flowers in her hair, as she had been on the beach, but holding a plastic refuse bag, picking up rubbish. She told me she'd specifically requested the job since she had no desire to dress up and be stared at. Even at the time that struck me as a disturbing comment. Why was this young woman so fearful of being watched? Mia told me about last year's Santa Lucia festival, the celebration of light on the darkest day of the year. The church decided to stage a specially commissioned play about the process of choosing the right girl to take on the role of Santa Lucia – the saint with candles in her hair. In this fictional play, there was the character of a bigoted choirmaster who selects the girl based on a stereotypical model of Swedish beauty. The girl he selects is a bully, but she's beautiful and blonde. The character Mia played was overlooked because she was black, even though she was the most pure of heart. During the ceremony, the bully girl at the front of the procession stumbles and her hair catches on fire because she uses so much hairspray. Mia's character puts out the flames, risking her own safety. It sounded like a peculiar play to me. Even more bizarre, after this play, about a fake Santa Lucia procession, they proceeded with the real Santa Lucia procession in which Mia was given the lead. Mia said the whole affair was excruciating. Since that embarrassment she'd vowed never to perform in front of an audience again.

During our conversation Mia reacted powerfully to the sight of someone behind me. I turned around and saw Håkan marching into the food tent. Mia ran after him. I followed and discovered, inside the tent, a great commotion. Håkan had a young man by the scruff of the neck, a handsome man in his early twenties, with long blond hair and a stud in his ear. Though the young man was tall and athletic, physically he was no match for Håkan, who pressed him up against the canvas, angrily accusing him of messing about with his daughter. Mia ran forward, grabbing Håkan's arm and telling him that she didn't even know this man. Håkan wasn't convinced, wanting an answer from the young man, who looked at Mia and started to laugh, saying if Håkan was talking about this girl he was crazy, because he didn't like black girls. In fact, the young man used an inexcusable racial slur which I will not repeat. Everyone in that tent must have despised him for it except for one person, Håkan, because he immediately calmed down, realising this young man was a racist. Whatever information Håkan had garnered from his spies was wrong. He visibly relaxed. As I've already said to you, nothing's more important to him than the concept of ownership. Instead of rebuking this young man for the ugliness of his remark Håkan apologised for falsely accusing him.

Mia was upset by this public confrontation. She ran out of the tent, dropping her bag of rubbish. I walked up to Håkan and suggested that he chase after her. Håkan stared at me with such hatred. He told me to mind my own business. As he passed me in that crowd, keeping his arms by his side, he clenched one hand into a fist and pressed it hard against my cunt, pushing his knuckles through my cotton dress, causing me to gasp, before moving off as if the gesture had been an accident. If I screamed he'd deny it. He'd call me a liar. Or he'd say the tent was crowded and he'd merely brushed past me. Back in the beer tent, I could still feel his knuckles on me as if I were made of dough and their impression would last forever.

• • •

I WONDERED IF MY MUM had used that word – cunt – in order that I might feel some of the shock she'd felt, simulating the lasting impression his knuckles had made on her. If so, she'd succeeded, since I'd never heard her say it before. Was there a secondary calculation? Perhaps she'd thought I'd become too comfortable. After the kindness and intimacy we'd just shared, she was warning me not to expect any protection from the truth, reminding me that, according to her, we were dealing with violence and darkness that she'd expose without censoring.

From her journal she pulled out a second invitation, expensively produced, placing the two contrasting invitations side by side on the table so that I might examine them.

> This is the invitation to the exclusive second midsommar party. I don't need to point out the difference in quality. Notice my handwritten name in elegant black calligraphy. They've included my middle name – Elin – but not Chris's middle name, strange because how did they obtain that information and why the inconsistency? I'd never shared it with anyone. It's not a secret, but it can't have been a thoughtless slip. It can only be interpreted as an implicit threat that they can unearth private information about me. This was Håkan's way of telling me that the investigative process cut both ways and if I was coming up against him I'd better be ready for the fight of my life.

•   •   •

I COULDN'T UNDERSTAND THE NATURE of the threat: 'Mum, what's there to find out about you?'

They could find out about Freja! If they did I'd be ruined. Those rumours had forced me from my home before. In the eyes of my parents I'd killed my best friend. It didn't matter that it wasn't true. Håkan would whisper those stories to his wife over dinner, certain she'd whisper it to her friends over coffee. Soon there'd be a hundred people whispering at the same time. There'd be looks and glances. I couldn't live among those lies, not again, anything except those lies. I'd try to be strong, I'd try to ignore them, but in the end, you can't shut out the world. I'd have no choice but to sell our farm.

Until those stories about Freja were uncovered my investigation would continue. I would not live in fear, and this midsommar party offered an opportunity to observe the community interacting. Though I expected the celebrations to be cautious at first, soon the drink would flow, tongues would loosen, indiscretions would surface, and I'd be ready to take note of what happened next. Unlike my stumbling appearance at Håkan's summer grill, where I was concerned with how I was being perceived, this time round I'd be the observer. I wouldn't waste a thought on my own reputation. I couldn't care less whether they liked me or not. My objective was to see which men latched on to Mia.

I promised not to waste time on description unless it was necessary. If I tell you that the sky threatened with a storm it will help you understand why that day was the most disturbing midsommar of my life. Any minute I expected the heavens to open, and consequently, there was a sense of apprehension. Moreover, in the hearts of many attending, there was a lingering feeling of resentment. The previous day the tourist party had been gifted the most perfect summer weather, splendid sun and bright blue skies. Revellers had drunk beer until late in the evening and dozed on the grass. On this day there was a chill in the air and bursts of blustery wind. Every element that the organisers could control was superior except the weather, a fact that fouled the mood.

I'd taken the decision to dress up in traditional Swedish folk dress, clasping a home-picked bunch of flowers, my hair tied into plaits. The use of my middle name had made me anxious. My outfit was an attempt to make myself a harmless figure of fun. If there were any suspicions that I was too close to the truth, this outfit would surely dispel them. They'd snigger at the woman wearing a blue dress and yellow apron. Chris protested that I was making a fool of myself. He couldn't see how it would bring us closer to the community. He didn't realise I'd given up on that ambition; it was a futile one and we'd never be considered one of them. More to the point, I didn't want to be part of that group. Unable to articulate these reasons for my silly appearance, I was forced to rebuff Chris's protests with unconvincing claims about how this was my first midsommar in Sweden for many years and I wanted to make the most of it. He was so frustrated he left our farm without me, catching a ride with Håkan. He said if I wanted to behave like a child he wanted nothing to do with me. As I watched him go, I wished we could've partnered on the investigation as we'd partnered on almost every-thing important in our lives. The reality was that I mistrusted him. So I set off on my own, in the folk dress, partnered instead with my cracked old leather satchel.

Arriving at the party, I tolerated condescending looks from a few of the wives. They spoke to me in gentle tones as if I were a simpleton, congratulating me on being so brave. As expected, the community rolled its eyes and dropped its guard. There was no denying that the location was picturesque. The party was held on a strip of land alongside Elk River, downstream from the salmon ladder, not far from the outdoor theatre where touring farces played to summer crowds. The land had been prepared with great care. There were luxury toilets and boutique food marquees. There were bouquets of summer flowers. Even more striking was the maypole, the exact same struc-ture used the day before but with the number of flowers doubled or trebled. It was so beautiful I was briefly blinded to the unfairness it represented. They could easily have used the same beautiful maypole for both midsommar parties. This celebration of life and summer was tainted with a meanness of spirit.

Elise was there, disdain in her eyes. Although I told you earlier that I wouldn't be blind like Elise, on some days, at my lowest ebb, I understood her choice and shamefully confess that wilful blindness appealed to me. What a relief it would be to close down my suspicious mind and divert my energies into worshipping this community. I wouldn't lose any more sleep, I wouldn't worry – I wouldn't spend a second longer asking what was happening up the river in the depths of the forests. Had I chosen blindness, I'm quite sure Håkan would've celebrated my choice, delighting in my surrender and rewarding me with a host of friendships. But blindness is not an easy path. It requires commitment and dedication. The price was too high: I would become an imitation of Elise. Perhaps she was imitating a woman before her, perhaps this pattern of blindness was generations old, women forced to empty their heads of questions or criticisms, playing a part that was as old as these farms – the part of loyal devotion – a role that would bring me acceptance, maybe even happiness of a kind. Except when I was alone. I'd hate myself. It's how we feel about ourselves when we're alone that must guide our decisions.

Like me, Mia arrived independently. Far more surprising was that also, like me, she was dressed up, wearing bridal whites with flowers in her hair and clutching flowers in her hands. They were the exact same clothes she'd worn on the beach except they were no longer pristine. The fabric was dirty and ripped. The flowers were shedding petals. She'd made no effort to conceal the scuffs on her clothes. It was as if on her walk back from the lighthouse she'd been attacked in the forest. At first, Mia ignored everyone, standing by the river, her back to the party, staring at the water. I let her be, not wishing to publicly break formation. Later, I noticed something wrong about the way she was moving. Her steps were too careful. She was overcompensating. Sure enough, my instinct was spot on, because when I eventually said hello to Mia her eyes were bloodshot. She was drunk! She must have brought her own supply, because they wouldn't have served her at this party. Of course, teenagers occasionally get drunk, there's no need to sensationalise it, but to be silent-drunk in the middle of the afternoon at an event like this wasn't frivolous or fun: it was the drinking of a troubled mind.

By the time we were set to dance around the maypole Mia was no longer able to hide her intoxication, or no longer wanted to. Other people less finely tuned to the nuances of her behaviour had begun to notice something was wrong. I could see Håkan making preparations to take her home. Such drastic action would cause a stir. He must have calculated that it was better to have a short controlled disruption rather than permit her to create a scene. I couldn't allow him to remove her from the party.

There was a reason Mia was drinking. I had a clear sense that she was becoming drunk in order to confront someone, to give herself courage. It was imperative I buy her enough time in order that she could carry out her plan.

I gently took hold of Mia's arm and guided her centre stage, calling everyone together. Improvising, I began talking about the history of the midsommar festival. With the entire party gathered around me, including Håkan, I explained how this was the night of the year when magic was strongest in Sweden, how our great-grandparents would dance as a fertility ritual to impregnate the earth and bring full harvests to the farms. At this point I handed each of the children a flower from my hand-bound bouquet and told them that, according to tradition, these flowers should be placed under their pillows and when they slept that night they'd dream of their future lovers, husbands and wives. There was giggling as the children accepted their flowers. To them I must have seemed like a harmless witch, but there was a motive behind my eccentricity. I reached Mia, handing her the remains of my bouquet. Now that I had spoken about lovers and husbands, how would she react? Mia held her flowers aloft. I was right! She was on the brink, ready to denounce this community and whatever secrets it was hiding. Everyone was staring at her, waiting to see what she'd do next. She threw the flowers high over her head as a bride might on her wedding day. We followed them as they arced into the air, the string around the stems loosening, flowers coming apart, breaking free, a comet of summer petals.

Håkan pushed forward, grabbing Mia by the arm, apologising to everyone. He was careful not to drag her or appear to manhandle her. She didn't resist, retreating towards his gleaming silver Saab. He put her in the front seat. She lowered the window and looked back. 'Tell us!' I wanted to shout to her – 'Tell us now!' As the car accelerated, her long dark beautiful hair blew into her face, concealing it entirely.

That was the last time I saw Mia alive.

• • •

THERE WAS NO EXCUSE NOT to test my mum's claim. Using my phone it would be simple to enter the name 'Mia Greggson' into a search engine. If the girl had been murdered there'd be newspaper articles and widespread public attention. I weighed up whether to be open with my mum. Announcing my intentions would only work if my mum knew articles existed. She might even produce hard copies from her journal. If there weren't newspaper articles she might panic, deducing that I couldn't believe her without them. She might run. Straightforward honesty, in this instance, wasn't noble – it was risky. I said:

'I want to check to see if Dad's plane has landed.'

Since Mark's interruption my mum had become unsettled. The apartment was no longer a safe place. She'd refused to sit down or take off her satchel. She paced the room. Her tempo was faster. As I picked up the phone she said:

'His plane will have landed by now.'

I opened a new page on a separate browsing window so that it was possible to flick back to Heathrow arrival information if my mum suddenly demanded to see my phone. With my precautions in place I typed Mia's name, my hands fumbling at the keys, doing a bad job of concealing my anxiety. My mum had so far proved perceptive.

'What does it say?'

'I'm still typing.'

I added the location of the alleged murder and pressed 'search'. The screen went blank. The connection was slow. My mum edged closer. She raised her hand, wanting the phone:

'Let me see.'

With an imperceptible flick of my thumb I switched the window to the airport's website and passed it to her. She stared at the screen intently:

'The plane landed twenty minutes ago.'

I could only hope she wouldn't notice or care about the icon at the bottom indicating that a second browsing window was open. She didn't own a smart phone. But her mind was so alert to trickery of any kind that she might figure it out or accidentally drag the other screen into view. She raised a finger, touching the screen. From my angle I couldn't tell if she was merely studying the list of inbound flights from Sweden. I was tempted to step forward, to ask for the phone back, but fearing this would give me away, I decided to hold my nerve and wait. My mum handed the phone back. She hadn't discovered the other page. By now the search on Mia would be complete. The information would be on my screen. But I couldn't look since my mum was speaking directly to me:

Chris will rush through the airport, hailing a taxi. He'll race across the city. His aim will be to take us by surprise. He won't call until he's outside the building. Once he's here it will be impossible to get away, not without a fight. Unlike last time I won't go quietly.

* * *

THE IDEA OF MY MUM AND DAD caught up in a scene of domestic violence was incomprehensible to me. Yet I now believed the inevitability of them coming to blows if they came face to face.

'Mum, we're leaving now.'

My mum double-checked to see if she'd left any evidence behind. The temptation to glance at my phone was powerful, but her movements were so erratic I was worried about being caught. I waited until she descended the stairs, following behind. I couldn't hold off any longer. I looked down at the screen.

The phone displayed a list of possible search results. They were from Swedish newspapers. I was shocked. I must have expected to see no results, no newspaper articles – a blank page. Though I'd promised to be objective and open-minded, deep down I must have believed that nothing had really happened and that Mia wasn't dead. I clicked on the top link. The page began to load. A fragment of image trickled down. I couldn't chance it any longer. I lowered the phone, sinking it into my pocket, just in time, as my mum turned around at the bottom of the stairs. I reached out and touched her shoulder, with no idea where we were going:

'Mum, where shall we go? You don't feel comfortable talking in public.'

'We can decide where later. We have to leave now.'

'And just stand on the street?'

My mum snapped:

'Are you trying to delay me? Is that your plan? Are you stalling so Chris can catch me?'

'No.'

'You're lying!'

The allegation was sharp.

'I don't want to see you fight with Dad. I want to hear the end of your account. That's the truth.'

My mum opened the front door. We left, walking out into the corridor. As though she were being pursued, my mum repeatedly pressed the call button for the lift. When she saw that it was rising up from the ground floor she stepped back:

'He might be in the lift! Let's take the stairs.'

I didn't argue, following her into the emergency stairway, where she hurried down, almost running. I called out, my voice echoing around the concrete space:

'Mum, I'm calling Mark. He has an office. Maybe he'll know somewhere we can talk. We need somewhere private.'

My mum replied:

'Hurry!'

I took out my phone and studied the screen. The local Swedish newspaper article was about Mia. There was a picture of her, just as my mum had described. The article declared that she was a missing person. I scrolled down. There was a reward for information. The article wasn't conclusive. It hadn't talked about a murder. But a missing person often preceded a murder. Nothing in the article contradicted my mum's account.

I dialled Mark. He picked up immediately. I said:

'My dad's on his way. His plane has landed. My mum won't stay in the apartment. We need another place to talk. Somewhere private. Somewhere my dad can't find us.'

'Are you sure you don't want to wait for him?'

'It would be a disaster.'

Mark found the solution immediately:

'I'll book you a hotel room. Order a cab. I'll call you back with the details. Are you okay? Is your mum okay?'

'We're okay.'

'Leave the hotel to me. I'll call you back.'

He hung up.

In contrast to my mum's speed, I moved like a man who'd had one too many drinks. Was I making the right decision or should I delay and allow my dad to catch up with us? After speaking to Mark my doubts resurfaced that I was the person to be in charge. I hadn't come up with the idea of a hotel room, an obvious solution to our problem. Even if I had, I didn't have the money to pay for it. My dad could be useful. If my mum was ill he knew more about her illness than anyone. On the other hand, a fleeting glance at the article offered no conclusive proof that my mum was delusional. Furthermore, it was hard to understand why my dad hadn't phoned when he arrived at the airport. The prospect of a violent confrontation was only minutes away. Allowing Dad to catch up with us would be an act of betrayal, a rejection of everything I'd been told. Whether I wanted the responsibility or not, it was mine. Without any evidence that her account was untrue, I'd take my mum's word on faith. Earlier she'd said that we have a duty to believe the people we love. In this case, she was asking for the space and time to finish telling me what had happened to Mia. I couldn't refuse her that.

I caught up with her at the bottom of the stairs:

'Wait.'

She stopped. I made a call to a local cab company. Without the name of a hotel I told them we were heading into the centre of London. They dispatched a car immediately. Meanwhile my mum stood on tiptoes, peering through the small glass panel into the communal space. Seeing it empty, she declared:

'We'll stay here until the cab rings. I don't want to wait on the street.'

The cab driver called a few minutes later and we edged forward into the communal areas, furtively skulking out of the building. There was a stretch of open ground between my apartment block and the main gates. With nowhere to hide we were exposed, unable to take any precautions against a chance encounter with my dad. I could feel the enormous strain even that short distance placed on my mum. Both of us were relieved to make it to the cab, but before I could suggest a plan, my mum leaned forward, addressing the driver:

'Drive to the end of this street and stop.'

The driver looked at me for confirmation. I was surprised by the request but I nodded. My mum whispered to me:

'Why did he need to check with you? Not because he knows there are allegations against my state of mind, he can't possibly know that. Why then? I'll tell you why. Because I'm a woman.'

The driver parked at the top of the narrow side street that ran between my apartment building and the main road. I suggested to my mum that the reason the driver had looked at me was because he found her instructions odd. My mum dismissed this:

'It's not odd. I want you to see him arrive.'

'Who?'

'Your father.'

'You want to wait here until Dad turns up?'

'It's important you see him for yourself. You're clinging on to a memory of Chris as an ordinary man. It's holding you back. But he's not the same man. You'll see that clearly from here. We can't risk being any closer. Once you see him you'll understand.'

I explained, in couched terms, our peculiar requirements to the now uneasy driver. We were buying his time. We'd wait at this spot for a while then we'd leave. My mum added:

'On our signal.'

The driver studied us carefully. No doubt he'd experienced plenty of bizarre and sketchy passenger requests. He phoned the cab company, who vouched for me. With the price agreed, he began to read his newspaper.

Outside my apartment, in the open, my mum's character radically changed. She wouldn't speak other than to utter a command or direction. She didn't relax, not for a second, her body twisted around, staring out of the rear window towards the main gates where a taxi would invariably pull up. I couldn't engage her in conversation. We waited in near silence, staking out my apartment building.

My phone rang. It was Mark. He gave me the address of an expensive hotel in Canary Wharf. He'd prepaid for the room and any incidentals. I wouldn't need a credit card upon checking in. He suggested waiting at the hotel, in the foyer, or the restaurant, to be on hand. I said:

'That sounds like a good idea.'

I ended the call and outlined the plan to my mum. We'd drive to the hotel, where she could finish her story without fear of being found. Canary Wharf was sufficiently far away. It was an unusual choice. My dad wouldn't expect us to go there, a usefully anonymous location, an area of London with no memories for us. My mum kept her eyes fixed on the main gate. As I pressed her for an answer, she suddenly grabbed my arm, pulling me below the window. A taxi passed by. With my face close to my mum's, we crouched in the nook between the seats. My mum held her breath. The other car's engine grew fainter. Slowly, she allowed us to rise up. We peered out of the rear window as if peering over the top of a trench. A black cab pulled over by the main gates. My dad stepped out.

It was my first sight of him since April. His body had changed. He'd lost weight. His appearance was ragged, paralleling many of the changes to my mum. Standing on the street, he lit a cigarette and inhaled as if his whole existence depended upon that intake of smoke. It was good to see him, I loved him very much, that emotion was strong, my instinct was to trust him, to leave my hiding place and call his name.

A second man stepped out of the cab. My mum exclaimed:
'Not him!'
The man put a hand on my dad's shoulder. I was so surprised I sat up, clearly visible until my mum pulled me down, hissing:
'They'll see you!'
The second man was of similar age to my dad but formally dressed. He wasn't a man I'd seen in any of the photographs or newspaper clippings. My dad hadn't mentioned that he'd be travelling with anyone, an omission so glaring I wondered if I'd failed to

listen to his voicemail message properly. This unknown man paid for the black cab, putting his sleek leather wallet into his pocket. I felt my mum's fingers tighten on my arm. She was afraid.

'Who is he, Mum?'

She spun around, touching the driver on the shoulder, imploring him:

'Go! Go! Go!'

Unaccustomed to playing the part of a getaway driver, the man took his time folding up his paper, much to the consternation of my mum, who appeared to want to scramble over the seat and take the wheel. I looked back to see my dad and his unidentified companion at the gates, in discussion. As our driver started the engine my dad looked up, in our direction, and my mum sank down again, out of sight.

'He's seen us!'

My mum refused to surface until I assured her, several minutes later, that we weren't being followed. Gently easing her into her seat, I asked:

'Who was that man?'

She shook her head, refusing to answer, putting a finger against her lips, just as she'd done on the train from Heathrow, just as she'd claimed Håkan had done when he'd visited. I found myself wanting to mimic the gesture, to explore it for myself. There was something about it I didn't understand.

My mum remained facing rearward for the journey, checking every car weaving through the traffic. The driver threw me a glance in the mirror, his eyes angled to ask if my mum was okay. I looked away. I didn't know – one moment I was sure she was sick with paranoia and fear. In the next moment her paranoia and fear seemed justified, and I found myself feeling it too, still wondering why my dad hadn't informed me there'd be someone with him when he arrived – a well-dressed stranger.

My phone rang. It was my dad. I looked at my mum.

'He'll be wondering where we are.'

'Don't answer.'

'I should tell him that we're okay.'

'Don't tell him anything about our plans!'

'I have to explain what we're doing.'

'Without any specific details.'

I answered the call. My dad was angry:

'The concierge said you just left.'

My mum's face was close to mine, listening to the conversation. I replied:

'Mum didn't feel comfortable talking there. We're going somewhere else.'

'Where?'

With urgency my mum waved at me not to tell him. I said:

'She wants to talk to me alone. I'll call you once we're done.'

'You're indulging her, Daniel. You're making a mistake. The more she convinces you, the more she convinces herself. You're making things much worse.'

It hadn't occurred to me that I could be aggravating my mum's condition. My confidence was faltering.

'Dad, I'll call you later.'

'Daniel—'

I hung up. He rang again. I didn't answer. He didn't leave a message. My mum was satisfied with my handling of the call. She said:

'It was nasty of him to suggest you're making me worse. He knows how to play people.'

Afraid I'd made a mistake, I said:

'No more personal attacks. Let's stick to facts. I'd say the same to him if he spoke that way about you.'

'Just the facts then. Why didn't he tell you he was with someone?'

I looked at her:

'Who was that man?'

My mum shook her head and once again put a finger to her lips.

Arriving at the hotel, I paid the driver. We stepped out, surrounded by the steel and glass lines of Canary Wharf. I escorted my mother into the reception, passing opulent flower arrangements. Members of the hotel staff were dressed in starched white shirts. I rushed through the paperwork, my mum beside me, her back pressed against the front desk, eyes on the main doors, expecting the conspirators to follow us. She took hold of my arm, apparently oblivious to the other people around, and asked:

'What if he phones the cab company to find out where they took us?'

'He doesn't know which cab company we used. Even if he did, or guessed, they won't give out that information.'

My mum shook her head at my naïveté:

'They can be bought like anyone else.'

'If he does come here, he couldn't find our room, the hotel won't tell him.'

'We should take another cab, a different taxi company, give them a false name, and ask them to drive us near another hotel, but not to the actual door, we can walk the rest of the way. This would make us impossible to find.'

'The hotel is paid for.'

Money seemed to make an impression. I added:

'Dad has been ringing and ringing. He wouldn't be doing that if he knew where we were.'

My mum considered the situation and with reluctance nodded. The staff had been pretending not to listen. I refused the offer of being shown to our rooms, taking the card key, explaining we had no luggage.

I knew better than to talk until we were safely in the room with the door locked. My mum would need to approve the new location. We were on the sixth floor. The room was modern, comfortable, and my mother was briefly distracted by the fact that it must have been expensive. She walked to the sofa seat set up in the window alcove, filled with soft bright cushions, offering a view upriver, towards the centre of town. Any pleasure was short-lived. She began making an examination of the room, lifting up the telephone receiver, opening every drawer and cupboard. I sat in the alcove and phoned Mark. He was already in the lobby. Unsure how to express my gratitude, I said:

'I'll pay you back.'

He didn't reply. The truth was that I had no idea how much it cost and couldn't afford to pay him back. Meanwhile, my mum moved from the bedroom to the bathroom, finally checking the hallway, looking at the map of the other rooms, the fire escape –

the exit routes. Finished, she placed her satchel of evidence on the coffee table, beside the fruit plate and fashionable bottle of spring water that had been left in the room.

I walked to the minibar, choosing a sugary caffeinated energy drink, pouring it over ice and sipping at it.

'Do you want anything, Mum?'

She shook her head.

'Why don't you take some fruit?'

She examined the bowl, selecting a banana. We sat in the window seat, more like picnic-goers than hotel guests, as she peeled and sliced the banana, sharing it between us.

'Mum, who was that man?'

*　*　*

M Y MUM OPENED HER SATCHEL, taking out the journal and removing a handwritten list of names. At a glance I counted six.

The man is on this list of suspects. I would've shown it to you earlier but I was sure you'd dismiss it as fantasy. However, this list is now coming to life. One of these people has followed me here, prepared to go to extraordinary lengths to stop me.

At the top, there's Håkan and Chris. Your father is a suspect. I'm sorry, but he is.

There's Ulf Lund, the hermit in the field.

There's the two-faced town mayor, Kristofer Dalgaard, I told you about him already – he betrayed my story about the elk to Håkan.

By the way, every name on this list, even Ulf, was at the midsommar celebration where Mia was drunk and the last place she was seen alive in public. These six men were standing in the crowd when she threw her flowers in the air. Reviewing the memory, I've tried to calculate where the flowers would've landed if they hadn't broken apart, if the string hadn't come undone, whose feet they would have dropped at. Though I can't be sure, I believe Mia was aiming at the next name on the list.

Stellan Nilson is a detective, one of the most senior officers in the region. He'll become very important to the events that follow. He's more like a brother to Håkan than a friend. They even look similar – tall, strong, serious. When they're standing together people often ask if they're related and they love the idea, they smile and say they should've been.

The last name on the list is Olle Norling, television and radio celebrity, a doctor, on paper, but he doesn't have a practice or any actual patients. He's a successful showman, an entertainer, and his circus act is soul-enriching wisdom, presenting health segments on popular television programmes, publishing books about losing weight by smiling fifty times a day, or other far-fetched claims about the power of the mind. He's a make-believe doctor, a snake oil salesman, adored by the public, who've fallen for his cultivated image as a gentle, caring wizard. In fact, he's risen to great heights by guile and shameless self-promotion. Dr Norling was the first to declare me insane:

'You're not well, Tilde.'

That's what he said, in English, shaking his head slowly from side to side, as though he could only possibly want the best for me.

One of these men is in London, right now, with Chris, chasing after me.

* * *

J UDGING FROM THE ENERGY WITH which she described him, I guessed:
'The doctor?'

Dr Olle Norling. Why is he here? Having failed in Sweden to institutionalise me, their plan is to try again. They haven't changed strategy; despite my release from the asylum and the real doctors declaring me fit and well, they're sticking to their approach to have me locked up, numbed by drugs, and my credibility destroyed. They're too late to stop you hearing the truth. Their only option is to break our relationship and compel you to join their group – to finish me off as a force that can bring them to justice. The conspirators rightly doubt your father's ability to get the job done. I don't know whether Norling originally came up with the idea of bringing my sanity into question. Norling was certainly the first to say it aloud, using his reputation and medical knowledge against me. The question of my state of mind was raised only when I refused to accept their explanation of what happened to Mia.

After midsommar I hoped to talk to Mia about that disturbing day. But there was no sign of her. I was scared. It was the summer holidays. She should be outside, on the land. I took to walking through the fields in the morning, at night, staring at Håkan's farm, hoping to see Mia on the veranda or at the bedroom window. But I never did.

A week later the answer finally came. I was awake early, working on our guest lodgings, painting the barn walls on top of a tall ladder, when I saw Håkan's gleaming silver Saab driving at great speed. Håkan isn't a brash and dangerous show-off. I'd never witnessed him reckless on the roads before. There had to be an emergency. I was expecting the car to race past our farm, stunned when it swung into our drive and he jumped out, running into our farmhouse, missing me altogether. I tightened my grip on the ladder, fearful I'd fall, because what other explanation could there be other than that something terrible had happened to Mia?

Hastily descending to the ground, I could hear raised voices. Through the window I could see Chris and Håkan in the kitchen. Håkan turned and bolted out of the house, back to his car. I dropped the paint, chasing after him, pressing a hand against the window, leaving yellow fingerprints on the glass. I needed to hear him say it. He lowered the window and said:

'Mia's gone!'

My next memory is of lying on the gravel drive looking up at the sky. Chris was supporting my head on his lap. Håkan's car was no longer in the drive. I'd been unconscious for only a small amount of time. Mia quickly came into my thoughts and I hoped the news had been a nightmare, maybe I'd fallen from the ladder, struck my head, maybe Mia was safe – except I knew the truth, I'd always known the truth. My enemies will tell you that my fainting was a watershed moment. My mind snapped and nothing I subsequently said or thought or claimed can be taken seriously. Sick words from a sick mind. Here's the truth. Fainting didn't mean a thing. I accept, it made me seem weak and vulnerable, but the sensation that came over me wasn't madness, it was an overwhelming sense of failure. I'd spent the past two months aware that Mia was in danger and I'd done nothing to protect her.

Håkan gave an account of what happened the night Mia disappeared. His explanation goes like this:

They'd quarrelled.

She'd been upset.

She'd waited until the household was asleep, packed two bags, and disappeared in the middle of the night, gone with no goodbye and no note.

That's what we were told. That's what the town was told and that's what the town believed.

Stellan the detective, Håkan's closest friend, arrived at his farm. I happened to be in the fields at the time. I saw his car in Håkan's drive. I timed them. After seventeen minutes Stellan the detective left, the men shaking hands, an investigation seventeen minutes long concluded with a pat on the back.

Håkan stopped at our farm the next day, explaining that the police had been notified in the major cities – Malmö, Gothenburg, Stockholm. They were looking for Mia. However, there was a limit to what they could do. She wasn't a child, chasing runaways was a difficult process. Repeating this information, Håkan dropped his head to indicate that he was lost for words, consumed with grief, or so we're supposed to believe. Chris comforted him, stating that he was sure Mia would come back, that this kind of behaviour was typical of teenagers. Their conversation wasn't real! It was an act – the two of them performing for me, Håkan playing the part of the heartbroken father, Chris feeding him cues. Except it was more than a performance, they were testing me. Would I walk up to Håkan and put my arm around his shoulder? I couldn't do it. I remained in the corner of the room as far from him as possible. If I'd been political and shrewd I would've embraced him, shed false tears for his false grief, but I don't possess his gift for deceit, so instead I made it perfectly clear that I didn't believe him, a brazen statement of defiant opposition. Looking back, I realise what a miscalculation that was. From that moment on I was in danger.

* * *

R ETURNING TO HER SATCHEL, my mum took out a poster. She unfolded it across the coffee table and sat back down beside me.

These weren't produced on Håkan's computer. He employed a professional printing company, using the highest-quality paper. Even the layout is stylish, more like a supplement pulled from the pages of *Vanity Fair* or *Vogue* magazine – the world's most extravagant missing person poster. They were everywhere. I spent a day spotting them and counted over thirty, wrapped around tree trunks, on a notice board on the beach, in the church and the shop windows along the promenade. The positioning was troubling to me because Mia wasn't going to be hiding in any of these places. If she'd run away, she'd be in one of the cities. If she'd run away, she was going to be far, far away, not here, not a mile from home. And if she'd run, she'd never have told a soul, because that information would've reached Håkan in a second, so these posters served no useful purpose except as a grand gesture that Håkan had done the right thing, that he was playing the part expected of him.

Look at the bottom of the poster—
A rich reward for useful leads and that isn't a misprint: one hundred thousand Swedish krona, ten thousand pounds! He might as well have offered a million dollars, or a chest of pirate gold; he knew it would provide

no new information. It was a crass statement about him:

'Look at how much money I'm prepared to pay! My love for Mia has a number attached to it and it's greater than any number you've ever seen on a missing person poster before!'

From your expression, you've interpreted these posters as evidence of his innocence just as you were intended to do.

·   ·   ·

I SHOOK MY HEAD AT MY MUM'S presumption that she always knew what I was thinking.

'I don't believe these posters prove he's innocent. They don't prove anything. You can argue posters both ways. If he spent no money, if he put up no posters, or if he only put up one tatty poster, you could accuse him of being callous. Or too riddled with guilt—'

'But I can't make a judgment about something that he didn't do.'

'My point is—'

You don't accept it as evidence. Fine. We won't accept it. We don't need it. You shouldn't doubt his innocence because I say so. You shouldn't doubt it because of these posters. Doubt it because Håkan's account of the night Mia disappeared doesn't make any sense. She supposedly fled the farm on 1 July. What did this sixteen-year-old girl allegedly do? Mia didn't own a car, no taxi was called, how did she leave a farm in the middle of nowhere in the middle of the night? She wasn't at the train station in the morning. Her bicycle was still on the farm. She didn't walk – there was nowhere to walk to, the distances were too great. I've escaped from a remote farm. Let me tell you, from personal experience, you need a plan. According to Håkan there was a gap of ten hours in which she could've disappeared, but those ten hours were a time when everything was shut down. For many miles in every direction the world turned dark, a population asleep, no shops open, no public transport.

Mia just vanished. That's what we were supposed to believe.

It was my duty to talk to the police and I approached them without discussing with Chris, wanting to discover how seriously they were taking the matter. I cycled through the centre of town. The shops were busy. The promenade was crowded. In the coffee shop where I'd eaten cake with Mia only a few weeks ago other people were sitting, drinking, laughing. Where was the grief for this lost girl? The pursuit of comfort is one of the great evils of our time. Håkan understood that perfectly, he understood that as long as there was no body, no evidence of a crime, no one would mind. Everyone would much rather believe that Mia had run off rather than consider the possibility that she'd been murdered.

The local police station was quieter than a library. It was preposterously clean, as if they did nothing but polish the floor and wipe the windows. Self-evidently these officers had never encountered any crime to speak of. These were novices. In Stockholm I might have had a chance, there might have been an ally, someone with experience of the darkness in men's hearts. Not here, these were steady, safe job-seekers, men and women who understood how to play the politics of a small town.

At the front desk I demanded to speak to Stellan the detective. I'd expected a long wait, several hours, but I'd barely read more than a page or two of my notes when Stellan called my name, ushering me into his office. Maybe it was because he looked so much like Håkan that he seemed so out of place in an office, with pens and paper clips. He gestured for me to sit down, towering over me, asking how he could help. I asked why they hadn't spoken to me about Mia's disappearance. He asked bluntly if I knew where Mia was. I said no, I didn't know, of course I didn't know, but that I thought that there was more to this than merely a girl running away. I didn't have the courage to spell out my hypothesis in the police station, not yet, not without enough evidence. What was interesting was that Stellan didn't stare at me like I was mad, or as though I was speaking nonsense. He stared at me like this—

* * *

M Y MUM GAVE ME A LOOK that could have meant she was sad, or that she was listening carefully, or that she was bored.

Like I was a threat! He was assessing how much of a problem I was going to be. This police station and its most senior officer had no intention of unearthing the truth. It was an institution working to conceal the truth. This case required someone who was sceptical – it required an outsider. I hadn't wanted to be one. But it was the role I was forced to play. I thanked Stellan for his time, deciding that the next course of action, the only logical course of action, in the absence of a functioning police force, in the absence of a search warrant, was to break into Håkan's farm.

* * *

A S I SAT, TROUBLED by the notion of my mum breaking into a house, her hands disappeared into the deepest pocket of the satchel. I couldn't see what she was doing until she slowly lifted them. She was wearing two red mittens, gravely stretched out for my inspection as if they were as conclusive as blood-soaked gloves. There was an absurdity about the moment, the disjunction between my mum's earnestness and the novelty mittens, yet I felt no urge to smile.

To avoid leaving fingerprints! These were the only gloves in my possession, thick Christmas mittens. I started carrying them in my pocket during the height of summer, waiting for my chance to break in. As you can testify, I've never done anything like this before. I wasn't going to sneak into Håkan's farm in the middle of the night as a professional thief might do. I'd be opportunistic, seizing a moment when both Elise and Håkan were out. Remember, this is rural Sweden, no one locks their door, there are no alarms. However, Elise's behaviour had changed since Mia's disappearance. She wasn't working. She sat on the veranda, lost in thought. Earlier I described her as always busy. Not any more— Before you interrupt again, I agree, it could be argued in many ways. Regardless of how you interpret the change in her character, it made it difficult to break in because she was at home much more.

One day I caught sight of Elise and Håkan leaving

together. I didn't know where they were going or for how long, maybe they'd be gone for minutes, maybe hours, but this was my only chance and I took it, abandoning my work on the vegetable garden, running through the fields, and knocking on their door just to make sure that the house was empty. There was no reply and I knocked again, asking myself, as I slipped on these thick mittens, whether I had the courage to open this door and walk into their house. As with all sensible people, I'll break the law if need be. However, that doesn't mean I find the process easy.

Try the mittens on.

Pick up that glass.

You see?

They have no grip. They're impractical. No professional burglar would ever choose them. Standing in front of their house I became flustered because I was wearing Christmas mittens in the middle of the summer, trying to break into someone's farm, and I couldn't even open the door. The smooth round steel handle didn't turn easily. I tried many times. In the end I had to clasp the handle with both hands.

Those first few metres inside, from the front door to the bottom of the stairs, were some of the most daunting steps I've ever taken. So ingrained were my Swedish customs and sense of household etiquette that I even took off my shoes, an idiotic thing for an intruder to do, depositing my clogs on the bottom step, announcing my presence to anyone who might return home.

I'd never been upstairs in that house before. What did I discover? Fetch a brochure for any mid-range furniture store and I could show you Håkan's bedroom. It was neat and proper with a pine bed, pine wardrobes, immaculately clean, no clutter on the bedside tables, no pills, no books, no piles of dirty clothes. The decorative touches were few and inoffensive, as if decided by a committee, acceptable local artists framed on the wall. It was a furniture show-room, not a real bedroom, and I say my next remark carefully, not as a criticism, but as an observation from someone married for forty years – I was quite sure, stand-ing in the middle of this bedroom, next to a vase filled with painted wooden tulips, that no one was having sex in here. It was a sexless space, and yes, you're right, I don't have evidence for that, but a person can tell a lot from a room, and it's my unsubstantiated observation that Håkan was looking elsewhere for his sexual needs. Elise must have surrendered to that fact, and for the first time I felt pity for her, loyal Elise, a prisoner of that pine bedroom. I'm quite sure the inelegant solution of sleeping around wasn't open to her. She was his. He was not hers.

By deduction the last room on the landing belonged to Mia. I peered inside, certain there was some mis-take – this couldn't be Mia's room. The furniture was identical to the previous room, the same pine wardrobe,

even the same pine bed as her parents. Mia hadn't per-
sonalised the room except for an elaborate mirror. There
were no posters, no postcards and no photographs. It
was a room unlike the room of any teenager I've ever
seen. What a lonely room it was, not a space where
Mia had been given freedom, no, it was decorated and
cleaned according to Elise's standards. The room felt like
an order – a command, she should become one of them.
Mia might have slept in that room but it didn't belong to
her, it didn't speak of her personality. It was no different
from a comfortable guest room. Then it struck me – the
smell! The room had been professionally cleaned, the
bed had been made, the sheets were fresh and pressed,
they were new, they hadn't been slept in, the room vacu-
umed – it smelled of lavender. Sure enough, in the plug
socket was an automated air-freshening device turned to
its highest setting. If forensics were called in to make an
examination I was sure that they wouldn't find even the
smallest particle of Mia's skin. This was cleanliness to a
sinister degree.

I checked the wardrobe. It was full. I checked the
drawers. They were full. According to Håkan she'd
packed two bags. With what? I asked myself. Nothing
much was missing. I can't say how many clothes were in
the wardrobe before she left, so can't compare, but this
didn't feel like a room that had been ransacked by a girl
on the run. There was a Bible on the bedside table – Mia
was a Christian. I have no idea if she believed in God

or not; certainly she hadn't taken the Bible with her. I checked the pages: there were no notes, no pages ripped out. I turned to the verse from Ephesians that Anne-Marie had stitched in the days before she killed herself. It was unmarked. Underneath the Bible was a diary. Glancing through, there were events listed, there were homework assignments, no references to sex, no boyfriends, girl-friends, no frustrations. No teenager in the world keeps a diary like this. Mia must have known that her room was being searched. She was writing this diary in the knowl-edge it was being read – this was the diary she wanted Elise and Håkan to read. The diary was a trick, a diversion to pacify a snooping parent, and what kind of teenager produces such a clever decoy document except someone with a great deal to hide?

I'd vowed to stay for no more than thirty minutes, but thirty minutes goes quickly and I'd found no evidence. I couldn't leave empty-handed. I decided to stay until I found something, no matter the risk! It occurred to me that I'd overlooked the mirror. It stood out as different, not an antique, not from a furniture store, but a piece of craftsmanship, handmade and ambitious – shaped like a magic mirror, wood swirled around oval-shaped glass. Standing close, I noticed that the glass hadn't been glued to the frame: there were steel clips at the top and bottom. They turned, like keys, and the glass fell cleanly from the frame. I jolted forward to catch it and prevent it smashing on the floor. Behind the mirror, carved into the wood, was a deep space. The person who'd crafted this unusual mirror had an ulterior motive. They'd created a hiding space, custom-made for Mia. This is what I found inside.

●　●　●

M Y MUM HANDED ME the ragged remains of a small diary. There was a front and back cover but the inside pages had been torn out. For the first time I experienced a powerful emotional response to my mum's evidence, as though this object retained some undeniable trace of violence.

Imagine the perpetrator in action, their powerful hands ripping the pages, the air full of words. Fire would have been a surer way to destroy this evidence, or tossing it into the depths of Elk River. This wasn't a rational attempt at concealment. It was a savage response to thoughts written in these pages, an expression of hatred carrying with it the implication of a crime to come, or a crime already committed.

Examine it for yourself.

Almost nothing remains, none of the written entries, only jagged fragments along the spine, paper teeth spotted with partial words. I've counted exactly fifty-five scattered letters and only three complete words.

Hans, the Swedish word for 'his'.

Rök, the Swedish for 'smoke', and please consider who smokes, and who doesn't.

Räd, not a complete word, caught on the rip, and there's no such Swedish word as *räd*, I believe the second 'd' was torn off, it should have been *rädd* – the Swedish for 'scared'.

*

The diary was too important to put back. But stealing the remains of Mia's journal was a provocation, an unmistakable signal of my intention to pursue the culprit and do whatever was necessary to discover the truth. When Håkan returned and found it missing, the most suggestive piece of evidence that Mia hadn't run away from home, he'd sweep through his farm burning incriminating clues. Logically, this had become not my first but my only chance of collecting evidence. I couldn't leave. Standing in Mia's bedroom, wondering where to search next, I stared out across the fields, seeing the bump in the land, the underground shelter where Håkan carved those obscene trolls, the location of the second padlocked door. Tomorrow the shed might be emptied or razed to the ground. I had to act now.

With the remains of Mia's journal in my pocket, I found a hand-carved key cupboard on the hallway wall. On farms there are always a vast number of keys, for various barns and tractors. I was going through them one by one, none of them were marked, it would take hours to try them all, so I ran to the toolshed, right next to the farm, stealing Håkan's bolt cutters. Still wearing my red mittens, leaving no fingerprints, I hurried to the underground shelter, cutting the first padlock and opening the door, fumbling for the light cord. The sight awaiting me was so disturbing I had to fight against my urge to run away.

In the corner of the shelter was a stack of trolls, piled up like a heap of bodies, horrifically disfigured, cut in half, eyes gouged out, decapitated, smashed and splintered. It took a few seconds for me to muster the willpower to walk past the mound of trolls, trampling on the woodchips, arriving at the next door, secured with a second padlock. It was a different kind of lock to the one on the external door, a far tougher brand. Finally, after a great effort, the blades sliced through the steel, I gripped the second door and pulled it open.

Inside there was a plastic table. On top of the table was a plastic case. Inside the case was a digital video camera. I checked to see if there was anything on the memory. It had been wiped. I was too late. The answers were gone. In their place were just more questions. The room was fitted with power sockets – five in a row. What for? The walls were covered with soundproofing foam. What for? The floor was spotlessly clean. Why, when next door was a mess? Before I could examine any further, I heard Håkan's voice calling out urgently across the farm.

I put the camera back and hurried to the outer door, opening it slightly and peering out. The shelter was visible from the farm. I was trapped. There were no trees nearby, no shrubs, and nowhere to hide. I could see Håkan at the toolshed. Foolishly I'd left the door open and he was examining the premises, no doubt wondering if he'd been robbed. He'd quickly notice his bolt cutters were missing. He'd call the police. There was very little time. As soon as Håkan's back was turned I ran towards the fields, as fast as I could. Reaching the edge of the wheat, I threw myself down to the ground, waiting among the crops, catching my breath until I found the courage to look up. Håkan was walking towards the shelter, only a hundred metres away. When he entered the shelter I took my chance and crawled away, flat on my stomach, using my elbows to pull me along.

Reaching the edge of our land, I realised that for some reason I'd kept both padlocks, so I buried them deep in the soil, took off my mittens, stuffed them into my pocket on top of the diary, and walked back, brushing myself down. I picked up the basket I'd left by the vegetable patch ready filled with potatoes, and entered my farm, saying aloud that I'd picked some fine-looking potatoes for dinner! Except Chris wasn't at home, so my alibi – they'd used a salmon as an alibi, why shouldn't I use a potato? – was wasted. I set about washing and peeling the potatoes, a huge number, trying to finish as many as possible so I could explain what I'd been doing this morning should I be asked.

An hour or so later, with a mountainous heap of potatoes beside me, enough for ten hungry farmers,

I heard Chris at the door and turned to tell him the innocent story of my morning, only to see the tall solemn figure of Stellan the detective standing at the entrance.

· · ·

M Y MUM WASN'T DONE with the mittens. She picked them up, pushing them into her jeans pocket so that part of the material was poking out.

The detective wanted to question me and the mittens were still in my pocket.

Like this!

With one bright red fingertip hanging over the lip, and underneath them was Mia's stolen diary. I'd buried the padlocks but forgotten about the mittens, and it was the middle of summer, so there was no reason to have them in my pocket. If they saw them I'd be caught because the mittens would lead to the diary. If they asked me to empty my pockets I'd be going to jail.

Stellan didn't speak much English. In this instance he needed to communicate in Swedish to be absolutely confident of what he was saying and what he was being told, so I asked Chris to hold off while we spoke. I'd translate at the end. I sat at the kitchen table with Stellan seated opposite me and Chris standing. Somehow it had taken on the appearance of an interrogation, these two men against me. Chris wasn't by my side, but next to the detective. I asked if this was regarding Mia. The detective said no, it wasn't about Mia – he was categorical about that, describing the break-in on Håkan's farm. Someone had cut his locks to the troll shed. I must have said something like, 'That's terrible,' before asking what had been taken, and he told me nothing had been taken, the locks had been cut but nothing was missing except the padlocks. I said that was curious, very curious, maybe the thieves were looking for something specific, angling Stellan towards a discussion of that second room, as sinisterly clean as Mia's bedroom, but he didn't take the bait. Instead, Stellan the detective leaned forward and told me that they didn't have theft in this part of Sweden. Incidents such as this were exceptionally rare. I didn't like the way he was looking at me. There was accusation and aggression. I didn't like the reference to 'this part of Sweden', talking about it as though he were a guardian of this realm and I was an outsider to be mistrusted, as though I'd brought crime into this area by the very fact of my foreignness, even though I'm Swedish born! I wasn't going to be intimidated by him, no matter his physical size or status, and so I mirrored his posture, also leaning forward, feeling the dense clump of mittens press against my upper leg, asking how he could be sure a crime had been committed when nothing had been taken. Stellan said that clearly there'd been an intruder since two padlocks were missing. And I retorted, pleased with my logic, that something being missing isn't proof of a crime. A young girl was missing – a beautiful young girl, Mia, was missing – but they didn't believe a crime had been committed. Why should this be any different? Why should they take the disappearance of two padlocks more seriously than a missing girl? Why was the case of the missing padlocks definitively and absolutely a serious crime the likes of which had never been seen around here? And the other, a girl gone in the middle of the night, with no trace of her, that was a family matter requiring only a few minutes of their investigative time? I didn't understand, two replaceable padlocks, which could be bought anywhere, two worthless padlocks no one loved, and they were acting as though we should be scared in our homes because a padlock had never gone missing before in these parts. Perhaps that was true, perhaps this was the safest place in the world for padlocks, but I couldn't help them with the mystery of the missing padlocks, as serious as the case might be. If they wanted my advice, I told them to dredge Elk River or dig up the land, search the forests, we had no missing padlocks here.

What were they going to do? Arrest me?

.　.　.

I WATCHED MY MUM DELICATELY remove a matchbox from the smallest pocket of the satchel. She balanced it carefully in the palm of her hand. With a push of her finger she opened one side. I saw a golden chanterelle mushroom cradled on a bed of cotton wool:

'A mushroom?'

'It's only one half of the evidence.'

My mum sat beside me, and it was one of the few occasions when I could see her struggling with how best to introduce her evidence.

> You and I often went hunting for chanterelles when you were a child. We were a formidable team. You were so quick among the trees, with an eye for where they grew. We'd forage for the entire day, returning home only when our baskets were brimming. But you always hated the taste even when I did no more than fry them and serve them on buttered toast. Once, you even cried because you were so disappointed that you couldn't join me in saying how delicious they were. You felt sure that you'd let me down. Of all the people in the world you can testify to my abilities: I've never picked a mushroom that was dangerous.

* * *

I NODDED MY AGREEMENT:
  'I've never known you to.'
My mum pushed for more:
'You find it hard to believe I could make such a mistake?'
'I find it hard to believe.'

After the police officer departed, Chris suggested I'd been under too much stress trying to prepare our barns for paying guests. I was working fourteen-hour days, seven days a week. He claimed I'd lost weight and that I needed to enjoy life in Sweden more. As though the idea were off the top of his head he suggested that we should go into the forests for a relaxing day foraging for mushrooms. I wasn't sure whether his proposal was genuine. He'd framed it so cleverly I had no reason for refusing. I gave him the benefit of the doubt, of course I did.

The next day it was raining outside. Chris said it didn't matter – keen not to cancel our plans. Since I didn't mind about a little rain, we cycled north, to the forests, the same forest where Teardrop Island was located. I tried not to think about the island, or Chris's visits there. Turning off the road, we cycled up a dirt track. The easily accessible areas were no good. We needed to go deeper, off the paths, into parts of the forest that hadn't been touched, the remoter spots. We left our bikes together under the cover of a tree next to Elk River. We took our cycle baskets, padded with newspaper to stop the bottom layer of mushrooms being crushed and destroyed. After a while we reached a slope of giant rocks, boulders the size of cars. Some were completely covered in moss. I couldn't imagine many people climbing the slope in order to find mushrooms, so I pointed to the top, saying that I was going to forage up there. Without waiting for a reply I began to climb, clambering over the stone, my feet slipping on the moss. At the top there was a view over a hundred thousand trees – firs, pines and silver birches as far as the eye could see, no roads, no people, no houses, no power lines, just the forests as they had been when I was a child and always would be, long after I'm dead. Chris joined me at the top, breathlessly admiring the view.

Chris has never taken foraging as seriously as me, or as you. He's half-hearted in his efforts. He likes to break and smoke and chat. I didn't want to be burdened by him. We agreed to meet back at the bikes, setting a time towards the end of the day. I quickly left him behind, and before long I'd found my first chanterelles, a tiny cluster of young mushrooms. I cut them with my special knife rather than ripping them out, so that they'd grow back. Within a few minutes I'd found a rhythm, hardly ever straightening my back as I swooped between the damp shady nooks where they pushed out of the soil. Then, tucked under the exposed root of an ancient tree, a golden treasure trove, twenty or thirty together, enough to make me exclaim with gratitude, as if the forests themselves had made me a gift. Without a pause for lunch, I stopped only when my basket was full, a satisfying heap, like the kind we'd always collected together. You would've been proud of me.

At the end of the day it was a long walk back. I was tired and happy – the happiest I'd been for some time, remembering the true reason I'd come back to my country, for feelings just like this. The light rain hadn't stopped and after several hours my hair was soaked. I didn't mind. I pressed my hair flat with my hands, squeezing all the rainwater out. I was quite sure Chris had stopped foraging long ago. He'd be by the bicycles, sheltered, perhaps with a fire burning, warm by the river – that was my honest hope.

When I reached the bicycles, there was no fire burning. Chris was sitting by the river, on the trunk of a fallen tree, smoking Håkan's weed, his back to me, hood pulled up. I placed my basket by the bicycle, beside his, which contained nothing, not a single mushroom, and joined him by the river. He turned round and smiled, which surprised me, because I'd been expecting him to be annoyed. He must have waited several hours. He told me to take a seat and offered to fetch a cup of tea from our Thermos. My hands had become damp and my fingers were stiff. I was looking forward to a warm drink. Several minutes passed, no tea arrived. Finally I heard him call out my name.

'Tilde?'

Something was wrong. I stood up and saw Chris standing by the bicycles, staring down at my basket. He seemed upset. Now the trap will be sprung, I thought. I didn't understand the nature of it but I could feel its jaws closing around me. My happiness had been complacency. Afraid, I slowly walked towards him, not sure what to expect. He crouched down and picked up my basket. Instead of chanterelle mushrooms it was full of these—

•   •   •

M Y MUM PUSHED OPEN the other side of the matchbox, reveal-ing a golden silver birch leaf suspended on a bed of cotton wool.

Leaves, Daniel!

Leaves!

The basket was full of leaves! Chris was looking at me with mock pity in his eyes. It took me a few seconds to absorb the implication. This wasn't a practical joke. He was claiming that I'd spent the entire day collecting leaves. I grabbed the top layer, crushing them in my hands, digging down to the bottom. Every chanterelle had gone. With a jerk of my wrists I threw the leaves into the air. Chris just stood there as they tumbled around us. The whole situation was preposterous. I couldn't have made such an extraordinary mistake. Then I remembered my knife. It was smeared with chanterelle stem. So I brandished the blade, purely as evidence. Chris lurched back, as if I were threatening him. Belatedly I understood the nature of the trap. Only one explanation remained – Chris had replaced the chanterelles with these leaves. He'd collected them while we'd been sepa-rated. He knew we'd separate. He knew he'd have time to return and make preparations. While I was waiting for tea, he'd made the swap. I cried out, demanding to know where the mushrooms were. I patted his pockets. The mushrooms were surely close by. Perhaps he'd pre-pared a hole and tipped them in, burying them, covering them with loose soil. I began to dig, like a dog searching for a bone. When I looked up I saw Chris coming towards me, arms out wide, as if to smother me. This time I did use the knife, I slashed the air and told him to stay back. He was trying to soothe me as if I were a startled horse, but the sound of his voice made me sick. I had to get away, so I ran into the forest. When I looked back he was running after me. So I ran faster, heading for higher ground, I couldn't beat him on the flat but I was a nimble climber, he was a smoker, I was fitter over long distances. He'd almost caught up, reaching out, finger-tips stretched towards the tails of my rain jacket. I cried out, reaching the base of the boulder slope, scrambling on all fours. I felt him grab my leg so I kicked out, kicked and kicked until I caught him in the face. It bought me some time. From the bottom of the slope he screamed my name, this time not as a question but furious:

'Tilde!'

My name echoed around the forest but I didn't look back, reaching the top and running as fast as I could into the woods, leaving Chris screaming from the base of the hill.

Eventually I collapsed with exhaustion, lying under a tree on the wet moss, the light rain on my face, trying to fully grasp the implications of the plan that had been launched against me. As the sky darkened I heard my name being called out, not by one voice but several. I cautiously followed the sounds back to the ridge of boulders and saw crisscrossing beams of the torches through the trees, counting them – one, two, three, four, five, six, seven – seven beams of light, seven people looking for me. It was a search party. In a matter of hours since my fight with Chris a search party had been mobilised. It was an overreaction. There was no need to recruit so many people unless you required witnesses, unless you required this staged incident to be logged officially. Chris had probably given a statement, shown them the bicycles, the basket full of leaves, marked it as evidence, shown them the spot where I'd slashed at him with the knife. He'd been quick and smart. I'd been wild-tempered and foolish.

Consider Chris's character. As you can testify, he's always hated the authorities, he's wary of doctors, and he's never trusted the police. If he were innocent he would've searched for me alone. What are the chances that he would have phoned the police to organise an official search party? The chances are zero. I wasn't hurt or lost – I'm an adult and in no need of being escorted out of the forest like a lost child. To reassert my authority and offer proof of my presence of mind, there was only one option. I'd set about finding my own way back to the farm. This would prove that I was competent. There's a legal phrase for this, a term I've heard a great number of times in the past few weeks, a Latin term – *non compos mentis* – not of sound mind. If I were found lost and cold, wandering in these forests,

I'd be declared not of sound mind. I wasn't lost, I was *compos mentis*, and once I'd located Elk River it was a simple case of following the fast-flowing water all the way back home.

It was midnight by the time I reached our farm. There were several cars in the drive. My enemies were waiting for me. I recognised Håkan's Saab, there was Stellan the detective's car. But the remaining car was a mystery to me. It was expensive and impressive. I was outnumbered. I briefly considered running away, but the thought was a childish one. I didn't have a plan. I didn't have my satchel or my journal. Most importantly, I couldn't abandon my responsibilities to Mia. If I ran, my enemies would only use it to support their argument. They'd claim I was acting erratically and illogically. I entered my farm, expecting an ambush. Even so, I was unprepared for what happened next.

The mysterious expensive car belonged to Dr Olle Norling, the celebrity doctor. While our shoulders might have brushed at parties, I hadn't, at that time, been worthy of his attention – this was the first occasion we'd spoken directly. Chris stood in the corner, his eyebrow fixed with a bandage. I guessed that was due to the injury I'd inflicted on him while trying to escape, a kick to the head. It was now part of the evidence against me, along with the silver birch leaves. I asked what was going on, not aggressively. I needed to be composed and articulate, not emotional. These men would catch me with emotion. They'd try to provoke me and then claim that I was hysterical. I didn't wait for an answer. Instead, I described our silly little argument in the forest. Feeling disgruntled, I'd walked home. That was the long and short of the matter, nothing more remarkable than that, so why were the police here, why were the detectives not looking for Mia, why was the great Dr Norling not hosting his radio show, or the powerful Håkan not dealing with his business empire, why were they gathered here, in our modest farm, as solemn as a wake?

Norling's first words were:

'I'm worried about you, Tilde.'

He spoke perfect English. His voice was so soft, like a cushion – you could rest your head and fall asleep on the sound of his allegations. He uttered my name like I was a dear friend. No wonder the public adores him. He could imitate the sound of genuine affection faultlessly. I had to pinch myself not to believe it. But it was a lie, the trick of a professional showman.

Seeing my enemies lined up against me, I absorbed the depth of their expertise. They were pillars of the community. And they had an insider, Chris, an ally who could provide them with a host of personal details, perhaps he already had, perhaps he'd told them about Freja. The thought terrified me. But what surprised me most was the presence of the rusted steel box in the middle of the room on a table in among the conspirators, the rusted steel box that I'd placed under the sink many months ago, the box I'd saved from the well diggers, the box I'd found a metre under the soil containing no more than the water-destroyed blank old pages. Why was this worthless old box in such a prominent place? Dr Norling noticed that I was staring at it. He picked the box up, offering it to me as though it were a gift. His soft kind voice commanded me:

'Open this for us, Tilde.'

I hated the way he said my name.

'Open it, Tilde.'

So I did.

•   •   •

FOR THE SECOND TIME my mum took out the rusted steel box from the satchel. She placed it on my lap.

Norling asked why I thought the box might be important. I didn't know. And said so. It made no sense. Norling didn't believe me, asking if I was sure. What a question! Of course I was sure. A person can always be sure of what they don't know. They might not be sure of what they know. But I knew nothing about the reasons these men were suddenly so deadly serious about a collection of water-damaged sheets of paper, crinkled and discoloured and more than a hundred years old, pages that had been entirely blank when the box was first discovered.

Go ahead and open the box.

Take out the pages.

Turn to the back.

You see?

They're no longer blank! They're covered in writing, beautiful old-fashioned handwriting, in Swedish, of course, traditional Swedish, old-fashioned Swedish. I was in shock. Was it possible I'd missed the writing on the back, presuming them all to be blank? It was so long ago I couldn't clearly remember whether I'd checked every page or not. Norling asked me to read them. I exclaimed, in English:

'This is a setup!'

I didn't know the Swedish phrase. Norling stepped

forward, edging closer, asking why I thought it was a 'setup', repeating the phrase in English, translating it for Stellan the detective, with a knowing glance as if the phrase supported his theory that my mind was racked with paranoia, my head choked with conspiracies. I stated that the pages had been blank when I'd discovered them. There'd been no writing. Norling repeated his request that I read the pages aloud.

Let me read these pages to you because your Swedish is not as good as it used to be. The translation will be rough. The Swedish isn't modern. I want to add, before I start, that no one is claiming these pages are authentic – neither me nor my enemies. Someone has written these pages recently, over the summer. They're a fabrication. That's not in dispute. The question you must answer is who fabricated them and why.

•   •   •

I STOLE A GLANCE AT THE HANDWRITING, elegantly composed in unusual brown ink that appeared to have flowed gracefully from a fountain pen. My mum caught my glance:

'I was planning to ask the question after I'd finished reading the diary to you. Since you're ahead of me, I'll ask now.'

She handed me a page:

'Is the writing mine?'

Using her journal, I compared the two, prefacing my judgment with:

'I'm not an expert.'

My mum dismissed this:

'You're my son. Who could be more expert? Who else knows my writing better than you?'

There was nothing similar about the two styles. I've never known my mum to own a fountain pen, let alone use one so fluidly, preferring disposable biros, often chewed at the end as she laboured over her accounts. More importantly, the writing didn't seem to be a deliberate distortion or crudely disguised. There were no erratic jagged letters. The writing expressed a nature of its own that was complete and consistent. I took my time, trying to find some connection, even if just on a single letter. I couldn't. My mum became impatient:

'Is it my writing? Because if you say no then you have to accept that I'm the subject of a conspiracy.'

'Mum, as far as I can tell, it's not your writing.'

My mum stood up, leaving the pages on the coffee table. She walked to the bathroom. I followed her:

'Mum?'

'I mustn't cry. I promised, no tears. But I'm so relieved. This is why I came home, Daniel. This is why I came home!'

She filled the sink with hot water and unwrapped the individual portion of soap, washing her hands and face. She took note of the neat stack of towels, using the top one, drying her face. She smiled at me, as though the world had been put to rights. The smile caught me by surprise, a reminder of her great capacity for happiness. Yet today it felt more like the appearance of a rare and exotic bird, glimpsed only briefly. She said:

'A weight has been lifted from my shoulders.'

If the weight had been lifted from her shoulders, it now rested on mine.

She turned the light off, returning to the main room, taking my hand as she passed me, guiding me back to the window, where we watched the last of the sun slip away.

> These pages are an elaborate deceit. Their purpose is to suggest that I'm the author and therefore unwell and requiring help. When I read them aloud, you'll appreciate the depth of their trickery. There are cunning references to my life. I won't need to point them out – you'll hear them. But the handwriting is nothing like my writing, and when you tell the police that simple fact then we have evidence, not opinion, evidence that my enemies are guilty. They claim these diary entries were the product of my sick imagination, that I'd created the journal of a fictional character, a woman living on our farm over

a hundred years ago, in 1899, a woman suffering from loneliness and isolation. It's a bold and creative attack, I'll grant my enemies that, far subtler than the mushroom trickery in the forest. However, they didn't count on you, they didn't take into consideration that I could escape Sweden and find you, my precious son, someone separate from the events of this summer to confirm that this is not my writing and I did not write this diary.

*   *   *

WITHOUT TAKING A SEAT, my mum picked up the pages. She took on the appearance of an actor reading the text to a stage play, but a play she had little respect for, communicating her contempt and distance from the words.

1st December – Life is lonely on this farm. I'm looking forward to the day my husband returns from his travels. Hopefully that will be any day now.

4th December – There's not enough dry wood to last another week. I will have to venture into the forest and chop some more, but the forest is far away and the weather is bitterly cold. There are deep snowdrifts. I will ration the remaining timber, hoping for the snow to ease and my husband to return.

7th December – The need for timber is desperate and cannot be put off any longer. Snow continues to fall. It will be hard to reach the forests and even harder returning with whatever timber I manage to cut. Once I collect the timber, I'll pile it on my sleigh and drag it back. I'll set out tomorrow regardless of the weather. I have no choice. I cannot wait any longer.

8th December – My first visit to the forest was a success. I dragged the empty sleigh up the frozen river since the snow is thinner on the ice than on the land. My progress was slow but steady. At the edge of the forest my intention was to search for trees that had fallen during the winter storms since these would be the easiest to chop for timber. After some time I discovered one such tree and chopped it up as best I could. Fully loaded, the sleigh was far too heavy for me to pull and I was forced to put most of the wood back. I'll retrieve the logs tomorrow. But I am happy and tonight for the first time in weeks I've enjoyed the warmth of my fire.

9th December – On my return to the forest to collect the remaining timber I saw a giant elk standing in the middle of the frozen river. When the creature heard the sound of my sleigh on the ice it turned and looked at me before disappearing among the trees. My joy lasted until I discovered that the timber I'd cut was missing. Someone had stolen it. There were footprints in the snow. It was desperately cold, so it shouldn't have been a surprise that other people were looking for timber, except our farm is remote, there's no one near us, and these footsteps went deeper into the forest, not back towards habitable land. Could someone live in these woods?

10th December – There was no sight of the elk today. I walked further than before. The deep snow makes it hard to find fallen timber and I was exhausted. I came back with very little.

11th December – I saw the footprints again. Even though they were heading further into the forest I decided to follow them, hoping to find my stash of timber or the person who'd stolen it. The footprints led me to an island in the middle of the frozen river. On this small island there was a timber cabin. It was much smaller than a farmhouse. There was no light in the windows and I'm not sure what purpose this cabin served. It was too small to be a home. Outside there was the timber I'd cut. I knocked on the door but no one answered. Seeing as the timber was mine, I took as much of it as I could. Nervous of being caught, I hurried away from that strange cabin.

14th December – For several days I've been too afraid to go back to the forest in case I encounter whoever lives in that cabin. However, my stock of wood was depleted and I was forced to return, determined to retrieve some more wood from the cabin. I'd confront the person who'd stolen my timber if necessary. Reaching the island, I saw light in the window of the cabin. There was a man inside. I was scared and decided this was dangerous. I hurried away, dragging my sleigh, except the steel runners scratched the ice and made a noise and when I turned back I saw the man outside the cabin. He began walking towards me. I was so afraid that I abandoned my sleigh, running as fast as I could, slipping on the ice, not looking back until I'd left the forest. It was foolish. Now I have no timber and no sleigh. I am in despair.

17th December – The farm is freezing. I can't keep warm. Where is my husband? There's no word from him. I'm alone. My fingers struggle to hold this pen. I must retrieve my sleigh. I will confront the man in the cabin. He has no right to keep my property. Why did I panic? I must be strong.

18th December – I returned to the island, and the cabin, ready with my axe to defend myself if need be. From a distance I saw light in the cabin window. Smoke rose from the chimney. I told myself to be brave. At the tip of the island I found my sleigh loaded with cut timber. It seems I was wrong about this man. He was not my enemy. He was my friend. Feeling great joy, I decided to thank him for the work he'd kindly done. Perhaps all he desired in return was my company. It must be lonely living in these woods. I knocked on his door. There was no reply. I opened the door. In front of me I saw a deformed woman, her stomach swollen, with arms as thin as sticks. I was about to scream when I realised that the woman was my reflection in a curved mirror. What a strange mirror to own! But there were more strange discoveries to be found in this cabin. There was no bed. Instead, there was a pile of wood shavings in the corner. There was no food in the cabin and no kitchen. What kind of home was it? I grew uncomfortable and left. I didn't want to thank this man any more. Back at the farm, making a fire of my own, I noticed that all the logs I'd brought home had faces carved into them. They were grotesque faces with awful eyes and sharp teeth. I couldn't keep them. They scared me. I threw them all onto the fire, a wasteful act, forming a pyre of burning faces. Suddenly I felt a terrible itch on my back as though a creature were chewing into my skin. I ripped at my shirt, throwing it to the floor, but no insect dropped out, just a curl of coarse wood shaving. I picked it up and tossed it onto the fire, promising myself that no matter how cold I became, I would never go back to that cabin. But I am afraid that I will go back. I'm afraid there is no choice. And I am afraid of what will happen when I do.

• • •

D URING MY MUM'S READING her contempt for the words had
softened. By the end, she'd become caught up in the story
and unable to maintain her original distance from the material. I
had the impression my mum was aware of the mixed signals she'd
been sending. No longer speaking with scorn, she returned the
pages to the box:

'That's the last entry.'

She closed the lid and looked at me:

'What do you make of it?'

The question was dangerous, the same as asking whether we
were going to the police, or the doctor's.

'It's elaborate.'

'That's how serious and determined my enemies are.'

'Could Chris really have written this?'

'It wasn't your father. It was Dr Norling. Håkan advised him.'

'Why would he agree to do it?'

'He's involved.'

'Involved in what?'

'Mia's only the tip of the iceberg.'

'You're going to explain what you mean by that?'

'Very soon.'

I returned to her chronology of events:

'What happened next? You're at the farm, in the living room.
There's the detective, the doctor. There's Chris and Håkan.
They've made you read these pages in front of them. They're
watching you. And then?'

I was scared. But I pretended to be calm. I refused to

take the bait and claim that they were written by Håkan. The diary was a trap. They wanted to provoke me. They expected me to become furious, claiming it was one of them. I had no evidence for their involvement. My tactic was to seem perplexed and a little stupid. I said these pages were a fascinating insight into life on this farm, as though I thought they were genuine. With a theatrical yawn, I then declared that I was tired, it had been a long day and I wished to sleep. Norling asked if I was prepared to visit him tomorrow, in his house, for a talk – just the two of us, no one else – and seeing as this was the only way I could get rid of everyone, I agreed. I'd happily see him tomorrow, after a good night's sleep. With that promise they left. I suggested to Chris that he spend the night in the unfinished guest lodgings, saying it would be impossible for me to sleep beside him after the way he'd behaved.

But I didn't go to sleep. I waited until it was late, three or four in the morning. I crept out of bed and turned on the computer, sending you an email. I was so panicked by the bright light of the computer screen I didn't have the courage to type for very long. There was so much I wanted to say. I was cautious because Internet searches aren't secure, they can be monitored and intercepted, nothing is secure, they can find out anything, even after it's deleted, it doesn't disappear, nothing ever disappears, so in the end I settled for a single word, your name.

•   •   •

THIS SUMMER OUR LIVES HAD INTERSECTED on only a tiny number of occasions. My dad had taken advice from Håkan and Dr Norling long before he'd even informed me of what was going on. In this war council of men gathered at the farm I'd had no seat and no voice. Either that was because, as my mum claimed, they were working together to cover up a crime, or because I'd so effectively written myself out of my parents' lives that my dad considered me of little use in this predicament. His reasoning would've been that I offered nothing and might myself have required attention when he had none to spare. Therefore believing in the conspiracy flattered me – it absolved me of responsibility, I'd been excluded for devious reasons rather than for deficiency of character. Troublingly, I wondered whether my mum had seen my absence as further evidence of a conspiracy against her. My absence offered her a hook from which to hang the notion that those men were set against her for a specific reason based upon local events. Up until this point I'd been ashamed of having played no part in events. But I was wrong. By not being there I'd played a very specific part. If everyone my mum loved had gathered in the farm that night, from both England and Sweden, could she have so conclusively believed that we were all against her? If I'd been there, with Mark by my side, there would've been no easy way for my mum to incorporate our support for my dad into her narrative, so far only hinted at, but which seemed to be about the sexual exploitation of a vulnerable young woman. I saw my name clearly in the otherwise blank email:

Daniel!

My reaction to her desperate email had been breezy compla-cency. I had no idea that I was being shaped in my mum's mind as the alternative to my dad, a loved one who'd believe her. Her conspiracy had already begun to live in me:

'I should've flown out to Sweden, Mum, after that email.'

My mum gestured for me to take a seat and I obeyed. She joined me:

'What's done is done. And I'm here with you now. We're almost at the end. There's only one last piece of evidence.'

My mum opened her purse, as though she were about to give me pocket money:

'Open your hand.'

I offered her my palm.

It's a human tooth. No animal teeth look like this, burnt black, no flesh or tissue remaining.

Now you're going to ask if I believe this is Mia's tooth. You want to ask the question because if I say yes, then you have your proof. I'm insane and you must take me to a hospital.

My answer is this—

It's a milk tooth, a child's tooth. Mia was sixteen years old so it can't be her tooth, and I never claimed it was.

The tooth came into my possession a few hours before Dr Norling's assessment. My appointment was sched-uled for the afternoon – he selected the time, not me, a fact that struck me as irrelevant, but this was of great importance, the sequence of events is crucial, a sequence they hoped would drive me mad.

With the morning at my leisure I decided not to work. I needed to be fully rested and have my wits about me. If I failed Dr Norling's evaluation then I was finished, as an investigator and as a free individual. My liberty was at stake, decided not by a fair audience but conducted by one of my enemies. Was I *compos mentis*? If I failed their tests they'd drive me from his beach house to the hospital, where Norling would personally oversee my admission. I couldn't skip the appointment even though it was self-evidently a trap. My absence would be taken as proof of madness and I'd be hunted down. So I'd attend, on time, punctual, well turned out – I'd attend and give them nothing – that was the key, give them nothing! Walk into their trap and wriggle right out! I wouldn't talk about murder and conspiracy, not a word, instead I'd discuss my plans for the farm, the barn conversion, salmon fishing, vegetable gardens, home-made jam, I'd play the part of a docile and harmless wife entirely at ease with her new life, challenged, yes, tired from hard work, certainly, but looking forward to many happy years. Give them nothing, not a furrowed brow, not a single allegation, not a dark thought, and then what could the doctor do?

My plan was a good one. I intended to spend the next few hours avoiding anyone who might disturb me.

I toyed with the boat. I swam. I was relaxing on the jetty, my feet in the water, when, in the distance, from the forest, I saw wisps of black smoke rising into the sky. I knew – I just knew – that the smoke was coming from Teardrop Island.

I jumped into the boat, barefoot, setting off upstream, using the electric motor at full speed, passing Håkan's farm, noticing that his boat wasn't docked. He must be on the river. Maybe he was already there. I pushed on, eyes fixed on the rising curl of smoke. As I reached the forest, there was a chemical smell. This wasn't a natural fire. It was a petrol fire. Up ahead, Teardrop Island was ablaze. The cabin at the back was engulfed in flames twice as high as me. Embers fizzled on the surface of the river but I didn't slow down, I took aim and rammed into the tip of the island, powering onto the muddy rim with a thud, jumping out, standing before the flames, cowering from the intense heat. Fortunately there was a container in the boat to shovel out rainwater, and I filled it from the river, throwing bucket after bucket at the base of the fire, plumes of steam erupting. Quickly the entire cabin collapsed. I used an oar to knock some of the burning planks into the river, where they spat and hissed.

My initial conclusion was an obvious one. The fire had been started for a simple reason – to destroy evidence. Almost certainly the people who'd started it were in the woods, watching the fire burn, and now they were watching me.

Let them watch!

I wasn't scared. With the island smouldering I set about carefully pouring water on the ash until the area cooled down. Once that was done, and the water no longer turned to steam, I raked through the remains, running my fingers through the ash and the sooty puddles, the black water, finding a lump – the tooth you now hold. If I were mad I would've jumped to some sensational conclusion, screaming out:

'Murder! Murder!'

I didn't. I sat on Teardrop Island, staring at the tooth, sat and sat, and thought and thought, and asked myself – what was this doing here? No corpse had been burnt on that island, where was the skull, the bones? The idea was ridiculous. Where had this tooth come from, this tiny tooth, this milk tooth, not Mia's tooth but the tooth of a young child? It was then that I realised the true purpose of the fire was not to destroy evidence but to destroy me. The tooth had been planted there, possibly with several others, a handful of teeth to ensure I found at least one. My enemies had planted this shocking and provocative evidence before setting fire to the island.

Consider the sequence. Why now? Why would they have started a fire now, today, in the morning? Why not wait until I was at Norling's house, by the sea, far away – I wouldn't have seen the smoke, there was nothing I could've done. As an attempt to destroy evidence the fire makes no sense! The discovery of the tooth was too easy. The real purpose of this fire had been to unsettle me before Norling's examination. They wanted me to walk into Norling's house stinking of smoke and ash, with mad sooty hair, clutching this charred tooth, they wanted me to declare the black tooth as evidence of murder – to cry out:

'Murder! Murder!'

A simple laboratory test would reveal it was the tooth of some little girl, safe and well on another farm. She'd brought it to the island to show a friend, or some such lie. Where would I be then? What could I say? I'd be sent straight to the asylum.

I shook my fist and cursed my enemies hiding among the trees. I wasn't the fool they thought me to be.

I'm no fool!

But they'd already won a small victory. I was going to be late for my appointment with the doctor. I hastily climbed back into the boat, noticing for the first time that one side of my foot was burnt from the hot embers, bubbling with blisters. It didn't matter. I had no time to spare.

Returning to the farm as fast as I could, late for my appointment, I stripped off, tossing my smoke-stinking clothes aside, and swam in the river, hastily washing myself. I couldn't wear those clothes again, so I ran naked to the farm, where I changed into fresh clothes, hiding the charred tooth in my satchel.

Chris was standing by the white van wearing his smartest clothes. When does your father wear anything other than jeans and a jumper? The reason was obvious. He was primed for his role at the hospital, for his appearance before the doctors and nurses, the devoted loving husband, wanting to appear at his best – which is to say, his most convincing. Gone were the T-shirts that stank of pot. Gone were the ugly old boots. Just as a mugger might borrow a suit that doesn't fit for a court hearing, Chris had dug out clothes he never normally wears. He didn't mention the smoke in the sky, didn't ask where I'd been, didn't pick up on the fact that I'd taken the boat. He studied me carefully, disappointed to find me *compos mentis*. He offered to drive. I didn't trust the offer. I expected there'd be another incident, some frightening item placed on the seat, something to shock me, so I refused. I said we had very limited petrol, which was true, very little money, which was also true. I was more than happy to cycle and mentioned some small details that needed attending to on the farm as though it was inevitable I'd be returning soon, life would continue, this was not the end! He'd dressed up in his best clothes for no reason. There'd be no visit to the asylum today!

Leaving the farm on my bicycle, I slung my satchel

over my shoulder, refusing to abandon it for their examination. I even dared to turn around, acquiring a knack for deceit, giving Chris a carefree wave goodbye, calling out a dishonest:

'I love you!'

* * *

I ASKED:
'Mum, don't you love Dad any more?'

Without pausing to reflect, she shook her head:

'No.'

'No?'

'No.'

'Of all the things you've said today, I find the idea that you don't love Dad the hardest to believe.'

My mum nodded, as if this sentimentality was to be expected from me:

'Daniel, this isn't about what you want to be true. I wanted to grow old on that farm with your father. I wanted to build the home I've dreamed about since I was a child. I wanted that farm to be our family's little corner of the world and for it to be so special that you'd start to visit us again in a way that you haven't done for a long time.'

I sensed no attack intended in her final comment. It was a matter-of-fact description of her dream. I said:

'Didn't Dad want the same?'

'Maybe once. But there was temptation. And he was tempted.'

'Mum, you said it yourself. You and Dad were an unbreakable team. It can't just be gone. In one summer, it can't be. I refuse to believe it.'

I was afraid that I'd overstepped the mark. To my surprise, my mum didn't seem annoyed:

'I'm glad you're defending him. I defended him too, in my mind, for months and months. I loved the man you know as your dad. But I don't love the man I discovered in Sweden. I could never love that man.'

'You believe he was involved in the murder of Mia?'

I'd pushed too far.

'Conclusions sound far-fetched without any context. This is why I asked you not to jump ahead. Allow me to tell it my way.'

It was late and the hotel would soon offer a turndown service, bringing ice to the room and making the bed. I said to my mum:

'I'm going to put a sign on the door so no one interrupts.'

My mum followed me as I hung the sign around the handle. She checked the hallway then pulled back into the room. I said:

'You were about to have your meeting with Dr Norling.'

Standing in the middle of the room, she closed her eyes, as though sending her thoughts back to that moment. I chose to perch on the edge of the bed, sensing that it was unlikely my mum would sit down again. As I waited, I couldn't help but reminisce about the times when my mum had read me a bedtime story. She opened her eyes:

Despite being late I cycled slowly, breathing deeply, wanting to recapture some of that early morning calm. My plan was a good one. All I had to do was pretend, smile, to speak like a contented wife and hard-working farmer, to talk about my hopes and dreams, to say how much I loved this area and remark how friendly the people were. Stick to the plan and I'd be okay.

Dr Norling lives by the sea, a house directly on the waterfront among the dunes and shrubs, the stretch of desolate coast where I'd go running. He had somehow managed to position his extravagant house on protected coastland – a house so intimidating that people didn't feel comfortable walking nearby. They sensed it must have protectors – keep away, the house communicated, because it could only have achieved planning permission by corruption and close connections with power. Ordinary people didn't live in houses like this. Approaching the grounds, I slowed down, but there was no need because the gate automatically sprang to life before I could dismount. He'd seen me coming. My confidence faltered. Could I really play the part of an unsuspecting wife and hold my tongue? I wasn't sure.

Outside the house I stood my bicycle on the gravel and waited. There was no doorbell to ring. There were two giant doors, enormous timber doors – castle doors – twice the height of a person. Simultaneously both doors gracefully opened and out he came, the renowned and respected Dr Olle Norling. He was dressed casually. His shirt was unbuttoned, slyly signalling that I had no reason to fear this appointment, a signal I reversed, understanding the exact opposite. I had everything to fear! Whereas Chris had been blind to my injuries, Norling noticed my awkward walk immediately, asking if something was wrong, but I assured him it was nothing – a splinter, might have been the lie I told, not wishing to mention the fire, a subject which must be avoided. I kept saying to myself:

Stick to the plan!

I was determined not to be impressed, a silly thing
to be determined about, and anyway, I failed. His house
was magnificent, not opulent, this wasn't gaudy wealth
to be dismissed with a roll of the eyes, it was simple in
style, minimalist, if you can apply the word minimalist
when confronted with those huge glass windows, cathedral windows pulling the sea and beach into the house,
and I wondered why I was so amazed when I cycled
along the coastal track with the exact same view. But
this was different, the windows were framing the sea
as if they were a private work of art, possessing what
cannot be possessed, turning private what was once
public – this view was power, and even though it wasn't
sunny, no dazzling blue sky, only a flat grey sea, I might
actually have gasped, not at the beauty but at the power,
the power to frame the sea. Only a handful of people in
this world have that power. Norling was one of them.

There was another person present, a man, a house-
keeper dressed in household livery, laughable if he
hadn't been so solemn. He was a handsome man, in his
thirties, with hair slicked to the side, like a butler from
1930s England, a blond butler, and he spoke to me in
deferential tones, asking if I required anything to drink.
I declined, too abruptly – defensive, fearful the drink
might be spiked. Norling missed nothing, immediately
asking for a bottle of water, two glasses, but specifying
that the bottle of water should be unopened and sealed

and no ice in the glass. I'd expected him to take me into a small room, somewhere intimate and intense, but he escorted me outside onto the decking, onto the sweeping platform sprawling over the sand dunes. There I faced my first test, the first of three. He took a match and lit a fire, a modern gas contraption in a copper drum surrounded by padded seats. Flames sprang up and Norling gestured to the chairs around it, positioning me directly beside these flames. You must accept that this was a reference to the fire on Teardrop Island because there was no other logical reason behind lighting it on a summer's day. He wanted me to see the flames and produce the charred black tooth, he wanted me to jump up and down shouting—

'Murder! Murder!'

But I did no such thing. Sticking to the plan, I took my seat, feeling the heat on my face for the second time that day, and forced a smile, remarking how pleasant this was, how very pleasant. I vowed not to react. There's no way he's going to catch me, there's nothing he can say or do, they've misjudged my mind, I'm not so fragile, not so easy to manipulate. They'd banked on the tooth turning me crazy. Instead, with my wits about me, I was demure and polite, complimenting him on the fineness of his house.

The doctor then asked if I'd prefer to speak in English. Håkan must have told him how much this insult irritated me, but I'd fallen for that trick once before, not again, and so I smiled, laughed, saying it was very kind of Norling to offer a choice of languages, but I was as Swedish as he was, our passports were the same, so it would be odd to communicate in English, as odd as two Swedes speaking to each other in Latin. He then gestured at the empty seats around the fire and told me he hosted many parties here. I thought to myself:

I bet you do, Doctor, I bet you do.

Sensing defeat, Norling attempted his second test, test number two, even more devious than the fire. He offered to show me the view through his binoculars set up on the decking, claiming it would allow me to study the boats out at sea. I was hardly in the mood but obliged, placing my eye on the lens, ready to say how pleasant, how very pleasant, only to be faced with a magnified view of the abandoned lighthouse, the old stone lighthouse where Mia had waited, dressed in bridal whites, the lighthouse where she'd hung the flowers on the door as a sign to an observer that she was inside. Those flowers were still there, wilted, dead and black, like the flowers by the side of a road where there's been an accident. Norling had set up the binoculars, chosen this view. The provocation was clever and strong. I took hold of the binoculars, searching and finding the place on the beach where I'd hidden behind a shrub. I would've been visible – that's why he didn't show that day. Slowly,

I straightened up, struggling to stick to the plan, but determined not to show any reaction. He asked me what I
thought. I said I found his view revealing – very revealing.

His two tests had failed. Disappointed, Norling
abruptly showed me inside, pressing a button, extin-
guishing the flames in the copper drum in an instant
like some wizard grown tired of his own spell, showing
me through the hallways past the cathedral windows,
into a study. This wasn't a room of intensive research,
not a real study messy with papers and notes and dog-
eared books, this was an interior design study, the kind
constructed with unlimited money. The books were as
beautiful as the view, floor-to-ceiling shelves with
antique library ladders to reach the highest point. At a
glance I saw books in several languages. Who knows if
he'd read them all, or if he'd read any, these books were
not to read but to be gawped at, propaganda for Norling's
mind. I considered the implication of the lighthouse.
Previously I'd thought Norling a disciple of Håkan, but
maybe I'd misjudged, maybe Håkan was a subordinate.
Norling indicated I should take a seat, there were several
to choose from, and I contemplated which to take, evalu-
ating their height and angle of recline, not wishing
to be slumped, or in a position of weakness. At this
point I noticed on the coffee table, carefully positioned
in the centre of the room – an article of evidence. It's one

you've already seen, one from my satchel. Can you guess which it was, can you guess what this man had on display in his third and final act of provocation?

*   *   *

I THOUGHT UPON THE ITEMS I'd seen and made a guess:
'The biblical quote from the hermit's farm?'

My mum was pleased. She reached into the satchel and placed the quote on the bed beside me:

'I stole it. But not from Ulf, from Norling!'

'How did the doctor have it?'

Exactly! Here it was, on his table! Spread out, the quote, with the mysterious coded message, stitched in the days before she hanged herself in the barn that no longer exists, before an audience of pigs. I grabbed it, forgetting my promise to remain calm, turning to Norling, fist clenched, and demanding to know who'd given it to him. Norling pressed home his advantage, relishing my emotional response, his soft voice tightening like hands around my neck, claiming that Chris had informed him about my fascination with these words, describing how I'd written out these lines many hundreds of times, how I'd mumbled them, chanted them like a prayer. Norling asked what these words meant to me, goading me to tell him what I thought was going on in this quiet corner of Sweden:

'Talk to me, Tilde, talk to me.'

His voice was so alluring, and he was right, I wanted nothing more than to tell the truth, even though I knew it was a trap. Sensing that my will was faltering, I closed my eyes, reminding myself not to speak, to stick to the plan!

Norling picked up the bottle of water. He poured me a glass. I meekly accepted the water even though I was worried that he might use mind-altering chemicals, invisible to the eye, with no taste, a chemical that might make me speak and incriminate myself. I was so thirsty I raised the glass to my lips and drank. Within seconds I felt an instantaneous and overwhelming urge to talk, not a compulsion that came from my heart but an artificial desire, chemically stimulated. The idea occurred to me that this room was rigged with video cameras, tiny cameras, the size of buttons, or hidden in the tops of pens. Despite my fears the urge to speak grew stronger and stronger. I tried to keep the words down but it was no good. If I couldn't control the urge to speak I could, at the very least, control the content of what I said, and so I spoke words that couldn't hurt me, a description of my vegetable garden, how it was the largest vegetable garden we'd ever planted, producing lettuces, carrots, radishes, onions, red onions, white onions, chives, and fresh herbs, basil, rosemary and thyme. I must have spoken for five, ten, twenty minutes, I don't know, but when I turned around Norling was seated in the exact same position, on that exquisite leather sofa, giving off the impression he was happy to wait forever. My defences crumbled.

I told him everything.

• • •

MY MUM PULLED A newspaper clipping from her journal, the second that she'd shown me so far. She placed it neatly on my lap. It was cut from *Hallands Nyheter*, dated late April, only a few weeks after they'd arrived in Sweden.

I don't need to translate it for you. It's a critical study of the adoption system, asking whether there needs to be a review of procedures following the suicide of a young girl. The girl was born in Angola, the same country Mia was adopted from, brought to Sweden when she was just six months old. Aged thirteen she killed herself using her adopted father's gun. The journalist discusses the difficulties of growing up as a young black girl in remote rural Sweden. The article caused a sensation. When I rang the journalist to ask him about the story he refused to talk, saying he didn't want to comment further. He sounded scared. He was right to be. This article only touches the surface of a much deeper scandal.

•　•　•

No MATTER HER AVERSION TO CONCLUSIONS, it was time to ask: 'Mum, what is this scandal?'

'You must be able to see it.'

Consistently she'd maintained a tight control over her account, precise and forceful, yet when it came to the conclusions, surely the most important part, I had the impression she'd much prefer to present them unshaped, like the model kits that required assembly. No matter how much guilt I felt over my lack of involvement during the summer, or over the last few years, I couldn't collaborate in her accusations:

'The police are going to ask direct questions. What happened? Who was involved? You can't imply. You can't ask them to infer. They weren't there. I wasn't there.'

My mum spoke slowly and carefully:

'Children were being abused. Adopted children were being abused. The adoption system has been corrupted. These children are vulnerable. They're seen as property.'

'Including Mia?'

'Particularly Mia.'

'Is that why she was murdered?'

'She was strong, Daniel. She was going to expose them. She was going to save other children from having to experience the pain she lived through. She knew if she didn't make a stand then it would happen again. And her story would be the story of other girls and boys.'

'Who killed her?'

'One of the men from my list, perhaps Håkan. She was his daughter, his problem, and he would've felt duty-bound to deal

261

with her. Or it might have been one of the others – an encounter gone wrong, perhaps one of them became obsessed with her. I don't know.'

'The body?'

'I can't dig up forests or dredge rivers. That's why we need the police to investigate.'

'But the scandal involved more than just Mia.'

'Not every adoption, not even the majority, but a minority, a significant minority. Earlier I showed you a map of Sweden. The cases aren't in one village or town. They're spread across a vast area. The journalist was right: the statistics don't lie. Their failure rate was too high. Look at the numbers, the numbers don't lie.'

I sat back on the bed and crossed my legs, using my limited Swedish to read the article. Under pressure my mum had given me her allegation in summary form. There was a paedophile ring wired into the adoption system. There was a conspiracy to cover it up. The article confirmed that there was an issue with integration and listed several examples of failure, including one loss of life. I asked:

'You believe the conspiracy involved many of the men you've spoken about – the detective, the mayor – even though they didn't have adopted children?'

'There were parties. That's how your father became involved. He was invited to one. That's a fact. I don't know what went on at these parties, so I'm speculating. Some took place in Norling's beach house. Others took place behind that second padlocked door. There was drink. They took drugs. One of the girls was brought out.'

'I don't know the others so I can't comment. But I know Dad.'

'You think you do. But you don't.'

My mum had connected a series of dots, some of which, I agreed, were highly suggestive and disturbing. However, the lines she'd drawn between them were her own. I tried to pull together the threads, searching either for an argument that could be clearly contradicted, or one that couldn't be dismissed as conjecture. I asked:

'The woman who killed herself in the barn?'

'She must have discovered the truth. She must have! That's what her message was referring to – "For-my-struggle-is-against-flesh-and-blood-against-the-rulers-against-the-authorities-against-the-powers-of-this-dark-world-and-against-the-forces-of-evil-in-this-earthly-realm." Maybe her husband was involved. She wasn't strong like Mia. She died of shame.'

'You can't be sure of that.'

'Everything I've told you connects to this conspiracy. Why were we brought to that location? Cecilia knew. But she was too frail to fight it. She understood that only outsiders could expose the truth.'

'Mum, I'm not saying you're wrong. It's also impossible for me to say you're right. Cecilia never told you that.'

Her response was strangely abstract:

> I told you earlier nothing is more dangerous than to be desired. I'll add this: nowhere is more dangerous than the space behind closed doors. People will always find a way to follow their desires. If no legal options exist, people will turn to illegal ones. Håkan and others created

an elaborate organisation to satisfy their needs. Mia was exploited. I'm not sure by how many. She wasn't a daughter. She was an asset. She was property. Now, please, Daniel, let's go to the police.

• • •

MY MUM FOLDED THE STITCHED FABRIC, packing it into her satchel. She was ready to leave. I placed a hand on hers: 'Sit with me, Mum.'

With some reluctance, she sat on the bed, so light and small in size that the mattress needed only a faint adjustment to her body weight. We were both facing forward, like two children pretending to ride a magic carpet. She seemed tired and sank her glance towards the plush carpet. Addressing the nape of her neck, I said:

'What happened next? You told your theory to Dr Norling?'

'Yes.'

'Did you claim that he was involved?'

'Yes.'

'What did he say?'

He didn't say anything. I sat there and he stared at me. His expression was blank. It was my fault. I told the story wrong. I started with my conclusions, presented in summary form, without the detail or the context. I've learned from those mistakes, which is why I've been much more thorough talking to you, beginning at the beginning, with my arrival in Sweden, following the chronology of events, not letting myself skip ahead despite your demands for quick answers.

During the time I'd been talking, the blond butler had entered the room. He was standing behind me, summoned in somehow, a panic button perhaps because Norling hadn't said a word. I asked if I could go to the bathroom, weakly at first, like a schoolgirl asking a teacher, then more assertively – I needed the toilet and they couldn't refuse me that. Norling stood up, agreeing to my request, the first words he'd spoken since my accusation. He gestured for the housekeeper to show me the way. I said that wasn't necessary, but Norling ignored me, holding open the study door. I followed the house-keeper, observing his sinewy arms. Suddenly I wondered whether this man might be an orderly from the hospital, in disguise as a butler, ready with drugs and restraints. He escorted me to the bathroom, not allowing me to deviate or wander off, and as I shut the door he looked into my eyes with pity. Or was it contempt – pity or contempt? They can be hard to tell apart.

I locked the door behind me, reviewing my predicament. Instead of saying nothing, I'd said too much. My only option was to escape. I examined the window, but, as with everything in that house, it was bespoke, it didn't open. The thick frosted glass couldn't be easily broken, certainly not without making a great deal of noise. There was no escape. I was still holding the stitched quote and I folded it neatly, slipping it into my satchel with no intention of returning it, one of the most important items of evidence I'd collected. There was no choice but to emerge from the bathroom and find another way out. I expected both men to be there, waiting, arms outstretched. But the hallway was empty. I peered down, seeing them outside the study in conversation. I contemplated running in the opposite direction, finding another way out. But Norling looked up and saw me, so I walked towards him. I'd simply explain that I was tired and that I'd like to go home. They had no legal power. They couldn't detain me. I laid down the challenge – I was going to leave.

I'm leaving!

Norling considered. He nodded, offering to drive me. Would it be so easy? I turned the offer down, explaining I wanted fresh air and would prefer to cycle. Norling gently protested, reminding me that I'd just claimed to be tired. I stuck by my decision, scarcely able to believe that my ordeal was coming to an end.

Even though they weren't open I walked towards the giant oak doors, waiting for these men to jump me, or stick me with a needle, but the manservant dutifully pressed a button and the great doors swung open and I exited into the sea breeze. I was free. Somehow I'd survived. I hurried down the steps to my bicycle.

Once I was on the coastal track, cycling fast, I glanced back. Norling's expensive car was emerging from his discreet garage like a spider creeping out of a hole. He was following me. I turned face forward and, ignoring the pain from my blisters, flattened my feet on the pedals and accelerated. Norling's car could've overtaken me, but he was shadowing me into town. I raced across the bridge, turning sharply onto the cycle path alongside the river, glancing over my shoulder as Norling was forced to drive on the main road. At last I was free of him, if only temporarily, because there was no doubt in my mind he was heading to the farm. Maybe the doctor needed Chris's consent in order to take me to the hospital. I skidded to a stop and asked myself why was I cycling back to the farm, what safety was there at this farm? My old plan was dead, I'd told them everything. Things couldn't carry on as normal, there was no going back to life on the farm, our dream was over, the farm, the barn, the salmon fishing, it was over. I'd been lying to myself, pretending somehow the two lives could coexist, but they couldn't. It was an investigation or denial, there was no compromise, and I'd made my choice.

I was alone. I needed an ally. The only person I could think of, since you were in London, the only person who might give me a fair hearing, far removed from the events in this community, was my father.

. . .

M Y MUM'S CHOICE SURPRISED ME:
'You haven't seen your father for fifty years. He didn't even know you were in Sweden.'

'I wasn't going to him because we were close. I was going to him because of his character.'

'Based on what? The man you knew as a child?'

'He wouldn't have changed.'

'According to you Dad has changed. And over the course of just one summer.'

'Chris is different.'

'Different how?'

'He's weak.'

Considering my dad had been accused of the most serious sexual crimes, I'm not sure why this insult struck me as particularly barbed. Perhaps it was the impression that of all the vices, my mum despised weakness the most. And, perhaps, because if Dad was weak then, surely, so was I:

'Your father is strong?'

'He's incorruptible. He doesn't drink. He doesn't smoke. He was a local politician. Whereas that might be a joke to some, in his part of the country that meant he was scrupulous and highly respected. His image and reputation were everything. It didn't matter that we were estranged. He'd be on the side of justice.'

'Mum, he thought you killed Freja.'

'Yes.'

'Why would you go back to him when you were looking for someone to believe you? You left him because he didn't believe you!'

269

Rather than talk over her shoulder, my mum rotated so that we were now both cross-legged on the bed, looking directly at each other, our knees touching, like two teenage friends baring our souls:

'You're right to query the decision. However, in this case, I wasn't being accused. This was about other people's crimes. And unlike last time, I had evidence and facts, dates and names. I was asking him to be objective.'

I dared a provocation:

'The only way this makes sense to me is if you accept that he correctly assessed the events of the summer of 1963. He got it right then. So you think he'll get it right now?'

My mum looked up at the ceiling:

'You believe I killed Freja too!'

'I don't, Mum. But if your dad got it wrong, why go to him now?'

My mum's eyes filled with tears:

'Because I wanted to give him a second chance!'

Since the rationale was an emotional one, I stopped being obstructive, only pressing for some understanding of the logistics. Maybe there'd been communication that I wasn't aware of over the summer:

'When were you last in touch with him?'

'He wrote to me when my mother died.'

About ten years ago, I remembered my mum reading the letter at the kitchen table, surrounded by the remains of our breakfast. I'd been at school. It had been the summer term. Worried that the news would distract me before my exams, she'd tried to hide the letter, but I'd caught sight of the Swedish over her shoulder and asked about it. To me, the news had seemed so remote from our lives. My grandmother had never visited or been in touch. She was a stranger to us. The letter had been sent after the funeral, giving my mum no chance to return and attend. Since that was their last communication I asked:

'Could you even be sure of his address?'

'He'd never move. He built that farm with his own hands. He'll die there.'

'Did you phone first?'

I decided not to. It's harder to shut a door in someone's face than it is to hang up a phone. So, you see, I had my doubts too. Obviously I couldn't cycle all the way there. My only option was to steal our van and drive across Sweden. I abandoned my bicycle in the fields, approaching the farm through the crops in case they were watching the road. If you doubted me earlier when I said Norling was following me, you were wrong. His car was at the farm, parked in the drive – that didn't surprise me. The problem was that he was parked in front of our van. There was no way out! I couldn't accept that this was the end. I'd take the wheel of that van and smash my way out, ramming Norling's expensive car onto the road.

At the window I peered inside, seeing Norling with Chris. There was no sign of Håkan but he'd be coming soon. I didn't need to go inside since the keys were in my satchel. I ran as fast as I could to the van, opening the door, slamming it shut and locking myself in. I started the engine and the old van shuddered noisily. Chris ran out of the farmhouse. As I backed up, he banged his fist on the door, trying to get in. I ignored him, putting the van into gear and accelerating straight towards Norling's car. At the very last second I changed my mind, driving around the car – otherwise he'd call the police and I'd be guilty of criminal damage. Instead, I drove onto my garden, my precious garden, crushing onions and marrows, months of work, straight into the hedge, bursting out onto the road. The van had lost a lot of speed and sat in the middle of the road. Chris was running after me. I could see him in the side mirrors, along with the damaged vegetables. The view was heartbreaking, but that dream was over – the farm was over. As Chris caught up with the van I accelerated away from him.

It was inevitable that they'd pursue me, in expensive cars, racing up and down the narrow country lanes, hunting me, and a white van would be easy to spot, so I drove fast, dangerously fast, picking roads at random.

Once I was clear, using a map of Sweden I plotted a route to my father's farm, estimating it would take six hours. It was a tiring journey. The van's difficult to drive, cumbersome and hard to handle. The weather changed markedly, from mild sun to bursts of rain. I crossed regional borders, leaving Halland and entering Västergötland, where I was forced to top up with petrol.

In the service station the man behind the counter asked me if I was okay. The sound of kindness almost made me cry. I declared that I was more than okay. I was excited. I was on a great adventure, the last adventure of my life. I'd been travelling for many months, that's why I looked a bit out of sorts, but I was almost home now.

In the service station bathroom I examined my reflection in the mirror, accepting that I'd lost a great deal of weight these past few weeks and had been neglecting my looks. Women are treated with suspicion if they neglect their looks, more so than men. Looks are important when trying to convince people of your sanity. I washed my face with a dollop of pungent pink soap from the dispenser, straightening my hair, taming the wild strands, scrubbing my fingernails, fixing my appearance as best I could for my father, a man who insisted on cleanliness. Just because we lived in the country didn't mean we lived like pigs, that's what he'd say.

The last of the daylight was fading and it would've been hard to navigate as a stranger in a foreign land with only a map. But this was my home. I wasn't a foreigner here. No matter that it had been fifty years, the countryside hadn't changed. I recognised the landmarks as if they were birthmarks, the bridges, the great family farms of the region, the rivers and forests, the quaint local towns that had to my eye as a child been like metropolises, home to exotic shops, a department store spread over three floors, bustling squares, expensive boutiques where sophisticates bought French perfume, and gloomy tobacco stores where men stocked up on cigars and chewing tobacco. Passing through now I saw a town asleep at ten, a single backstreet bar with a shamefaced façade catering to the handful of people who didn't go to bed when the sun went down.

I drove down the country road where I'd ditched my bicycle in the fields and where I'd caught the bus all those years ago, retracing my escape route, past my father's wildflower meadows, turning towards his farm. It was just the same, the small red farmhouse, built by my father's own hands before I was born, flanked by a customary flagpole, backed by ponds and redcurrant bushes, a single dim light over the door swirling with gnats and mosquitoes, the only light for miles around.

Stepping out of the van, I waited. There was no need to knock because in these remote parts the sound of a passing car was unusual enough to bring a person outside and my father surely heard the van approach. He would've waited by the window, watching the road, to see what direction the van would take, shocked to see it come towards the farm, shocked again when it stopped outside his front door, an unexpected visitor – late at night.

As the door opened, I felt a desire to run away. Had I

made a terrible misjudgment coming here? My father was wearing a suit jacket. He always wore a jacket and waistcoat around the house, formally dressed unless he was working in the fields, never casual. I might even have recognised the suit, brown and coarse. But his suits had always looked the same – heavy, itchy and uncomfortable, pious clothes for a pious soul. Everything was familiar apart from the decay – that was new. The redcurrant bushes were overgrown except for one that had died. The ponds were no longer pristine, dense algae strangling the water lilies. The barn's paintwork was chipped. Machinery for tending the fields had begun to rust. In contrast to his surroundings, my father looked in excellent condition, still upright and strong, eighty-five years old, an old man but not a frail one, not weak, alive, incredibly alive – vigorous and sharp-witted. His hair was white and neatly cut. He'd been to a local hair salon. He was taking care of himself, wearing essence of limes, the only fragrance he ever used. He said my name:

'Tilde.'

No hint of wonder, or amazement, my name, the name he'd chosen, spoken as a heavy declaration, a fact that brought him no joy. I tried to mimic the sound, except I couldn't keep the wonder out of my voice:

'Father!'

I'd left this farm on a bicycle and fifty years later returned in a van. I explained that I wasn't here to argue, or fight, I wasn't here to cause trouble. He said:

'I am old.'

I laughed and said:

'I'm old too!'

We had that in common, at least.

The inside of the farm was 1960s Sweden, imperfectly preserved, like a forgotten jar of jam at the back of a larder, spotty with mould. The accumulation of grime saddened me. My father had been obsessed with hygiene and immaculate presentation. But my mum had been in charge of keeping the farm clean. He'd never lifted a finger in that respect. Since her death he hadn't adopted her chores. The result was that while he appeared meticulously groomed, around him the farm had sunk into squalor. In the bathroom the showerhead was rusted, the grouting was black, the plughole was clogged with hair, and there was a tiny fragment of shit bobbing in the toilet. And the smell! It was the same, a building in the middle of the countryside with the freshest air in the world, yet the air inside was musty and stale because the windows are triple-glazed with seals to keep out winter's bitter cold. My father never opened the windows, even in the summer. The house was a closed space, the door never wedged wide to let in a breath of fresh air. You see, my father hated flies. Fifty years later there were still strips of flypaper in every room, some thick with dead or dying flies, some new, and my father couldn't sit if there was a fly in the house, he'd chase it until it was dead, chase and chase, so no doors were ever opened for longer than need be, and if you wanted fresh air you went outside. This smell, whatever it was – flypaper and old furniture and electric-heated air – this smell, for me, was unhappiness. I began to feel restless as we sat in the living room, breathing this smell, beside a television that must have been bought after I'd run away – a huge black cube with two steel antennae jutting up, like an oversized insect head, with a single curved eye, almost certainly the first and only television he'd ever bought.

It didn't feel like we hadn't seen each other for fifty years. We didn't need to talk about the years that we'd missed. They weren't relevant. He didn't ask questions. He didn't ask about you. He didn't ask about Chris. I understood. Some wounds can't be healed. I'd humiliated him by running away. He was a proud man. The faded newspaper articles about his white honey were still on the wall. My behaviour had been a stain on his reputation, or if not a stain, then a question, he'd fathered a disturbed daughter. I hadn't intended to upset him by running away. It wasn't his fault about Freja. None of those issues could be discussed. It fell upon me to explain myself.

Why was I here?

Not for casual chitchat. Not to pretend that we could fix the past. I needed his help with the present. I began describing the events of this summer, told in nowhere near the detail you've heard today. However, I made a much better attempt of it than my effort with Dr Norling.

I started at the beginning, not with my conclusions. I tried to give some of the detail and context, but I didn't take my time, it was late, I'd driven for six hours, my mind wasn't focused, I skipped around, compressed months into minutes. While making these mistakes I learned vital lessons about how the story needed to be told in order to be believed, lessons that I've put into practice today. Summaries were no good. Without evidence my words seemed vague and unsubstantiated. That was when I realised I needed to structure my case around articles of evidence from my satchel, and also to use my journal notes to support my spoken words, to give them substance. I needed a chronology. I needed context. And numbers wherever possible. Everyone trusts a number.

I spent no more than an hour to reach my allegation that Mia had been murdered to cover up sexual crimes that had infected local government and law enforcement. At the end, my father stood up. He said nothing about the events, or the allegation, not a word in support or in attack. He said I could sleep in my old room – we'd talk tomorrow when I was rested. I accepted that sleep sounded like a good idea. I was exhausted. I needed a fresh start and a clear mind. I'd tell my story better tomorrow. I'd explain there was evidence. I'd have a second chance. And he would too.

My bedroom had been redecorated, leaving no trace

of me. I was fine with the changes, because people move on, even parents, they move on from their children, and my father explained that the room had been used as a guest room after I left, kept ready for the church, which frequently sent visitors to his farm, where they lodged, sometimes for weeks at a time. He was never lonely. Good for you, I thought. I wouldn't wish being lonely on anyone.

I lay on top of the bed, fully dressed, deciding to make sure my father didn't call Chris while I was sleeping. He hadn't believed me, my father – I sensed that much. I was no fool. If there was one reaction I knew very well it was my father's disbelief. After an hour of lying on the bed I moved to the living room beside the only telephone in the house, waiting to see if my father would sneak out of his bed at night to make the call. In the chair by the phone, in the dark, I must have shut my eyes for a few minutes, because I remember dreaming about Freja.

At dawn there was no sign of my father. He hadn't made the phone call. I'd been wrong. He hadn't betrayed me! He'd been telling the truth when he said we could talk over breakfast, perhaps he intended to tease out details I'd omitted. It was a new day in our relationship.

I went to the kitchen – there were coffee cups in the cupboard that hadn't been cleaned properly, and I boiled a pot of water, intending to wash every cup and plate in the cupboard, to scrub the sink, to give the room a clean, to throw away the flypaper on the windowsill, and change this smell. While doing this I called out to my father, asking him if he wanted his coffee in bed. There was no reply. I knocked on the door. There was no reply. It was late for the country. He was a man who woke up at dawn. I tried the handle to his room, only to find the door was locked.

Outside the farm I tapped on the glass of my father's window. The curtains were closed. I didn't know if he was hurt or sick, and I spent countless minutes going back and forth between the window and the door, calling his name, until I heard the sound of a car. I stood on the porch with a hand over my eyes, sheltering it from the rising sun. Dr Norling was driving towards the farm.

Chris must have guessed my plan and called before I'd arrived. My father would've called him back when he'd heard the van and told them to come in the morning, he'd keep me here, betraying me before he'd even heard a word, believing my husband over me, a man he'd never even met. I could have run, I suppose, or jumped in the van and made a getaway. I didn't. I sat on the edge of the pond, took off my shoes and socks, and sank my feet into the water, shackles of algae forming around my ankles.

When they arrived we didn't say very much. They treated me like a child. I was docile and obedient. They put me in the back of the car, binding my arms in case I should strike them during the journey, or try and jump out as they were driving.

Norling drove me home. Chris took the van, following behind. He said it would be too upsetting to drive with me as his prisoner. I never saw my father. He didn't emerge from the locked bedroom. He must have decided that my fears about Mia were no more than reconstituted guilt about my involvement in Freja's death – that's what he believed, I'm sure of it, that this was madness of my own creation, the madness of a murderer imagining another murder, unable to come to grips with my own crime, drowning Freja in the lake, holding her head under the water until she could speak no more. He still believed it. Fifty years on, he still believed me to be a murderer.

• • •

M Y MUM CLOSED HER JOURNAL and placed it on the bed in front of me:

'It's yours.'

She was relinquishing possession of her most treasured article of evidence, her notes and clippings, her photographs and maps, entrusting them to me – soulmates sharing a secret diary. I wondered if this thought was in her mind too – had she been searching for an ally, a term that sounded strategic, or, more emotionally, had she been searching for a confidant? I recalled my mum's description of her time with Freja in the forest, swapping stories, vowing to be friends forever, believing even in the existence of trolls merely because the other said so. I placed one hand flat on top of the journal as though stopping its secrets from bursting out:

'What about the asylum in Sweden?'

'Daniel, I'd end my life rather than go back to a place like that.'

I opened the journal at a random page, not reading but running my fingertip over the heavily indented notes. I came to the conclusion that the threat was real, my mum would consider suicide should she ultimately fail in her attempts at justice. The idea remained beyond my comprehension. I couldn't manage a response of any kind. My mum elaborated:

'The building was clean. The doctors were kind. The food they brought was acceptable. But to be a person no one believes, a person no one listens to, a woman considered incapable – I've never been that woman. I will never be her. If placed in that situation again, I'll prove capable of taking my life.'

'Mum, you'd never allow me to talk like that.'

She shook her head:

'I wouldn't be your mother in a place like that.'
'Would I still be your son if I was committed?'
'Of course.'
'What would you do if our positions were reversed?'
'I'd believe you.'

I put the journal down and took hold of my mum's hand, turning it upright, like a palm reader, tracing the lines with my finger:
'Tell me about the hospital.'
'I don't want to talk about that place.'
I ignored this:
'Did they drive you straight there?'

No, they drove me back to the farm. Chris had convinced Dr Norling to attempt treatment at home. Don't believe this was an act of kindness. They needed to make it seem like the hospital was the last option and that they'd tried everything. It would've looked suspicious otherwise. The farm was transformed into a prison. Only Chris had the keys. The computer was disconnected so I couldn't email you. I had no access to the telephone. They laced my food with toxins, not to kill, but psychedelic fungi from the forests to send me mad. They wanted me to cry out that I could hear voices in my head, to be wild with outlandish visions, to claim that the soil of our farm was speckled white with the ground-up bones of children, or to point towards distant dark trees with a trembling hand and declare that dangerous trolls were watching us. I refused to eat anything that wasn't sealed. Even so, there are ways round this, syringe needles pierced through packaging. My tongue turned black. My gums turned black. My breath turned rotten. My lips turned blue.

One day, when Chris was out shopping, I was studying the evidence I'd collected and he returned, taking me by surprise. He lost his temper, attacked me, and threw the stitched quote into the fire. I snatched it out, saving it just in time, holding it by the tongs, still burning. That was when he decided to have me committed. There was a risk I might burn the farm down, so he said.

Together with Dr Norling they took me to the asylum. It was a clever plan. Once you've been checked into an asylum your credibility is destroyed. It doesn't matter if you're released the next day. It doesn't matter if the doctors declare your mind okay. A lawyer could always ask, in front of a judge and jury, whether you'd ever been in an asylum. That said, the stay at the hospital turned out to be a blessing. Before I was admitted, I was beaten. My father's second betrayal had emptied me. My fight was gone. I didn't believe I'd ever have the strength to try and convince another person again. That night the doctor told me Chris's account of my childhood, with the implication I'd been involved in Freja's death. I was so outraged I spent every waking hour writing a truthful account, the testimony you've read. It was enough for the doctors to let me go. Their professional confidence restored me. I'd been a sentimental fool to turn to my father, chasing after second chances. It was you I needed to speak to – my son, my precious son! You'd listen. You'd be fair. You were the one I needed. As soon as I realised that, I was as happy as I'd been for many months.

I caught a taxi from the hospital. Everything I needed was in my satchel, passport and debit card. I didn't care how much it cost. I bought a ticket on the first flight out of Sweden. This time I'd tell the story properly, supported with evidence. This time I'd tell it to someone who has always loved me.

•   •   •

I LET GO OF MY MUM'S HAND.

   'Mum, do you trust me?'

'I love you very much.'

'But do you trust me?'

She thought upon the question for a while, and then she smiled.

· · ·

A SNOWSTORM HAD SWEPT ACROSS the south of Sweden, delaying flights, and by the time my plane touched down at Gothenburg's Landvetter airport it was nearly midnight. To cramped and irritable passengers the pilot announced that it was exceptionally cold for mid-December, even by Swedish standards. The temperature was minus fifteen degrees. A few unhurried snowflakes were still falling. The sight soothed many of the frayed tempers on board. Even the overworked stewardess took a moment to enjoy the view. We were the last flight in. The airport was nearly empty except for a lone figure at passport control. By the time I was waved through, my bags were on the carousel. I exited customs, passing families and couples reunited. The sight of them reminded me of my last occasion at airport arrivals and the sadness I felt caught me off guard.

Four months had passed since my mum had been committed. She was being held in a secure hospital in north London. It couldn't, on any level, be claimed that she was being treated. My mum was refusing medication. As soon as she realised the doctors weren't going to release her she stopped speaking to them. As a consequence she was undergoing no meaningful therapy. Recently she'd begun to skip meals, believing that the portions were spiked with antipsychotics. She mistrusted water from the taps. Intermittently she'd sip from bottled juice only if the seal was unbroken. She was frequently dehydrated. Her physical symptoms, so upsetting when I'd picked her up at the airport in the summer, were worsening. Week by week her skin stretched tighter around her skull as if her body was retreating from the world. My mum was dying.

While I'd never doubted the detail of my mum's account, I questioned her interpretations of events. I hadn't gone to the police, worried that if the substance of the allegations didn't check out, if the officers called the Swedish police and heard there'd been no murder, it might result in serious consequences to my mum's liberty. I'd wanted the three of us, my dad included, to talk to a doctor, an independent figure who couldn't possibly be accused of corruption. In the end, my solution, the hospital, had achieved the exact result I'd been trying to avoid – imprisonment.

During the night drive across London my mum had held my hand. She'd presumed I'd arranged a hotel car to take us to a police station, and though I didn't lie, I didn't correct her, not out of cowardice, but as a practical measure. She'd spoken excitedly about her dreams for the future, about how the two of us would spend time together and become close again. So assured was her trust in me that when the car eventually parked outside the hospital she'd been unable to understand that I'd betrayed her. She told the driver he'd made a mistake and taken us to the wrong address. She was so suspicious of everyone else, yet she'd trusted me. When she grasped that there'd been no mistake, her whole body seemed to tremble with anguish. I'd been her saviour and supporter, the last person she could turn to. In the end, I'd behaved like all the others – her husband and father and now her son. In the face of such a blow, her resistance was remarkable. This was a setback, no more. I was no longer her ally. I was no longer her son. She didn't run or panic. I guessed her calculations. She'd already convinced doctors in Sweden, she could do the same here. If she tried to run she'd be caught, declared insane, and trapped forever. She let go of my hand and took the satchel from me, dispossessing me of her evidence and journal. She placed the strap over her shoulder, calmly stepping out of the car, head held high. She was ready to make her case, to craft a new allegiance. As she coolly assessed the asylum, I couldn't help but admire her strength, displaying more courage in a level-headed glance than I'd ever displayed in my life.

During the admission process she wouldn't look at me. I was forced to mention the threats she'd made to her life and wept as I did so. To my display of emotion she flicked her eyes dismissively to the ceiling. In her mind I was play-acting, and badly too, 'false tears' and 'false grief', as she'd described it earlier. I could hear the thoughts in her head:

'Who would've thought he was such a convincing liar?'

She was right, I'd grown good at lying, but not in this instance. When the doctors escorted her into the ward she didn't say good-bye. Down that stark white corridor, I called out that I'd see her soon. She didn't turn around.

Outside the hospital, I sat on a low brick wall, my legs hanging over the street sign, waiting for my dad. He arrived in a cab, disoriented and exhausted. Up close I saw how lost he was, incomplete without my mum. When he hugged me I was worried he might collapse. Dr Norling accompanied him, delicately fragranced and immaculately dressed, reminding me of a dandy from a bygone era. He apologised for not informing the staff at the Swedish asylum that my mum could self-harm or possibly inflict harm on others. His tactful restraint had been prompted by my dad's well-intentioned request to downplay her condition so that she might stay in an asylum for as short a time as possible. As a result the staff underestimated her risk profile – a term I'd hear over and again. When my mum had threatened to take legal action they'd allowed her to go free. They had no grounds to hold her. Technically she was a voluntary admission. She was well behaved. Her written account of the past was coherent. Norling had travelled to England to put right his mistakes. While I sensed that he was primarily concerned with his own reputation, I could hazard no darker motive. He spoke to the English doctors with great gusto, performing for them. I didn't warm to him, despite the fact he'd done so much to help. My mum's description was accurate, he was vain and pompous, but he struck me as an unlikely villain.

The hospital itself was clean. The doctors and nurses were dedicated and warm. There was a visiting room where my mum often sat on the window ledge, staring outside through a sealed window that didn't open and couldn't be smashed. Her view, over the barbed-wire perimeter fence, was into a park. Out of sight there was a children's playground, and the sound of their laughter could often be heard during the summer. It had fallen silent as winter set in. Mum didn't turn when I entered the room. She would not look at me, nor would she talk to me, or my dad. Once we were gone she told the nurses that our visits were motivated by a desire to ensure her allegations were being discredited. I didn't know what theory she'd created to explain my involvement. She was contemptuous of antipsychotic medications, considering the pills to be an admission that the events of the summer were not as she described. She equated taking medicine with giving up on the adopted children who needed her help. The doctors couldn't compel her to take the drugs. They required my mum's consent. My mum didn't accept that she was ill. A wall surrounded her mind and we couldn't knock it down. Initially, in therapy, she'd laid out the evidence and repeated her allegations. Now she remained silent. If there was a new face, whether they were staff or a patient, she told her story again. Each time the account grew longer. Her storytelling skill improved, as if she were in hospital only because she hadn't properly set the scene or characterised one of her suspects. Without exception the other patients believed her. Some of them approached me during my visits and reprimanded me for not solving the case of murdered Mia.

Days and weeks passed in this way. Sometimes I would go alone, sometimes with my dad, occasionally with Mark. He'd always wait outside, feeling it improper to see my mum in this state before she knew his identity or why he was there. Initially we were optimistic. My mum would get better and we'd become stronger and closer as a family. The gaps between us would close. But in the eyes of my mother there was no return from my betrayal. The permanence of this position has slowly settled upon me. I feel a kind of grief.

One day, in late autumn, as I paced the visiting room, troubled by the change in season and the lack of progress, I said impulsively:

'I'm going to Sweden. I'll find out the truth for myself.'

It was the only time my mum reacted. She turned around, looking directly at me, assessing my claim. For a few seconds her eyes were the same as when she'd seen me at the airport – there was hope. For a few seconds I was her son again. She raised a finger to her lips, pressing it against them as though gesturing me to be silent. Crouching by her side, I asked:

'What does that mean?'

Her lips opened slightly, ready to speak. I saw her black-tipped tongue. Then a change came over her. She dismissed the sincerity of my inquiry. Her lips closed.

'Mum, please? Talk to me.'

But she wouldn't. It was a reminder that no matter how ill she was, her powers of perception were sharp. I hadn't seriously considered the idea of going to Sweden when I blurted it out. My focus up until that day had been the doctors, the therapy and treatment.

Afterwards I discussed the idea with my dad and Mark. Their introduction to each other had been an unspectacular one, carried out in the saddest of circumstances. They'd shaken hands, as if a business deal had been agreed. My dad had thanked him for his help. When we were alone, my dad had apologised if he'd ever done anything to give the impression that he wouldn't have accepted me for who I am. I found his apology excruciating, offering my own apology instead. He was in turmoil, not at the revelation, but at the years of secrecy, exactly as I'd imagined. Despite the sadness, finally he'd met Mark. I could stop lying. However, none of us were able to celebrate without Mum. It was impossible to comprehend celebrating anything as a family without her. Neither Mark nor my dad

thought going to Sweden was a good idea. There was no mystery
to unravel. Mia had been a young unhappy girl who'd run away
from home. If I went to Sweden I'd become caught up in an impossible quest, a distraction from the real concern – trying to convince
my mum to engage with medication and therapy. Worse still, it
would indulge her delusions rather than challenge them and it
might do harm rather than good. I dropped the idea, or at least I
dropped it from conversation, because I'd begun to learn Swedish
again, spending many hours reading my old textbooks and reminding myself of vocabulary lists, brushing up on a language that I'd
spoken fluently as a child.

As the darkest night of the year approached, the doctors discussed
the possibility of feeding my mum intravenously, outlining the
legalities and moral implications. At this point I openly declared
my intention to travel to Sweden. Mark saw it as denial, in many
ways typical of me, running away from problems – a form of
escape. My dad was so distraught at the deteriorating health of my
mum that he no longer opposed my idea, willing to consider anything. My plan was to discover what had happened to Mia. No
matter what the truth might be, there was a possibility of engaging
with my mum again if I brought back fresh information. New evidence would be the only provocation she'd respond to. I was sure
of it. Though Mark disagreed, once he saw my mind was made up
he stopped putting forward counterarguments and loaned me the
money to make the trip. Initially I refused, proposing to borrow it
from the bank, but this angered Mark to such an extent that I swallowed my pride. There was no work on the horizon. The design
company that employed me was teetering on the brink of

bankruptcy. I hadn't worked on a project for months. I was broke. And in my more depressive moments, I did wonder if maybe I was running away.

Rationing out the money, I estimated that I'd have enough to survive for three weeks if I was frugal. Mark couldn't take the time off work but he planned to fly out for Christmas should I not return before then. He did well to hide his doubts. His mind was rational and disciplined. He dealt with matters that could be tested in a court of law. I acted on feelings. My gut was telling me that there was truth in my mum's account.

•   •   •

I exited the airport, into the freezing night, contemplating the long journey ahead. My rental car was a sleek and powerful four-by-four, chosen by Mark to cope with the extreme weather. I didn't own a car in London and felt like a fraud behind the wheel of this magnificent vehicle. But I was grateful for his choice. Conditions were challenging. The motorways hadn't been completely cleared. As a temporary measure a single lane had been carved out, banked with the day's snowfall. I was obliged to drive slowly, stopping at several service stations to buy black coffee, hot dogs with sweet mustard, and salted liquorice. At four in the morning I finally turned off the motorway, following narrow country lanes until the navigational computer declared that I was at my destination.

The driveway to the farm was filled with snow. I had no intention of digging it clear and backed up, ploughing the car at speed into the knee-deep snow, hearing it compact under the tyres. Opening the car door, I stepped out, staring at the shuttered farmhouse. After so many broken promises, I was finally here. A wedge of snow balanced on the thatched roof, crumbling at the edge. An oak tree huddled over the two-hundred-year-old house, as if the pair enjoyed an ancient allegiance. The snowfall was untouched. The menace my mum had perceived in this landscape was absent, or at least invisible to me. The extraordinary quiet that she'd found suffocating was wonderful, the openness of this world seemed the exact opposite of oppressive, and only the distant red lights of the wind turbines – rat eyes, as my mum had called them, stopped me from entirely discounting her nightmarish reconstruction of this landscape.

Glancing around, I quickly identified various locations she'd mentioned in her account – the converted barn for the paying guests who never came, the stone outhouse where the slaughtered pig had hung. I took a guess at where the vegetable garden must be, hidden under the snow, as was the damage caused when my mum had driven the van roughshod across the garden to escape. Only the break in the hedgerow revealed the trauma of that day.

Inside the farm there was evidence of a hasty exit. A full mug of tea sat on the kitchen table. The surface had frozen. I cracked the thin brown ice with my finger, swirling the liquid beneath. With the tip of my finger I tasted it. There was no milk and it had been sweetened with honey. Neither of my parents drank their tea this way. Accepting that this was a trivial deduction, I suddenly felt despondent at my chances. The trip was a grand gesture, flamboyance concealing powerlessness and despair.

Despite the long journey there was no chance I could go straight to sleep. It was too cold. My mind was too active. I lit a fire in the steel heart of the farm, a magnificent wrought-iron stove, the joints clicking as the metal warmed up. Sitting in front of it, I caught sight of a devilish face carved into the wood. I grabbed the tongs, pulling out the log, only to find that I'd mistaken a gnarled knot for a nose.

In the hope of calming my thoughts, I searched the shelves for a book to read, discovering my mum's Bible. I turned to Ephesians chapter 6, verse 12. The page was unmarked. Putting it back, I saw the collection of troll stories my mum had read to me as a child, the out-of-print book with just the single illustration of a troll lurking in the woods. It had been many years since I'd seen this book and, feeling fondness for it, I browsed through the stories by the fire. Even after all this time, I knew them by heart, and as I read the words I heard my mum's voice. It made me too sad and I put it to one side. Stretching out my hands in front of the flames, I wondered what I honestly hoped to achieve.

In the morning I woke slumped in front of dead embers. My body had curled to the shape of the chair and I stood up awkwardly. When I looked out the window the snow's brightness hurt my eyes. After showering, imagining muddy water running over my back, I brewed strong coffee. There was no food except for hundreds of jars of home-made pickles and jams that my parents had stocked up in preparation for the long winter. Eating delicious blackberry jam that dripped off the spoon, I sat at the kitchen table, taking from my bag an empty notebook and sharpened pencil – the tools of an investigator. I looked at the items with scepticism. On the top of the first page I wrote the date.

It was obvious that I should start with Håkan. My dad had rung his friend in advance of my arrival, informing him of my intentions, only to be told there was no news about Mia, no developments, and there was nothing to be achieved by coming here. My dad had recently taken the decision to sell the farm. Left with only a thousand pounds, he was living in Mark's apartment, in the study. He had no plans, sustained only by hope that my mum would improve. As she grew worse, he too weakened. They were an unbreakable team, united even in their deterioration. Though I had many concerns about selling the farm, they were vague and superstitious in nature, and from a practical perspective I had no grounds to oppose the sale. To my parents, the farm was a place of grief: I felt that keenly, standing under its old timber ceilings. Håkan was maintaining his generous valuation when he could easily have dropped the offer and exploited our predicament. He was a gracious victor. At the beginning of the new year the farm would be his.

I didn't want to meet Håkan in my current mood, unsettled and downbeat. My instinct was to trust my mum's account of his character, particularly since my dad was often blind to people's faults. It was perfectly possible Håkan had been nice to Dad and horrible to my mum. I had no doubt this formidable man would consider me as slight and inconsequential. But I was curious to know what he made of my objective. Delaying our encounter, I decided to look around town and stock up on groceries. I had fond memories of shopping with my mum in Swedish stores and loved many of the popular foodstuffs that were only available here. I was sure my confidence would grow again once I'd eaten well, stocked the pantry, and made the farm a more welcoming base.

With the back of the car filled with groceries, I took a stroll through the centre of town, along the main promenade mentioned by Mum. As the day was already beginning to fade, electric Advent candles set on automatic timers turned on in the windows. I paused outside the coffee shop called the Ritz where mum and Mia had spoken. Without any clear sense of why, I entered and browsed the array of cakes and open sandwiches, layered with prawns, sliced egg and clumps of beetroot salad. The woman behind the counter looked me up and down, making no attempt to hide her interest in my appearance. I didn't own a wide collection of warm clothes. Trying to wrap up against temperatures of minus fifteen for the first time in my life, I was improvising with mismatched layers and a jacket I'd found in a charity shop, a corduroy duffel coat, a far cry from the high-tech branded snow jackets most people here dressed in. Pretending not to notice that I was being inspected, I selected a bottle of mineral water, a cheese sandwich and, on a whim, the same cake my mum had shared with Mia, a Princess Torta, a sponge layered with thick white cream and a thin layer of green marzipan. The first few mouthfuls were delicious, but it quickly became too much, the texture too soft, like eating sweetened snow, and I pushed it aside, hoping the owner wouldn't be offended. Sitting back in my chair, I saw the missing person poster of Mia pinned to the notice board. Other posters and cards had begun to encroach around the perimeter, signalling that it was old news. I stood up, walking close to the board, studying it intently. There were perforated tags that could be ripped off with Håkan's telephone number. None had been taken.

When I turned around, the woman behind the counter was staring at me. With irrational certainty I knew that she was going to phone Håkan as soon as I left the café, the kind of statement my mum had frequently made and the kind I'd challenged. It was a feeling, and no more than that. But I'd bet any money I was right. Picking up my jacket, I fought the desire to say, 'Fuck you too,' as I left the premises, throwing up the hood of my corduroy jacket with a touch of defiance.

Arriving back at the farm, it was only four in the afternoon, but daylight was already gone. I'd been warned about the depressing effects of the winter darkness, particularly staying on my own in a remote area. Consequently I'd bought a great number of candles. There was comfort in their light compared with electric bulbs. Opening the car boot, I paused. To my side I saw a line of footsteps in the snow, deep tracks emerging from the fields. Leaving the groceries, I followed them to the front door. A hand-delivered letter was pinned to the timber frame.

Daniel

I dropped the envelope into my pocket, returning to the car and carrying the groceries inside. With a cup of tea and several candles burning around me I broke the seal. Inside was a cream card, the margins of which were lined with Christmas elves. It was from Håkan, inviting me to take a glass of mulled wine at his farm that evening.

Like my mum, I fussed over my appearance, in the end opting for smart clothes. I decided against bringing my pad and pencil since I wasn't a reporter interviewing a subject and contemplated whether it was absurd to have brought them to Sweden at all. I set off early, wanting to arrive on time and unsure how long it would take to walk. Reaching the enormous pig barn that marked the turnoff, I considered the bleak industrial building my mum had described. Under a layer of snow everything looked tranquil, but the smell was unpleasant and I didn't linger. Walking down the long drive meticulously cleared of snow, I realised that I should've brought a gift. I thought about returning to the farm, but I had nothing to offer. I couldn't make a present out of one of my mum's preserves.

Håkan's house was a welcoming sight. There were electric Advent candles in every window. Hanging above them were decorative Christmas lace curtains, elves wrapping presents and elves hunched over bowls of porridge. I could feel myself relax and fought against the sensation. I kicked the snow out of my boots, knocking on the door. It was opened by Håkan. He was nearly a head taller than me. His frame was broad. He smiled and shook my hand, allowing me to register the strength in his grip. As I left my boots in the hall, he spoke to me in English. Though my Swedish wasn't fluent, I politely told him that I'd prefer to speak Swedish. It was my version of a strong handshake, I suppose.

Showing no reaction, he took my jacket, holding the corduroy duffel coat up to the light, examining it briefly before placing it on a peg.

We sat in the living room beside an elegantly decorated tree. Stitched fabric gingerbread hung from the branches. On the top, instead of an angel, there was a stiff paper star. The electric lights were wrapped in a cotton-like fluff that transformed the sharpness of the bulb's filament into a diffuse glow. The tree stand was hand-carved, three carefully chiselled troll faces, their wart-spotted chins stretching down to form the legs on which the tree stood. Beside it were a number of presents wrapped in glossy gold paper with red silk bows. Håkan said:

'They're for Mia.'

The individual components of this room were splendid. But for some reason it was like being inside a depiction of a perfect Christmas scene rather than a real home.

Though I'd been talking to Håkan for several minutes, Elise, his wife, only appeared to serve us mulled wine. She emerged from the kitchen, giving me a nod of the head, carrying a tray with two ornamental glasses, a bowl of shredded almonds and diced raisins, and a steaming jug of mulled wine. In silence she deposited some almonds and raisins into the bottom of my glass, filling it with wine and offering it to me. I accepted, thanking her, finding it strange that she avoided eye contact and didn't join us, retreating to the kitchen once she'd finished.

Håkan clinked my glass and proposed a toast:

'Let's wish your mother a quick recovery.'

With a touch of provocation, I replied:

'And may Mia come home soon.'

Ignoring my remark, Håkan said:

'The mulled wine is an ancient family recipe. People ask me for it every year but we never give it away. It's a secret blend of spices and different types of alcohol, not just wine, so be careful, this stuff carries a kick.'

I could feel the liquid warming my stomach. Though prudence told me I should take no more than a sip, I quickly finished the entire glass. The shredded almonds and raisins formed a sweet, delicious mulch. Toying with the idea of using my finger to scoop it out, I noticed tiny wooden spoons on the tray intended for exactly that purpose. Håkan remarked:

'Coming to Sweden is a touching gesture. Perhaps the gesture on its own will be enough to help poor Tilde. In practical terms, I don't understand what you think you can achieve.'

His reference to my mum as 'poor Tilde' irritated me and I was sure that it had been intended to.

'I hope to bring a fresh pair of eyes to events.'

Håkan picked up the jug and filled my glass:

'This trip is not for my benefit.'

I took a sip from my second glass of mulled wine. I wanted to see him react to the question, even though I already knew the answer:

'Is there any news of Mia?'

He shook his head:

'No news.'

His free arm fell lank by the side of his chair, his fingers brushing the gold paper of the present nearest to him. Though the touch had only been gentle, the present moved, and the thought popped into my head that it was empty, no more than a gift-wrapped box. His silence felt like a challenge. Would I cross the line and press further into a subject he clearly had no desire to discuss? I accepted the challenge and said:

'You must be worried. She's very young.'

Håkan finished his glass but didn't refill it, signalling his desire that I should leave soon:

'Is she young? I started work on this farm when I was just nine years old.'

It was a curious response.

As we said goodbye, I made a snap decision to visit the underground shelter where he carved his trolls. Hearing the door close behind me, I walked up the drive, but once out of sight I doubled back, crouching through the snow-covered fields, sneaking up to the side of the house, below the kitchen, where I remained for a minute or two, attempting to listen to Håkan and Elise's conversation. The triple-glazed windows allowed no sound to pass through. Giving up, I hurried onward, reaching the shelter. The outer door was locked. A new padlock had been bought. It was thick, with toughened rubber around the arch, unbreakable for an amateur snoop. I set off, returning home through the fields and snow. Uneasy, I looked back towards Håkan's farm and saw him at the bedroom window. Electric candles flickered about his waist. I couldn't say if he saw me or not.

The next morning I woke while it was still dark, intending to fully exploit the brief period of daylight. Surrounded by candles I ate a breakfast of sour milk yogurt with pumpkin seeds, sliced apple, and ground cinnamon. Having taken care to wrap up warm, I stepped from the farm into knee-deep snow. Reaching Elk River, I discovered that the water had completely frozen over. In his rush to leave the farm my dad had forgotten about the boat, supposed to be pulled onshore for the winter. The river now encased it, the propeller locked within ice, the hull under strain, cracks clearly visible. In the spring the ice would melt and this boat would leak and sink to the bottom. It had been bought, my dad told me, not as a vessel to collect clues but because elderly Cecilia had been suffering from dementia. According to Håkan, she'd become irrational – there were days when she believed she was a young woman with many happy years on the farm ahead of her.

I stepped down from the jetty into the boat. As described by my mum, the engine was fitted with an LED panel. But it was dead: there was no charge, not even enough to operate the display. I turned my thoughts to the ice fragment my mum had found in the salmon's gill. She'd been right, on that night she had felt ice – my dad had bought the fish. However, it was not for the reason she suspected. Elk River contained no salmon. The salmon ladder built to bypass the quaint hydropower station had failed. It was poorly designed. The salmon no longer migrated upstream – there were no magnificent fish to be caught, just thrashing eels and vicious pike. In his haste, excited by the farm's bargain price, my dad had assured my mum that the river was good. The many fishing books that declared the river excellent had been written before the construction of the hydroelectric station. Realising his mistake too late, he'd tried to cover it up, worried about the additional stress that the revelation would cause my mum, coming so soon after the problems with the well. It was a miscalculation motivated by the best intentions. Håkan had paid for the salmon, selecting one from a local fishmonger, an imposter fish from the waters of Norway.

I threw a clod of frozen dirt over the ice, attempting to judge the thickness. Unable to decide, I swung my legs over the side of the boat and used my foot to test it. The ice didn't strain. I put my other foot down and stood up, ready to fall back into the boat if the ice should crack. The ice was deep and strong. I began the long walk to Teardrop Island.

My progress along the frozen river was slow. My footsteps were careful. It took over three hours to reach the edge of the forest and I regretted not bringing food or a hot drink. On the cusp of the forest I paused briefly, standing before the landscape featured in my mum's book of trolls – timeless and mythic. The sky was a dull white and an icy mist hung about the trees. In places, the river split around boulders and the ice took on strange shapes, swirls and splashes frozen midflow. The snow was crisscrossed with animal tracks, some of which were wide strides, creatures as large as elks. Maybe my mum had encountered one in the water – maybe it had passed so close she could've reached out and touched its mane. Certainly Teardrop Island was a real place. I gripped the same branch that had caught my mum's attention. There were lines on the tree trunk where visiting boats had moored.

Exploring the island, I brushed away the snow to find the

blackened timber stubs where the fire had blazed. My dad claimed it was a well-known spot where teenagers screwed around and smoked pot. The fire hadn't been accidental. My mum had started it. They'd discovered a fuel canister in the boat. Her discarded clothes on the riverbank stank of petrol. As for the milk tooth, the charred tooth – her final shocking evidence – it had come from her own mouth. It was my mum's milk tooth, kept, along with various other knick-knacks from her childhood, in an ornamental wooden music box. My dad believed it likely that the whole box had been thrown into the fire. Mum had watched it burn, standing so close her skin blistered, every item disappearing except for the tooth, turning from white to black.

At the farm that night I worked through the backlog of post. Among the junk mail, and a small number of overdue bills, I found a pair of tickets to the Santa Lucia festival in town, a festival of light on the darkest night of the year, the counterpoint to the midsommar celebrations. It was typical of my mum to have bought the tickets so far in advance. She was organised and methodical, and more importantly she would've been petrified of missing out. The entire town would be there, including many of my mum's suspects.

In advance of this gathering, I spent the next few days chasing information on Mia. I spoke to teachers at her school, shopkeepers on the promenade, and even passing strangers on the street. People were baffled by my interest. Many knew about my mum. Her story had been whispered across town. But they failed to grasp why I was inquiring about someone else's daughter. On every level my efforts were amateurish. At one point, I even offered my spare Lucia ticket in exchange for information. Without any authority, I cut a pitiful figure, laughable were I not so desperate. My most promising appointment had been with Stellan the detective in the sleepy police station. Unlike my mum, he'd kept me waiting, and agreed to speak to me only while walking from his office to his car, bluntly repeating Håkan's assertion that there was no news. Hopeful that I might have more success with the kindly hermit, I'd paid Ulf a visit. He'd opened the door but refused to allow me inside, giving me nothing other than a glimpse of the space on the wall where his wife's final stitched fabric quote should have hung.

That night, when I spoke to my dad, he informed me that my mum had passed out from dehydration. The doctors were asserting that under the Mental Capacity Act she didn't have the right to refuse liquids or food. If they took the decision to use a saline drip and she pulled it free from her arm, she would be restrained. Later, speaking to Mark, he was largely silent. He was hoping I'd make the decision to come home without being told.

On the brink of giving up, I jotted down possible flight times to return to London. That evening there was a knock on the door. It was Dr Norling. The charm and eloquence were gone, although the delicate sandalwood fragrance remained. He was abrupt to the point of rudeness, saying he couldn't stay long:

'You shouldn't have come. You'll achieve nothing. Tilde needs to return to reality. She doesn't need more fantasy.'

He gestured at my empty notebook on the table:

'This is fantasy.'

He added:

'You know that, don't you?'

There was a mild threat in his question, as though he were eyeing the issue of my sanity, like mother like son. That was the moment I decided to stay.

Had my mum remained in Sweden, Santa Lucia would surely have been a key event in her chronology, containing, in her eyes, some incident of great importance. I intended to arrive early in the hope of selecting a seat at the back, observing local society as they entered, trying to imagine which relationships my mum might have reacted to.

The church was located in a historic square, the oldest and highest point in town, perched on a small hill. With white stone walls and a high white tower, the building seemed to rise up out of the snow more like a natural phenomenon than a man-made structure. Doubting that I, a stranger, could possess a valued ticket, the woman at the front primly told me the event was sold out. When I produced a ticket she checked it carefully before begrudging me admission.

Inside there was no electric light, just the flicker of a thousand candles, lighting up walls decorated with biblical scenes painted on timber planks stripped from the hulls of old fishing boats. The leaflet I'd taken from the entrance informed me that this church was once a place where wives and sons and daughters would pray for the safe return of their husbands and fathers from the stormy sea, a perfect location to pray for the return of a missing daughter or, in my case, a mother present and missing at the same time.

On my lap, hidden inside the song sheet, was a re-creation of my mum's list of suspects. The mayor was the first suspect to arrive, with the admirably political intention to meet and greet the attendees. He saw me and studiously ignored me – the only chink in his otherwise incessant jocularity. The front row of seats had been reserved and the mayor took his place, with the remaining seats filled by, among others, the detective and the doctor. The church was full when Håkan entered, accompanied by his wife. I could tell that he enjoyed having the eyes of the whole town follow him to his reserved space at the front.

Once these important society figures had been seated the service began. A procession of young men and women dressed in bridal white flowed through the aisle, the men holding gold stars on sticks, the women holding candles, singing as they slowly walked, assembling into rows at the front of the church. The lead girl wore candles mounted in a steel ring, a crown of flames in her blonde hair, the Saint of Light, a role that Mia had played in last year's ceremony. The service lasted an hour. The congregation celebrated light and warmth not as an abstract idea but as a powerful need, a missed loved one. Despite the obvious opportunity, no mention was made of Mia. The omission was striking. There was surely calculation behind it, rather than mere oversight; a request had been made, and the priest had agreed not to raise the matter. It hardly qualified as evidence but it jarred, particularly with Håkan seated at the very front, and particularly since Mia had been the last to play the role of Santa Lucia.

After the service I waited outside by the line of flickering lanterns laid in the snow, keen to catch a word with Håkan. Through the church doors I could see him talking with members of the community, shaking hands, more like a statesman than an ordinary citizen. Upon seeing me he paused, too self-controlled to show a reaction beyond the pause itself. He eventually emerged with his wife. As I stepped up to Håkan he turned to Elise, ordering her ahead to a private reception. She glanced at me, and perhaps it was my imagination, but there was something in that look, not pity, or hostility, but something else – remorse, or guilt. It was the briefest of moments, I could have been mistaken, and she hurried up the candlelit track.

Håkan's civility was unconvincing:
'I hope you enjoyed the service.'
'Very much. It's a beautiful church. But I was surprised we didn't pray for your daughter's safe return.'
'I did pray, Daniel. I pray for her every day.'
Håkan had joined my parents in refusing to shorten my name to Dan. Fighting my instinct to avoid conflict, I recalled something my mum had said:
'I'm struggling with how Mia left your farm. She couldn't drive. She didn't take her bike. She can't have walked. There was no public transport. Now that I'm here, I understand how remote it is.'

Håkan stepped sideways, into the snow, isolating our conversation. He lowered his voice:

'Your father and I became close over the summer. He was worried about you. Do you mind me telling you this?'

It wasn't enough for Håkan to attack me. He wanted my permission to do so.

'Go ahead.'

'According to him, your career was going nowhere. After the opportunities provided to you, none of which your parents enjoyed, you hadn't thought for yourself, following in their footsteps, taking the easiest possible course. He wondered if your failure was why you'd cut yourself off from your family. You rarely phoned. You never visited. When I heard Chris repeat your excuses I thought to myself – that man is lying. He doesn't want to come. Chris was hurt by your absence. Tilde was too. They couldn't understand what they'd done wrong. They feared there was a chance you wouldn't come at all this year. But the part I find the hardest to believe is that you actually believed they were rich! Could this really be true?'

I was ashamed and considered making a qualified reply, defending myself, but in the end decided for a simple admission:

'It's true.'

'How? I knew as soon as they arrived that they were struggling. That's why I'd always pay for your father when we drank together, that's why when we invited them to parties we never asked them to bring anything expensive, like salmon or meat.'

Amid my humiliation, the mystery of why he'd asked my mum to bring potato salad was solved. It was an act of charity, with a touch of condescension. Håkan paused, assessing my reaction. I was unable to protest. Having completed his attack, he now turned to his defence:

'No one is more upset about Mia than me. I have done everything expected of me. To have my role publicly questioned by a man who did nothing for his parents, a man who wasn't even aware that his mother was shouting murder at every shadow, well, it is offensive. You're upsetting my wife. You're insulting my friends.'

'No insult was intended.'

Putting on his gloves, Håkan had the demeanour of a man disappointed that the fight had been so one-sided. But before he left I quickly added:

'All I want are some answers, not for me, but for my mum, and right now, despite your efforts, there are none. We don't even know how Mia left your farm.'

Perhaps Håkan saw in me a flicker of my mum's belief, because it was the only time I witnessed him lose control over his words:

'You couldn't even spot that your own parents were broke. What use could you be? This visit isn't about helping your mother and it certainly isn't about helping me. You feel guilty. You're trying to feel better about yourself. But you're not allowed to do it by nosing around in my life, in my community, insinuating that we've done something improper. I won't have it!'

Composing himself, Håkan gave one final twist of the knife:

'Unlike many here, I don't believe there's any shame in losing your mind. And maybe she didn't know it, but I like Tilde. She was strong. Her problem was that she was too strong. She shouldn't have fought me so hard. There was no reason for it. She got it into her head that I was her enemy. I could've been a friend. I see your mother in your face. But I see none of her strength. Chris and Tilde have brought you up to be soft. Children rot when they're indulged in too much love. Go home, Daniel.'

With that, he left me standing in the snow.

Driving back to the farm, I felt no anger towards Håkan. His remarks had not been unfair. However, on one important point he was wrong. I wasn't motivated by guilt. My task was not pointless. There were answers here.

At the farm I set about trying to find the words my mum had written on the walls. I hadn't seen them anywhere during my week. Searching in earnest, I eventually noticed that a cabinet had been moved. There were small scratches in the wood floor around the base of the legs. Pulling it back, I was disappointed to see just one word:

Freja!

One name, surrounded by space, just like the email she'd sent me –

Daniel!

I'd already discussed with my dad the issue of my mum's handwriting, wanting to know who'd written the lost diary, the disturbing journal found in a rusted steel box. My dad had explained that my mum was ambidextrous. Over the summer, he'd caught her, late at night, writing on the old papers uncovered in the ground.

She'd composed the fictional diary with elegant brown ink and using her left hand.

I picked up the phone, calling my dad. He was surprised by the lateness of the call. Without any of the usual pleasantries, I asked:

'Dad, why did you move the cabinet to cover up the writing on the wall? Why didn't you want anyone else to see it?'

He didn't reply. I continued:

'You didn't pack up the farm. You left the boat to freeze in the river. But you took the time to cover up one word.'

He didn't reply. I said:

'Dad, when you phoned me from Sweden to tell me Mum was sick, you said that there was a lot I didn't know. You said Mum could become violent. But she wasn't violent over the summer. And she didn't hurt anyone. What were you referring to?'

Silence again, so I asked:

'Dad, did Mum kill Freja?'

Finally he replied:

'I don't know.'

He added, barely audible:

'But if she did, it would explain a great deal.'

• • •

Unable to sleep, I climbed out of bed and dressed. I made a Thermos of strong coffee and on the embers of the iron stove warmed a roll filled with several thick slices of mild Swedish cheese, allowing it to soften. I packed a small bag, bringing with me a change of clothes and my notebook and pencil, carrying them as mascots, symbols of intent, rather than items being put to any practical use. Leaving the farm on the darkest night of the year, I drove across country, northwards and east, towards the great lake where my mum had swum and where Freja had drowned. For much of the journey I was the only car on the road. When I arrived at my grandfather's farm it was the break of dawn, with a sky evenly split between night and day.

From my mum's description of life on this farm my grandfather must have heard my car approach. It took just a single knock for him to open the door, as though he'd been waiting behind it. In this way, the two of us met for the first time. His hair was an attractive white, the hair of a goodly wizard, but it had been slicked down, forming uneven greasy icicles. At eight in the morning he was dressed in a black suit and waistcoat, with a grey shirt and a black tie – funeral attire. An inappropriate desire to hug him came over me, as though this was a reunion. He was a stranger unknown to me for my entire life, yet he was still family and family had always been precious. How could I not feel warmth towards him? Whatever problems there'd been in the past, I wanted him to be part of our small circle. Right now I needed him. With my mum in hospital, he was our only connection to the past. It might have been my foreignness, or my familiarity – maybe, as Håkan claimed, I had a touch of my mum in my face – regardless, he knew who I was. He said, in Swedish:

'You've come looking for answers. There are none here. Except for the one you already know to be true. Little Tilde is sick. She's always been sick. I fear she will always be sick.'

He called my mum 'Little Tilde' without contempt or affection. There was a studious blankness about his voice. His sentences were polished, as if pre-prepared, spoken with so correct a balance of gravitas that they felt devoid of any emotion.

I entered my grandfather's farm, built with his own hands when he was younger than me. Laid out over one floor, with no stairs or cellar, it was old-fashioned and surprisingly snug considering how much land he owned. The décor hadn't been changed for several decades. In the living room I noted the smell my mum had referred to, she'd called it the smell of sadness – stale air singed by decrepit electric heaters and curling flypaper. While he prepared coffee I was left alone and studied the walls, the awards for his white wild-meadow honey, the photographs of him and my grandmother. She was plainly dressed and sturdy, reminding me of Håkan's wife. As for my grandfather, evidently he'd always taken pride over his appearance. His clothes were well tailored. Unquestionably he'd been handsome, and immensely serious, never smiling, even when being handed a trophy, a stern father, no doubt, and an upright local politician. There were no photos of my mum on the walls. There was no trace of her on this farm.

Returning with the coffee and two thin ginger biscuits, each lonely on a separate plate, I could smell his lime cologne for the first time and wondered if he'd dabbed some on while waiting for the coffee to brew. He told me that guests were arriving from the church to stay in his spare room, so unfortunately he could give me no more than an hour. It was a lie, one he'd devised in the kitchen in order to limit the amount of time I could talk to him.

I had no right to be upset. I'd shown up unannounced and unexpected. Nonetheless, to be set a time limit was a rejection and
hurtful. I smiled:

'No problem.'

While he poured the coffee I offered a brief account of my life
by way of introduction, hoping he'd latch on to some element of
interest. He picked up his gingerbread biscuit and snapped it neatly
in two, placing both halves beside his coffee. He sipped the coffee,
ate one half of the biscuit, and said:

'How's Tilde now?'

He wasn't interested in me. There was no point wasting time on
trying to build a connection. We were strangers. So be it.

'She's very ill.'

If he couldn't offer emotion, I'd settle for facts:

'It's important that I find out what happened in the summer of
1963.'

'Why?'

'The doctors believe it could help with her treatment.'

'I can't see how.'

'Well, I'm no doctor . . .'

He shrugged:

'The summer of '63 . . .'

He sighed:

'Your mum fell in love. Or in lust, I should say. The man was
ten years her senior, he was working on a nearby farm, a summer
labourer from the city. Little Tilde wasn't even sixteen at the time.
The relationship was discovered. There was a scandal—'

I sat forward, raising my hand to interrupt as I'd done when my
mum was telling her version of events. I'd heard this story before.

But it had been told about Freja. Perhaps my grandfather had muddled the names.

'Don't you mean Freja fell in love with the farm labourer?'

My grandfather was suddenly alert. So far he'd addressed me with a melancholy weariness, not so now:

'Freja?'

'Yes, my mum told me that Freja fell in love with the farm worker. Freja – the girl on the nearby farm, the girl from the city, that scandal was about Freja, not my mum.'

My grandfather was troubled, rubbing his face, repeating the name:

'Freja.'

'She was my mum's closest friend. They ran away together once.'

The name meant something to him. I couldn't tell what.

'I can't remember the names of her friends.'

I found the remark extraordinary:

'You must remember! Freja drowned in the lake! My mum never got over the idea that you believed she was responsible for Freja's death. That's why she left. That's why I'm here.'

He looked up to the ceiling, frowning, as though there were a fly that had caught his attention. He said:

'Tilde is sick. I can't unpick her stories for you. I won't sit here trying to make sense of her nonsense. I've done enough of that in my life. She's a liar. Or a fantasist, take your pick. She believes her own stories. That's why she's ill.'

I was confused, partly by the vehemence of his reaction, mostly by the inconsistency. I said:

'I shouldn't have interrupted. Please finish telling me what happened.'

He was only partially soothed by this request and concluded his summary with a new-found briskness:

'Your mum's head was full of dreams. She imagined living happily ever after on a farm, with her lover, just the two of them. The rules of society and decency be damned! The farmhand had told her romantic lies to persuade her to sleep with him and she'd believed them. She was gullible. After the affair was terminated, the farmhand was sent away. Tilde tried to kill herself in the lake. She was rescued from the water, spending many weeks in bed. Her body recovered, her mind never did. She was shunned. She was an outcast. At school her friends disowned her. The teachers gossiped about her. What did she expect? She shamed me terribly. I was disgraced. I put aside my dreams of running for a national government post. The scandal ruined my ambitions. Who would vote for a politician with a daughter like that? If I can't bring up my own child what right do I have to make the laws for others? I found it hard to forgive her. That's why she left. It's too late for regrets. Consider yourself lucky she suffered a breakdown this summer and not sooner, when you were a child. It was only a matter of time.'

It was remarkable that my mum had brought me up with such love and affection – she couldn't have learned those sentiments from him.

Even though we'd been speaking for only forty minutes of the allotted hour my grandfather stood up, ending our talk:

'You must excuse me. My guests will be here soon.'

In the gloom of the hallway he gestured for me to wait. At a side cabinet, using a fountain pen dipped in a pot of ink, he wrote his telephone number on a card:

'Please don't turn up uninvited again. If you have any questions, ring. It is sad that it must be this way. We are family. And yet we will never be family. We lead separate lives now, Tilde and I. She chose that way. She must live with the decision. As her son, so must you.'

Outside I walked to my car, turning back for one last glance at the farm. My grandfather was at the window. He let the curtain fall, a declaration of the finality of this goodbye. He wanted me to understand that we'd never see each other again. Taking out my keys, I noticed a smudge of ink on my finger from where I'd clasped his card. In the daylight I saw that the ink wasn't black, it was a light brown.

• • •

In a nearby town I booked into the only available accommodation, a family-run guesthouse. I sat on the bed and studied the brown ink smudge on my thumb. After having showered and eaten a cold meal of potato salad, rye bread and ham, I phoned my dad. He knew nothing about Mum's alleged affair with the young farm-hand. Like me, he queried my grandfather's memory, reiterating that Freja had engaged in the affair. I asked for the name of my mum's old school.

Situated on the edge of town, the school building appeared to be new, the old premises demolished. I worried that too much time had passed. The school day was over and there were no children in the grounds. I rattled the gate, expecting it to be locked shut, but it swung open. Inside I wandered the corridors, feeling like an intruder, unsure whether I should call out. I heard the faint sound of singing and followed it upstairs. Engaged in an extracurricular class, two teachers were leading a singing rehearsal with a small group of students. I knocked on the door, quickly explaining that I was from England and looking for information concerning my mother, who'd attended this school over fifty years ago. The teachers were young and had only worked at the school for a few years. They explained that I wasn't authorised to access the school records so there was nothing they could do to help. Despondent, I remained at the door, with no idea how to overcome this obstacle. One of the women took pity on me:

'There is a teacher from that time. She's retired now, of course, but she might remember your mother, and if she does, she might agree to talk to you.'

The teacher's name was Caren.

Caren lived in a village so small I guessed there were no more than a hundred houses, a single shop, and a church. I knocked on the door, relieved when it opened. The retired teacher was wearing knitted moccasins. Her home smelled of freshly baked spiced bread. As soon as I mentioned my mum, Caren reacted:

'Why are you here?'

I told her it would take time to explain. She asked to see a photograph of my mum. I showed her my phone, finding a photograph taken in the spring before she'd left for Sweden. Caren put on her glasses and studied my mum's face before saying:

'Something's happened.'

'Yes.'

She didn't seem surprised.

*

Her home was warm, but unlike the electric warmth in my grandfather's farm this heat was welcoming, emanating from a log fire in the living room. The Christmas decorations were hand-made. There'd been no decorations in my grandfather's house, not even an Advent candle in the window. In further contrast with my grandfather's farm, there were photos of her children and grandchildren on the walls. Despite her telling me that her husband had passed away last year, this was a home full of life and love.

Caren made me a cup of honey-sweetened black tea, declining to speak while making the tea and forcing me to be patient. We sat by her fire. Steam rose from the bottom of my trousers, wet from the snow. With a touch of the schoolteacher about her, Caren instructed me not to rush, to tell her everything, in the proper order – her prescriptions reminding me of my mum's rules for narration.

I told the story of my mum. At the end, with my trousers dry, I explained that I'd travelled here to test my theory that the death of Freja, accidental or not, might be a defining event at the centre of my mum's illness. Caren stared into the fire while speaking:

'Tilde loved the countryside more than any child I've ever taught. She was far happier playing in a tree than in a classroom. She'd swim across lakes. She'd collect seeds and berries. Animals adored her. But she did not make friends easily.'

I asked:

'Except for Freja?'

Caren turned from the fire, looking directly at me:
'There was no Freja.'

. . .

Under a full moon I returned to my grandfather's farm, parking far
enough away that the engine couldn't be heard. I walked through
snow-covered fields, arriving at the clump of trees near his farmhouse,
the place where my mum had constructed a shelter and where, she'd
told me, she and Freja had spent time. A hundred or so pine trees
grew among moss-covered boulders, a pocket of wilderness that
couldn't be farmed. And though my mum had described climbing a
tree and looking down on Freja's farm, there were no buildings nearby.
I decided to climb anyway, to see the world as my mum had seen it.
The branches of the pine tree were at right angles to the trunk, like
rungs on a ladder, allowing me to reach two-thirds of the way up
before they became too fragile. Perched there, looking out across this
landscape, I saw that I was wrong. There was a building nearby, much
smaller than a farm, camouflaged by thick snow. From high above I
saw the spine of the roof – a black notch cut into the blanket of white.

As I climbed down, the building once again disappeared from sight.
I walked in its rough direction and before long I could, beyond the
heaps of snow, distinguish timber walls. It had been built using silver
birch wood. By its size I guessed it was a toolshed or workshop, probably connected to my grandfather's farm by a dirt track. There was
a rusted padlock on the door. Using the edge of my keyring, I
unscrewed the hinge from the timber, removing the padlock and stepping inside.

*

Having found the cabin under the light from a full moon, for the first time I needed my torch. Directly in front of me I saw a distorted reflection of myself. My stomach appeared swollen, twisted around the curved side of a giant steel container. This was where my grandfather collected his white honey. The space was functional. The only decorative item was an elaborately crafted cuckoo clock on the wall. It no longer told the correct time. I toyed with it until the mechanism sprang to life. There were two doors, one on either side of the clock face, one high and one low. When the clock chimed, the doors opened at the same time, two timber figures emerging, one male and one female. The man was at the top, he stared down at the timber woman and she stared up at him. Instinctively I added the dialogue:

> Hello up there!
> Hello down there!

The couple returned inside the clock and the cabin was silent again.

Around the back of the steel drum I saw, hanging on a peg, my grandfather's beekeeping outfit, the protective clothes he'd wear when retrieving honey from the hives. The outfit was made from white leathery material. Placing the torch on the floor, I dressed myself in the clothes, the trousers, the top and gloves. I put on the hat with the black protective netting, turning to study my distorted reflection. Before me was the troll my mum had described, with dinosaur-thick skin, pale webbed hands, extended fingers, and instead of a face, a single huge black eye that stared and stared and never blinked.

*

Taking off the outfit, I noticed a second locked door. I didn't bother with stealth, kicking the door with the sole of my heavy boot until the timber fractured. Squeezing through, I shone a light on a floor covered in wood shavings. There were saws and chisels – this was the place where my grandfather would repair and restore the beehives. It was also the place where he made cuckoo clocks. There were several incomplete clocks on the floor and a stack of half-finished timber figures. Faces jutted out of planks of wood. I held one in my hand, running my finger over the long curved nose. A few of the figures were fantastical creatures, exhibiting an imagination I would never have associated with my grandfather. This was a space to be creative, where he could shut the door on the world and express himself. Crouching down, I picked up a coarse coil of wood.

I don't know how long my grandfather stood at the entrance, watching me. On some deeper level I'd known he was coming, perhaps my kicking down the door had been a way of calling him, beckoning him from the farm. With a deliberately unhurried pace, I finished my examination of the workshop, imagining that he'd used fear before, when bringing my mum here, but he wouldn't have fear at his disposal now. I crushed the coarse coil of wood in my hand as I heard him shut the outer door.

I turned, raising my torch. He waved the light out of his eyes. I obliged, lowering the beam. Even in the middle of the night, hearing me outside, he'd put on a suit. I said:

'You brought my mum here. Except she wasn't Tilde, you gave her a new name. You called her Freja.'

327

'No.'

He was going to deny it. I felt a flush of anger, about to present the evidence, when he added:

'She picked the name. She'd read it in a book. She liked the way it sounded.'

It was an astonishing detail, hinting at complicity. I paused, re-evaluating this formidable man. An expert politician, he'd signalled his approach. He wouldn't deny the allegations. Far subtler, he intended to transfer some of the responsibility onto my mum. I couldn't allow it:

'You told her a story – your story. You would play her husband. You ordered her to play your wife. This place, you said, would be your farm.'

I waited for him to speak but he said nothing. He wanted to know how much I'd figured out.

'Tilde became pregnant. With your child.'

The teacher, Caren, had told me about the disgrace my mum had suffered because of her pregnancy. Though she'd been kind towards Tilde, many others hadn't. So effective had been my grand-father's lies that Caren still believed, even today, that it was the farm labourer's fault:

'You blamed a local farmhand. He lost his job. You're an important man. All your lies were believed. They became the truth.'

'They are still the truth. Ask anyone old enough to remember, and they will repeat my story.'

The power to commit a crime, and the power to get away with it, and while I couldn't stomach to think of him still drawing pleasure from the memory of the first crime, he evidently still relished the power of being believed.

'Did my mum speak to your wife? Or try to? And she refused to believe her?'

He shook his head:

'No, my wife believed Tilde. But she hated her for telling her the truth. She preferred my lies. It took her a little longer than everyone else, but, in the end, she learned to forget the truth. Which is something Tilde should have learned too. My wife and I lived on this farm, happily married, loved by everyone around us, for over sixty years.'

'What happened to the baby?'

As soon as I asked the question the answer came to me. Finally I understood my mum's overwhelming desire to protect Mia – an adopted daughter.

'She was given away.'

I said:

'What now, Grandfather?'

I watched as he pressed a finger against his lips, the gesture my mum had showed me in the hospital – the clue she'd asked me to seek out. It didn't mean silence: it meant he was deep in thought. I wondered if he'd pressed a finger against his lips while devising the various elements to his role-play scenario, signalling some new fiction would soon be forced upon her. For this reason she'd come to dread his finger against the lip. Eventually he took his finger away, placing his hands in his pockets, taking on the appearance of a man at ease:

'Now? Now nothing. Tilde is in an asylum. No one will believe a word she says. She's sick. She will always be sick. She talks of trolls and other nonsense. This matter is over. It was over a lifetime ago.'

He considered my mum's hospitalisation a victory, providing
him with certainty that he'd never be exposed. What could I do?
I'd not come for retribution. I'd come for information. Thoughts
of violence flashed through my head, but they weren't real, they
were ideas, and childish ones at that, clutching for resolution when
in truth I was powerless. My only aim was to help my mum.
Revenge was not my intention, nor was it mine to claim.

As I walked to the door, it occurred to me that one missing detail
might be useful to know:

'What name did you give yourself? She was Freja. And you
were ... ?'

'Daniel.'

The reply caught me by surprise. I stopped, looking him in the
eye as he added:

'She named her only child after him. Whatever you think of me,
she must have enjoyed her time here a little.'

It was a lie, an improvisation, a vicious one – a glimpse of his
cruelty, and his creativity, since viciousness can be creative too. My
grandfather was a storyteller and a masterful one, stories told first
out of desire, then out of self-preservation.

Sitting in my car, resting my head on the steering wheel, I told
myself to drive away, to start the engine and leave, but when I
closed my eyes I saw the burnt tooth, a remnant of my mum's
childhood that couldn't be destroyed no matter how hard she tried,
and I stepped out, walking to the boot, reaching for the spare canister of petrol.

*

Before my courage left me, I hastened back through the snow using the footprints as a path to the silver birch cabin. Working quickly, I used a stick to clear the roof of snow. Expecting my grandfather to return at any moment, I poured the petrol over the wood shavings and cuckoo clocks, over the tools and the work-bench, over the protective clothing and under the steel drum. I stood on the threshold, my hands shaking as I tried to light a match. Eventually, holding the burning match, I asked myself if this was the right thing to do and if anything would be gained. The flame descended towards my fingertip. But I couldn't decide. The flame singed my skin and I dropped it harmlessly into the snow.

'Give them to me.'

My grandfather was standing next to me, his hand outstretched. I didn't understand the request. He repeated the instruction:

'Give them to me.'

I gave him the box of matches. He lit a match cleanly, at the first attempt, holding it at eye level:

'You think I'm a monster. Look around you. There's nothing here. What else was I supposed to do with a frigid wife? I was a good father for fourteen years. And a bad one for two.'

My mum had described Freja as being a woman not a girl. On the cusp of adulthood, with breasts and an awareness of sexuality, she'd caught my grandfather's eye. She'd blamed her transforma-tion for his. When describing the imagined villainy of my dad, she'd stressed that he'd changed, become another person, abruptly, over the course of one summer – just like her father had done in the summer of 1963.

*

With a flick of the wrist my grandfather tossed the match inside the cabin. The petrol flames were quick to spread, the woodchips and shavings were first to take, then the half-finished timber faces. The waxy protective clothing melted slowly, the troll's skin burning green and blue. As the fire grew, the metal drum warped and buckled. Soon the walls were ablaze and then the roof. We were forced to step back from the intense heat. A plume of smoke blocked out a patch of stars. I asked:

'Will someone come?'

My grandfather shook his head:

'No one will come.'

As the roof collapsed my grandfather said:

'I stopped making honey a long time ago. Customers always preferred their honey to be yellow. My white honey was a delicate taste, wasted in tea or on bread. People would buy one jar, for the novelty, and leave it in their larder, untouched. It broke my heart. Tilde understood my pain better than anyone. To properly appreciate it she would only ever eat it on its own. She used to list which flowers she could taste.'

We stayed there together, by the fire, grandfather and grandson, warmed by the heat. It was the most time we would ever spend together. In the end the snowmelt extinguished the flames. Without a parting word, he returned to his farm, alone, to the smell of electric heaters and flypaper, and no matter what he claimed about his happy-ever-after ending, I didn't believe it.

Driving away from the farm I imagined my young mother pedalling along this road as fast as she could manage with the coins she'd saved up in her pocket. I drove past the bus stop where she'd waited, visible for miles around, standing beside nothing more than a metal pole with a schedule attached, where no more than a handful of buses passed each day. I imagined the relief she'd felt as she'd paid the fare and taken her seat, at the back, looking out the rear window to see if she was being followed. She'd carried with her a wooden music box full of trinkets, including a tooth, memories of this place – memories of those fourteen happy years, and the saddest of stories about the other two.

I followed the same route her bus had taken out of this region, the main road south, passing a sign that marked the end of the province. Behind this sign was an outcrop of rocks some thirty metres high, the tops of which were spotted with trees. Among the fringe of vegetation, near the cliff face of the tallest boulder, I saw a magnificent elk. I braked sharply and parked the car. Much of the circumference of this outcrop was steep, but I found a point where I could clamber up the rocks towards the summit. At the top was the elk. The creature didn't flinch even as I clumsily approached. I touched its back, its neck and antlers. The elk was made of sculpted steel, legs fixed to the rock with rusted bolts, head upright in a protective gaze over this land.

Driving overnight, I stopped frequently to brush my face with snow in order to stay alert. By the time I reached the farm it was the morning, too early to phone London, and anyway, I hadn't slept and doubted whether I could provide my dad with more than a summary. I decided to sleep for a few hours before calling. When I woke, I'd slept unbroken for an entire day.

Fresh snow had fallen. My tracks over the past week had been filled in. Feeling as if I'd emerged from hibernation, I lit a fire and warmed porridge on the stove, spicing it with a pinch of powdered cloves.

I made the call at eleven in the morning, for some reason waiting until it was exactly on the hour. My dad was silent for the majority of the conversation. He might have been crying. I couldn't be sure. He made no sound. It occurred to me that I hadn't cried, nor expressed any emotion, unless the pouring of petrol over the silver birch cabin could be called expression. When I spoke to Mark, he ascertained that my granddad had lit the fire – I could hear him silently constructing my defence case. Having heard the details of what happened, he asked:

'How are you doing?'

All I felt, at that point, was acute awareness that my discoveries were incomplete. The gap in my knowledge was like a missing tooth in my mouth – a gummy space my tongue couldn't adjust to. To Mark's ear, my reply didn't match up to his question:

'I'm not ready to come home.'

'But you have the answers?'

'No.'

He nudged the word back at me, trying to understand:

'No?'

'I don't believe the connection between the two summers is just in my mum's mind. Something happened here, something real. I'm sure of it.'

Mark's rational mind couldn't make the jump. My claim was unsubstantiated and seemed to run contrary to my discovery. However, he no longer gave off the impression of wanting to contradict me, trusting my assertion that the two summers formed a circle. One unlocked the other.

I drove past the tourist beaches; my destination was the deserted coastal wilderness where my mum had regularly run. Carrying a small backpack, I set off through brambles and dunes, wrapped up against a bitter sea wind. I wore the hood of my corduroy jacket up, tied securely around my neck to stop it blowing down. Eventually, through watering eyes, I saw the stub of an old lighthouse.

The waves had lined the rocks with black ice. At times it was so slippery I was on my hands and knees. Cold and bruised, I reached the door where Mia had once hung her flowers. There were none there now, replaced by an arch of icicles where the sea had splashed. I hit the door with my shoulder, icicles falling around me, smashing on the rocks.

Inside, there were cigarette ends and beer cans. Much like at Teardrop Island, teenagers had reclaimed this space as their own, far from adult eyes. I'd been here before, in my first week, and found nothing. But something had struck me as odd. The ground was dirty – the lighthouse had been abandoned – yet the interior walls were freshly painted.

I took off my bag and, from the Thermos, poured a hot sweet coffee, clutching the cup for warmth. My plan was to remove the top layer of paint, exposing whatever was underneath. In a hardware store, far from the local area, I'd discussed the project. Without access to power I'd been forced to opt for chemical stripper. After my coffee, feeling revived, I targeted several areas at once, exposing fragments of a mural. One particular spot caught my eye, a patch of bright colours – a bouquet of summer flowers. Concentrating on the area around the flowers, slowly I revealed a painting of Mia, dressed in midsommar white. There were flowers in her hair and flowers underfoot. In my haste I damaged the painting. Despite being far from a professional restoration job, it was good enough to offer a sense of the mural's exceptional artistic quality. Though I'd seen her picture on the missing person poster, this mural gave me my first real sense of Mia as a person. She was proud and strong, also a dreamer, head aloft, as she ambled through the forests.

I recalled Mia's escape in the middle of the night, and my mum was right, it didn't make sense, unless Mia had help. Someone picked her up – a lover. My guess was the person who'd painted her on the walls of the lighthouse. Raking over my mum's account, it struck me that Mia's lover might be the man who'd used a racial slur at the first midsommar party, described as a young man with long hair and an earring. Why would he go to the extreme of using racist language anyway? His comments were intended to throw Håkan off track. Mia had run out of the tent not because she was insulted, since she knew his racism was a necessary deception, but because she was furious at Håkan's interference. The fact that this man was working as temporary help during the summer tourist influx suggested that he was a student.

*

Mark had a friend who worked in a contemporary gallery in east London, and in collusion with him, using his email address, I messaged every university and college art facility in Sweden, attaching a series of photos I'd taken of the mural in the abandoned lighthouse, explaining that the gallery would like to arrange a meeting with the artist responsible. The results trickled back over several days – negative, until an email arrived from a teacher at Konstfack, the University College for Arts, Crafts and Design, the largest art school in Sweden, located just south of the capital. He was sure the mural was by one of his former students. The artist was a recent graduate. Had the academic been of a suspicious mind he might have wondered how a private gallery in London knew about an abandoned lighthouse in the south of Sweden, but I'd calculated that the flattery and excitement generated by the email would overcome most doubts. A meeting was set for Stockholm. The artist's name was Anders.

I drove up the night before, checking into the cheapest room in a grand hotel near the waterfront, spending much of the night rehearsing my part, reading profiles of obscure new artists. The next morning I waited in the lobby, facing the main doors. Anders arrived early, tall, handsome, dressed in skinny black jeans and a black shirt. He wore a stud in his ear and carried a portfolio under his arm. We chatted for a while about his art. My appreciation for his talent was genuine. However, I told many lies about myself, marvelling at how good at lying I'd grown over the years. But something had changed. I hated every lie I told. Only the prospect of failure stopped me from telling the truth. Mia might not want to be found. If I risked the truth, Anders might walk out.

*

Playing my part, I made steady progress towards my request to see the art for real – the actual paintings, too large to bring to my hotel. I presumed he wouldn't be able to afford a studio. He'd paint at home, and if Mia had run away with him then she'd be there too, or at least some evidence of her. The trap worked. He sheepishly explained I'd need to come to his apartment, apologising that it was a long distance from the centre since he couldn't afford the high costs of Stockholm. I said:

'The hotel can arrange a car.'

I paid for our coffees with a hundred-krona note, noticing on the money not some famous face, an inventor or politician, but a honeybee. Anders was already moving away from the table when I said in Swedish:

'Wait.'

I remembered the clean smooth snow outside the farm and my hope that this could be a new beginning. I wouldn't build this discovery on the back of lies.

I began my story with the request that Anders not leave until I was finished. He agreed, confused by my change in tone. I watched his anger develop as I revealed how I'd tricked him. I could see he was tempted to leave but, a man of his word, he remained seated. His anger softened into sadness as I summarised my mum's relationship with Mia and the events after Mia left. By the end of my account his anger had mostly dissipated. An element of disappointment remained that he had not yet been discovered as an artist. I assured him, as a layman, that my appreciation was genuine, as was that of the gallery owner whose email address I'd hijacked. Finally I asked if I could speak to Mia. He told me to wait in the foyer. He was going to make a call. Strangely, it didn't even cross my mind that he might not return. I closed my eyes and waited, feeling lighter despite the risk I'd just taken.

We arrived at a residential block far from the centre of town. Anders muttered:

'Artists should live in poverty.'

He was a romantic, the kind of temperament to inspire a girl to run away from home. We walked up the icy concrete stairs in single file since only the middle of the stairway had been gritted and the lift was out of order. Reaching the upper floor, he took out his keys. With a joke about owning the penthouse he showed me inside. Anders said, now speaking in Swedish:

'Mia will be back soon.'

I waited in their living room, surrounded by his paintings. They owned very few items of furniture, no television, only a small radio plugged into the wall. To pass the time he began to paint. Thirty minutes later there was the sound of a key in the door. I walked into the corridor and saw Mia for the first time. She looked older than sixteen, heavily wrapped up against the cold. I could feel her eyes searching for my mum in my features. She shut the door, taking off her scarf. As she removed her winter coat, I saw that she was pregnant. I almost asked who the father was but caught myself in time.

The three of us took a seat in the small kitchen, the patterned linoleum floor squeaking under our chairs. We drank black tea sweetened with white sugar since honey, I guessed, was an unaffordable luxury. About to hear the truth of this summer, I was scared that maybe my mum had simply been wrong. Mia said:

'I didn't run away. Håkan asked me to leave. After I told him I was pregnant he arranged an appointment for an abortion. If I wanted to stay on his farm, as his daughter, I'd have to behave in a way that he found acceptable. He claimed he was concerned for my future. He was. But mostly he was concerned with his reputation. I was a disgrace, no longer the kind of daughter he wanted. I didn't know what to do. Anders and I don't have much money. We're not fools. Could we be parents? I almost gave in, I almost said yes to the abortion. One night, I saw your mum walking through our fields. I didn't know what she was doing there. But I remembered our long talks. She was so different from everyone else. She'd told me the story about how she left her farm, when she was just sixteen, she had nothing, and she'd made her way to England, and started a business, and a family. I thought – this is a woman I admire. She's so strong. Everyone bows down to Håkan, but not her. He hated her for it. I told Håkan that if I couldn't keep the baby then I'd leave. Part of me was sure he'd change his mind once he saw how serious I was. But he accepted. He didn't even talk to Elise. She was my mum and she didn't have a say in my future. She was upset. She writes to me every week. She visits regularly too, and whenever she does she fills the fridge with food. She misses me very much. And I miss her.'

Mia's voice broke with emotion. There was real love for Elise.

'She's a good person. She was always kind. But she'll never stand up to him. She's his servant. And I didn't want to grow up like her.'

I asked if Mia had cut up Håkan's wooden trolls in anger. She shook her head. By deduction, it could only be one other person:

'Then it was Elise.'

Mia smiled at the thought of her mum taking an axe to Håkan's trolls and said:

'Maybe, one day, she will leave him.'

I queried Mia's drunkenness at the second midsommar party. She shook her head. If she'd seemed drunk it was because on that day she'd discovered that she was pregnant. She was in a daze. The next ten days were spent as a prisoner on the farm – the worst ten days of her life. Once she'd made her decision, Håkan came up with a plan. He wanted her to disappear. He didn't want to explain anything to the local community. He couldn't stomach the shame.

Mia said:

'His idea was to stage a runaway story so that he could be a victim.'

My mum was right on both counts. To escape from a remote farm you needed a plan, but the plan hadn't been Mia's, it had been Håkan's. And there had been a conspiracy. Stellan the detective had been told that Mia wasn't a missing person. No one was looking for her. The posters had gone up only in places where they were useless. Håkan transferred money into Mia's account at the end of every month. He paid for the apartment. He could visit any time he liked. To date, he hadn't.

At the end of her account I asked whether there'd ever been any element of danger. My mum had been convinced Mia was in peril. On this crucial point Mia shook her head:

'Håkan never touched me, never hit me, never laid a finger on me, he wasn't like that. He never even raised his voice. If I wanted a new set of clothes he'd buy them the same day. He'd give me anything I wanted. He called me spoiled. He was right. I was spoiled. But he didn't love me. I don't think he understands love. To him, love is control. He'd go through my belongings. He found my diary inside the mirror that Anders had carved for me. He put the diary back in order that I'd keep writing in it and he could keep reading it. When I realised what he was doing, I ripped the whole thing up and put it back for him. That made him angry, as if it belonged to him.'

I asked about the suicide of Anne-Marie and the hermit in the field. Mia shrugged:

'I didn't know her well. She was close to Cecilia, the woman who sold your mum the farm, and Cecilia blamed Håkan for her suicide, but I don't know why. Possibly Anne-Marie was sleeping with Håkan. It's no secret that Håkan has affairs. To him, everyone's wife was fair game. Elise knew it. Anne-Marie was devout, when sober. You saw all those biblical quotes, right? But no one flirted more than her if she drank, she'd do it in front of her husband, she'd torture him with it, she always thought he was a big stupid oaf of a man. She was horrible to him when drunk and guilt-ridden when sober. Underneath it all, she was just really sad.'

'Why does Håkan want our farm so much?'

'No reason, other than he owns the land around it. He'd look at the map and your farm was a blotch on his kingdom, a pocket of land that he didn't control. It was a blemish. It infuriated him.'

'He's going to own it soon.'

Mia thought about this:

'Like him or not, it's hard not to respect a man who always gets what he wants.'

I imagined Håkan gloating over his map, but that was not a battle for me to fight.

Mia had been speaking for an hour. She and Anders were both wondering what more I could want. I asked them to wait while I made a call. I left the apartment and, standing in the cold concrete walkway, phoned my dad. He pointed out bluntly that Mum wouldn't believe anything he told her, or anything I said:

'Mia needs to come to London. Tilde needs to hear it from her.'

After our conversation, I called Mark, asking if I could use the remaining money to buy Mia and Anders a flight to London. During our conversation Mark's tone was different. I'd experienced many warm sentiments from him but never admiration. He agreed to the buying of the tickets. I told him that I loved him and that I'd see him soon.

Inside the apartment, I presented my plan:

'I'd like you to come to London. Your flights, a hotel, they'd be paid for. Even so, I'm asking a lot of you. Mia, I need you to speak to my mum. I need my mum to see you. It's not enough for me to repeat this information, she won't believe a word I say, or a word my dad says, she hasn't spoken to me since the summer, she won't speak to me, she won't listen to me, she needs to hear it from you.'

They discussed the matter. Though I didn't hear the conversation, I imagined Anders was reluctant, worried about stress, since Mia was six months' pregnant. They returned, and Mia said:

'Tilde would have done it for me.'

On the flight to London Mia saw my mum's Bible and her

collection of Swedish troll stories in my bag. As she reached for them, I was convinced the Bible had caught her eye. Instead, she took hold of the troll storybook, examining the illustration:

'This is Tilde's, isn't it?'

'How did you know?'

'She wanted to loan it to me. She said there was one story in particular she was keen for me to read. Your mum was wonderful to me but I never figured out why she thought I'd be interested in reading more troll stories. I've heard enough of those for a lifetime. I promised to pick the book up but never did.'

I was surprised by my mum's emphasis on one particular story, curious as to which one she might have been referring to. She'd never singled one out before. I flicked through, assessing each one. In the middle of the volume I came across a story called 'The Princess Troll'. Reading the opening lines, I realised they were new to me. I couldn't hear my mum's voice, despite being convinced she'd read the entire book aloud many times. Checking the rest of the collection, I established that this was the only story she'd skipped. According to the appendix, a part of the book I'd never explored or known existed, this troll legend was one of the oldest. There were numerous versions to be found in Germany, Italy and France, in volumes of fairy tales by Italo Calvino, Charles Perrault and the Brothers Grimm. The Swedish variant was of an unknown origin. I set about reading it for the first time.

•   •   •

THE PRINCESS TROLL

Once there was a great king who ruled his kingdom justly. By his side was a queen more beautiful than any other woman and a young daughter lovelier than any child in the kingdom. The king lived happily until his queen was struck gravely ill. On her deathbed she made him promise that he would only remarry a woman as beautiful as her. When the queen died the king went into mourning, convinced he would never remarry. His courtiers insisted that their kingdom required a queen and that he must search for a new wife. Mindful of his promise, the king could find no woman as beautiful as his wife.

One day the king was staring out of his castle window. He saw his daughter playing in the royal orchard. She'd come of age. She'd grown to be as beautiful as her mother. The king jumped to his feet and declared that she would be his next wife. The courtiers were aghast and implored him to reconsider. A wise fortune-teller predicted such a marriage would bring ruin to the kingdom. The daughter pleaded with her father to think again, but he would not. The wedding date was set. The daughter was locked in the tower so that she might not run away.

The night before the wedding one of the courtiers, fearing the kingdom was about to be cursed by such a wicked act, helped the daughter escape into the enchanted forest. On the morning of the wedding the king found his daughter missing. He executed the courtier. He then sent his army out into the forest to search for her.

The daughter was sure to be found. She begged the enchanted forest for help. A mushroom answered her cry. If the princess promised to tend the forest the mushroom would help her. There was one condition. She must never have any contact with people again, devoting herself to the natural world. The princess agreed and the mushroom blew magic spores onto her face, turning her into an ugly troll. When the king's army found her lurking behind a boulder they recoiled and continued their search elsewhere.

The princess troll spent many years tending to the forest and became friends with the birds and the wolves and the bears. Meanwhile her father's kingdom fell into ruin. The king was turned mad by his quest to find his missing daughter. Eventually, with his castle crumbling, his treasury empty, the mad old king had no more servants to command or citizens to rule. He set out into the forest to find his daughter for himself. He spent months crawling through the moss, chewing on bark, until finally the king collapsed. He was on the brink of death.

The princess troll heard news of her father's condition from the birds. She visited him but dared not approach too close. Seeing the troll's yellow eyes among the trees, the king asked the troll to bury him so that his body would not be ripped apart by ravens and that he might, in death, at last know peace again. The princess troll's heart was pure. She remembered her love for her father and thought she must grant him this final wish. However, as soon as she gave a nod of her head her promise was broken and she was transformed, returning to the lovely shape of a princess, more beautiful than ever before.

The sight of his daughter rejuvenated the sick king. He staggered to his feet, chasing after her. The princess called out for help. The wolves and the ravens and the bears answered her cry and ripped the king apart, each taking a piece of his body to the far corners of the forest to feast upon.

Afterwards, the princess bade sad farewell to her forest friends and returned to the castle. Order was returned. The princess married a handsome prince. In attendance at the wedding were the bears and the wolves. The castle roof was covered in birds. The enchanted forest turned its leaves gold in celebration.

The kingdom was restored to greatness again and the new queen ruled justly and lived happily ever after.

• • •

I EXCUSED MYSELF FROM THE SEAT and stood in the galley at the back of the aircraft. In Sweden I'd remained composed, refusing to dwell too deeply on the emotions embedded in my discoveries, concentrating on the procedure of gathering facts and the goal of presenting them to my mum in hospital. Yet as I read this story I couldn't help but picture my mum sitting on my bed, her fingers lingering on this story before skipping over these pages, refusing to read them, afraid she might be unable to mask her feelings, afraid I might ask a question or catch a glimpse of the sadness that she'd spent much of her life concealing, not only from us, but also from herself. I should've read these stories for myself a long time ago and wondered if my mum had secretly wanted me to. She could easily have discarded the book but she'd kept it close, returning to this collection time and again, communicating its great importance while also refusing to reveal why. I thought upon the way in which we'd always shared in each other's happiness, believing it would make the moment burn brighter and longer, but sadness can be shared too, perhaps sharing makes it burn briefer and less bright. If so, I had, at last, that to offer.

Mark picked us up at the airport. I explained to him that I'd quit my job. In the new year I was going to search for another career. Had the idea been outlandish Mark would've expressed reservations. He accepted the announcement without protest, suggesting to me that he'd been thinking along similar lines for some time. He asked:

'What do you want to do?'

'I need to find out.'

*

347

My dad was waiting at the hospital. He greeted Mia with a hug.
I saw desperation in his face. I felt it in his body, too, when
he hugged me – the loss of weight, the tension. Though he wanted
to go straight through, I suggested we eat some lunch together. I
didn't want anyone to feel rushed. And I had one last matter to
put to Mia.

We found an old-fashioned café near the hospital. They served
our meal with a plate of ready-buttered slices of soft white bread
and steel pots of tea brewed so strong that Anders actually
laughed when it was poured. Aside from that welcome burst of
lightness, no one spoke much. Weighing on my thoughts was the
way in which danger had been such a particular part of my
mum's conception of events. It wasn't just unhappiness. She'd
perceived a young girl in jeopardy. There'd been a villain. Breaking the silence, I asked Mia again, had she ever been in danger
of any kind? She shook her head. However, there was something
she hadn't told me. I suspected the reason was because she hadn't
told Anders.

I decided to take a chance, handing Mia the collection of troll stories, pointing out the one my mum had wanted her to read. A
little perplexed, she began to read. She must have been close to my
mum, because she cried upon finishing it. I promised that I'd never
ask her again, repeating my question one final time:
　'Were you ever in danger?'
　Mia nodded. Anders looked at her. This was news to him too.
I asked:
　'What happened?'

'The mayor was a creep. Everyone knew that. He'd make comments about my body, about my legs, my breasts. He'd go to the toilet and leave the door open, standing there, hoping I'd pass by. I told Håkan. I told Elise. She admitted the mayor was a dirty old man. But he was a supporter of Håkan. He'd do anything Håkan asked. So Håkan told me that I should dress less provocatively around him.'

I remembered the first time my mum had seen Mia and said:

'At the summer grill, in May, you stripped down and went swimming, in front of all the guests.'

'That was my way of telling Håkan I'd wear whatever I wanted and wasn't about to cover up because the mayor was a disgusting bastard or because Håkan told me to. The principle's good, right? But the mayor was too stupid to understand it. He thought I was flirting with him. Later that summer, I was reading at my desk, late at night, and I looked up to see the mayor standing at my door. Håkan had been playing cards with some friends and he was driving one of them home because they'd drunk too much. Håkan was never drunk. Never. But he encouraged other people to get drunk. Anyway, Elise was out. Somehow the mayor and I were alone in the house. I've never been afraid of that man before, he just struck me as pathetic, but that night I was scared. He was leaning on the doorframe. I forced a smile and told the mayor I'd make him some coffee. I wasn't sure he was going to let me out of the room because he didn't move so I took his hand, pretending to be playful, pulling him out of the room, because I knew on some level he thought I wanted him and it would only be when I made it clear that I didn't that he'd become dangerous. I told him we could both have a drink, not coffee, something alcoholic, and he said that sounded nice. As soon as he put a foot on the stairs I turned and ran. The door to my room didn't lock but the bathroom door did and I slammed it shut and bolted the door, shouting out that I didn't feel well and I was going to take a bath, he could help himself to coffee or whatever he wanted. He didn't say anything. But I could hear his footsteps come towards me – I could hear him on the landing. I wondered if he was going to kick the door down, it wasn't a sturdy door and the lock was just a latch. I saw the handle turn, I saw him push against the latch. I waited, holding a pair of nail scissors. He must have stood there for five minutes. Then he walked away. But I didn't leave the bathroom. I stayed in there until Håkan came home.'

The mayor was the fourth name on my mum's list of suspects.

Anders took Mia's hand, asking softly:

'Why didn't you tell me?'

'Because you would've tried to kill him.'

I added:

'Mia, when you talk to my mum, can you start with this?'

My mum's ward was entered through two secure doors, the severity of her condition expressed by the heavy clunk of locks opening and closing. My dad had persuaded the doctors to delay using the drip, holding out until I returned. It was agreed that Mia should go in alone since we didn't want my mum feeling ambushed. Mia was happy with this arrangement, showing great strength, apparently unfazed by her surroundings or by the patients wandering the corridors. She was a remarkable young woman. Anders kissed her. A nurse escorted Mia into the visiting room.

*

I took off my watch to stop myself counting the minutes. I was seated next to Mark, who was seated beside my dad, seated beside Anders, the four of us side by side, none of us able to read a newspaper, or check our phones, none of us able to pass the time except by staring at the floor or the walls. Every now and then the nurse would update us. She'd check through the viewing window in the door, reporting back that Mia and my mum were seated close together, holding hands, deep in conversation. They hadn't moved from this position. When the nurse returned for the fifth time, she addressed us as though we were a single family:

'Your mum wants a word.'

ABOUT THE AUTHOR

Tom Rob Smith graduated from Cambridge University in 2001 and lives in London. Born in 1979 to a Swedish mother and an English father, his bestselling novels in the *Child 44* trilogy were international publishing sensations. Among its many honours, *Child 44* won the International Thriller Writer Award for Best First Novel, the Galaxy Book Award for Best New Writer, the CWA Ian Fleming Steel Dagger Award, and was longlisted for the Man Booker Prize and shortlisted for the Costa First Novel Award and the inaugural Desmond Elliott Prize. The forthcoming film adaptation of *Child 44* stars Tom Hardy, Noomi Rapace, Gary Oldman and Vincent Cassel.

Tom Rob Smith

CHILD 44

NOW A MAJOR MOTION PICTURE STARRING
TOM HARDY, NOOMI RAPACE, and GARY OLDMAN

Moscow, 1953. Under Stalin's terrifying regime there is no such thing as crime, and who dares disagree? Secret police officer Leo Demidov has spent his career arresting anyone who steps out of line. Suddenly his world is turned upside down when he uncovers evidence of a killer at large. Now, with only his wife at his side, Leo must risk both their lives, to save the lives of others.

AN INTERNATIONAL BESTSELLER IN OVER 35 LANGUAGES

OVER 2 MILLION COPIES SOLD

NOMINATED FOR 17 INTERNATIONAL AWARDS, WINNER OF 7

TOP 100 THRILLERS OF ALL TIME – NPR

Paperback ISBN 978-0-85720-408-0
Ebook ISBN 978-1-84739-808-6

Tom Rob Smith

THE SECRET SPEECH

FROM THE AUTHOR OF INTERNATIONAL BESTSELLER *CHILD 44*
THE MULTI-MILLION SELLING TRILOGY CONTINUES . . .

Moscow, 1965: a society trying to recover from a time when the police
were corrupt and the innocent arrested as criminals.

Detective Leo Demidov, former Secret Police Officer, is forced to ask
whether the wrongs of the past can ever be forgiven. Trying to solve a
series of brutal murders that grip the capital, he must decide if this is
savagery or justice.

Quickly it becomes apparent that Leo himself – and his family – are in
danger from someone intent on revenge. Desperate to save those he
loves, he is offered salvation from an unexpected source – and at a
terrible price.

Paperback ISBN 978-0-85720-409-7
Ebook ISBN 978-1-84737-715-9

Tom Rob Smith

AGENT 6

THE HEART-RACING ADVENTURE THAT BEGAN IN *CHILD 44*
AND *THE SECRET SPEECH* REACHES ITS EPIC CONCLUSION

Moscow, 1965. When Leo Demidov's worst fears are realised and a
tragic murder destroys everything he loves, he demands only one
thing: that he is allowed to find the killer who has struck at the heart of
his family.

Crippled by grief, his request denied, Leo sees no other option than to
take matters into his own hands, even though he is thousands of miles
from the crime scene.

In a thrilling story that takes us from the backstreets of 1960's New York
to the mountains of Afghanistan in the '80s, Leo will stop at nothing as
he hunts down the one person who knows the truth: Agent 6.

Paperback ISBN 978-1-84739-674-7
Ebook ISBN 978-1-84737-976-4